PRAISE FOR COLLEEN COBLE

"*The Lightkeeper's Bride* is a wonderful story filled with mystery, intrigue, and romance. I loved every minute of it."

> — Cindy Woodsmall, *New York Times*
> best-selling author of *The Hope of*
> *Refuge*

"Colleen Coble has long been a favorite storyteller of mine. I love the way she weaves intrigue and God's love into a story chock-full of carefully crafted characters. If you're looking for an awesome writer—I highly recommend her!"

> — Tracie Peterson, best-selling author of
> *Dawn's Prelude*, Song of Alaska series

"Colleen delivers a heart-warming romance—and plot twists that will keep you guessing until the final pages! Perhaps best of all, her novels call us to a deeper, richer faith."

> — Tamera Alexander, best-selling author of
> *The Inheritance*, regarding *The*
> *Lightkeeper's Daughter*

"*The Lightkeeper's Daughter* is a maze of twists and turns with an opening that grabs the reader instantly. With so many red herrings, the villain caught me by surprise."

> — Lauraine Snelling, best-selling author of
> *A Measure of Mercy*

"A high stakes, fast-paced romance. I loved it!"

> — Mary Connealy, best-selling author of
> *Montana Rose*, regarding *Lonestar*
> *Homecoming*

The Lightkeeper's Bride

OTHER NOVELS BY COLLEEN COBLE INCLUDE

The Rock Harbor series

Without a Trace

Beyond a Doubt

Into the Deep

Cry in the Night

The Aloha Reef series

Distant Echoes

Black Sands

Dangerous Depths

Alaska Twilight

Fire Dancer

Midnight Sea

Abomination

Anathema

The Lonestar Novels

Lonestar Sanctuary

Lonestar Secrets

Lonestar Homecoming

The Mercy Falls series

The Lightkeeper's Daughter

THE LIGHTKEEPER'S BRIDE

A Mercy Falls Novel

Colleen Coble

THOMAS NELSON
Since 1798

NASHVILLE   DALLAS   MEXICO CITY   RIO DE JANEIRO

Published in Nashville, Tennessee, by Thomas Nelson. Thomas Nelson is a registered trademark of Thomas Nelson, Inc.

Thomas Nelson, Inc., titles may be purchased in bulk for educational, business, fund-raising, or sales promotional use. For information, please e-mail SpecialMarkets@ThomasNelson.com.

Publisher's note: This novel is a work of fiction. Names, characters, places, and incidents are either products of the author's imagination or used fictitiously. All characters are fictional, and any similarity to people, living or dead, is purely coincidental.

KING JAMES VERSION is in the public domain and does not require permission.

Library of Congress Cataloging-in-Publication Data

Coble, Colleen.
    The lightkeeper's bride : a Mercy Falls novel / Colleen Coble.
       p. cm.
    ISBN 978-1-59554-266-3 (pbk.)
    1. Brides—Fiction. 2. California—History—1850–1950—Fiction.
3. Domestic fiction. I. Title.
PS3553.O2285L523 2010
813'.54—dc22   2010025951

Printed in the United States of America

10 11 12 13 14 RRD 6 5 4 3 2

For Jen

I treasure your friendship and constant support. Love you!

Jehovah-Shalom—the Lord our Peace

ONE

THE LAPEL WATCH on her blouse read half past nine when Katie Russell removed the skates from her boots and dropped them inside the door of the Mercy Falls Telephone Company. She pulled the pins from her Merry Widow hat, then hung it on a rack. Smoothing the sides of her pompadour, she approached the switchboard in the room down the hall. "Has it been busy?" she asked the woman in front of the dangling cords.

Nell Bartlett sat with her stocking feet propped on the railing of the table that supported the switchboard. Her color was high and her voice clear and energetic as she answered a question then disconnected the line. A faint line of discontent lingered between her brows as she eyed Katie. "It's your shift already?"

Nell was unmarried and still lived with her ailing mother, though she was thirty-five. On the street she dropped her gaze and barely whispered a hello, but in front of the switchboard she came alive. Whenever she entered the office, she removed her hat, let down her hair, and took off her shoes.

"It is indeed," Katie said, approaching the switchboard. "Has it been busy?"

"Not too bad. I only received three calls last night." Nell's tone indicated her displeasure. "But the rings have increased quite nicely this morning." She rose and stepped away from the seat in front of the switchboard but kept one hand on the top with a proprietary air.

Katie settled herself in the chair and donned the headset. Nell slipped her shoes back on, wound her hair into a bun, then put on her hat. Out of the corner of her eye, Katie watched her scurry from the room, her mousy identity back in place.

Katie peered at the switchboard then forced herself to put on her hated glasses. She nearly groaned when the light came on at her own residence. She plugged in the cord and toggled the switch. "Good morning, Mama."

Her mother's voice was full of reproach. "Katie, you left before I could tell you that Mr. Foster called last night while you were out gallivanting at the skating rink."

Katie bit back the defense that sprang to her lips and kept the excitement from her voice. "What did he say?"

"He asked to speak with your father and they went to the library."

Such behavior could only mean one thing. Heat flooded Katie's face. "He asked Papa if he could court me?"

"He did indeed! Now you mind my words, Katie. You could not make a better match than this. You need to quit that ridiculous job and focus on building your social ties."

Katie opened her mouth then shut it again. Another light flashed on her switchboard. "I must go, Mama. I have another call." She unplugged the cord over her mother's objection. Her parents didn't understand how important this job was to her. She thrust the cord into the receptor. "Operator," she said.

"Fire! There's a fire," the man on the other end gasped.

Katie glanced more closely at the board, and her muscles clenched. The orphanage. "I'll call the fire department, Mr. Gleason. Get the children out!" She unplugged and rang the fire station with trembling hands. "Fire at the orphanage, hurry!" She rushed to the window and looked out to see smoke billowing from the three-story brick building down the street. People were running toward the conflagration. She wished she could help, too, but she turned back to the switchboard as it lit up with several lights. Moments later she heard the shriek of the fire truck as it careened past.

She answered the calls one by one, but most were people checking to make sure she knew about the fire. The morning sped by. She relayed a message out to the North house and managed to chat a few moments with her best friend, Addie North. One call was Mrs. Winston asking the time, and Katie realized it was after one o'clock. At the next lull, she removed her sandwich from the waxed paper and munched it while she watched the board.

The light for Foster's Sawmill came on. She plugged in. "Operator."

Bart Foster's deep voice filled her ears. "I'd recognize that voice anywhere."

Katie pressed the palm of her hand to her chest where her heart galloped. "Mr. Foster, I'm sorry I missed your call last night."

"I had a most rewarding chat with your father," he said, a smile in his voice. "Did he tell you?"

Her pulse thundered in her ears. "He did not."

"Excellent. I wish to tell you of our conversation myself. Might I call tonight?"

"Of course." She wasn't often so tongue-tied. All her dreams of respectability lay within her grasp. From the corner of her eye, she saw her boss step into the small room. "I won't be home until after seven. Will that be too late?"

"Of course not. I shall call at seven thirty."

"I look forward to it. Did you wish to place a call?"

"Someone must be there since you are not quite yourself." The amusement in his voice deepened. "Connect me with your father's haberdashery, please. I'll see you tonight."

"Of course." She connected the cord to the shop then turned to face Mr. Daniels.

.

"I just stopped by to commend you on the way you handled the fire call, Miss Russell. You kept your head about you in a most admirable fashion."

She stood to face him. "The children? Are they all out safely?"

He nodded. "I just came from the site. The building is a total loss, but everyone is safe, thanks to your quick call to the fire department that I was told about. Well done. I'd like you to consider more hours. You're the best operator I have. People like you, and you're most efficient."

She couldn't stop the smile that sprang to her lips. "Thank you, sir. I'm honored. I love my job."

"Then you'll increase your hours? I'd like you to work six days a week."

She realized the plum that had been thrown into her lap. These were tough times, and jobs for women were scarce. But her parents—especially in light of Bart's courting—would be less than pleased.

"Katie?"

"I would like nothing better, Mr. Daniels, but I fear I'm going to have to cut my hours instead. Nell will be delighted with the extra work."

❦

Will Jesperson brushed off his hands and surveyed the gleaming glass on the Fresnel lens in the light tower. Whether he'd done it properly was up for debate, but he liked the way the sun glinted through the lens and lit the floor of the tower. He glanced outside again. He'd found it hard to keep working when he would rather study the clouds and the waves from this vantage point.

Beautiful place, this rocky northern California shoreline. He still couldn't believe he had landed such a perfect job. Instead of pursuing his hobby once a week, he could do it every day. There were weather balloons in the shed just waiting to be used. He eyed the rolling clouds overhead and held up a finger. The wind was coming from the north. Was that common here? He'd have the time and equipment to find out.

He stepped outside and leaned against the railing. The beauty of the rolling sea transfixed him. Whitecaps boiled on the rocks poking up from the water at the mouth of the bay. Seeing them reminded him of his grave duties here: to save lives and warn ships of the dangers lurking just below the surface of the sea. Squaring his shoulders, he told himself he would keep the light shining bright—both here at the lighthouse and in his personal life. God had blessed him with this position, and he would do his best to honor him with his work.

He removed his pocket watch, glanced at the time, and then stared back out to sea when he heard a man yell. Were those shouts of alarm? Through the binoculars he saw a ship moving past the bay's opening. A puff of smoke came from a smaller boat trailing it—*gunfire?* The small craft caught up to the ship, and several men clambered up the mast.

Pirates. Will pressed against the railing and strained to see when he heard more shots across the water. Additional men poured onto the ship and were already turning it back toward the open ocean. He had to do something. Turning on his heel, he rushed toward the spiral staircase. The metal shook and clanged under his feet as he raced down the steps. He leaped out the door and ran down the hillside to the dinghy beached on the sand.

The pirates shoved men overboard, and he heard cries of pain. He clenched empty fists. No weapon. Still, he might be able to save some of the men thrown overboard. Shoving the boat into the water, he put his back into rowing, but the tide was coming in and the waves fought him at every stroke.

He paused to get his bearings and realized the ship was moving away. The smaller boat, attached by a rope, bobbed after it. Something whizzed by his head and he ducked instinctively. A hole appeared in the side of the boat behind him. The pirates were firing on him. His hands dropped from the oars when he saw several bodies bobbing in the whitecaps. Men were already drowned.

The wind billowed the sails and he knew he had no chance of intercepting the ship. But he could save the men that he could reach, then inform the authorities of what he'd seen. He grasped the oars and rowed for all he was worth.

❧

At 3:03 a light came on and Katie answered. "Number, please." The caller, a man whose voice she didn't recognize, sounded breathless.

"Is this the operator?"

She detected agitation in his tone. "It is. Is something wrong?"

"Pirates," he said in a clipped voice. "Just off the lighthouse. They shot some sailors and dumped others overboard."

She sprang to her feet. "I'll contact the constable. Do you need further assistance?"

"I need a doctor at the lighthouse. I've got two injured men. The rest are—dead. I couldn't get their bodies into the boat, but they're washing up onshore now." His taut voice broke. "I had to leave the men on the shore to get to a phone, but I'm heading back there now. Tell the doctor to hurry."

"Right away," she promised. She disconnected the call and rang the doctor first. Saving life was paramount. The constable would be too late to do much about the pirates. With both calls dispatched, she forced herself to sit back down, though her muscles twitched with the need for activity. She reminded herself she'd done all she could.

The switchboard lit again. "Operator," she said, eyeing the light. The call originated from the bank.

"R-10, please."

She plugged in the other end of the cord to ring the Cook residence.

Instead, she heard Eliza Bulmer pick up the phone on the other end. "I'm sorry, Eliza, we seem to have a switched link somewhere. Would you hang on until I can get through to the Cooks?" Katie asked.

"Of course, honey," Eliza said. "I just picked up my wedding dress, and I'm trying it on. So if I don't say much, you'll know why."

"You're getting married? I hadn't heard. Congratulations."

"Thank you." Eliza's voice held a lilt.

"Just leave the earpiece dangling, if you please."

"I can do that."

There was a *thunk* in Katie's ear, and she knew Eliza had dropped the earpiece. Katie waited to see if the ring would be answered at the Cook residence but there was only a long pause. "There's no answer, Eliza. You can hang up," she said.

The other woman did not reply. If the phone were left off the hook, it would go dead. Katie started to raise her voice, but she heard a man's voice.

"You said you had something to tell me. What is it? I need to get home."

The voice was familiar, but Katie couldn't quite place it. It was too muffled.

"Honey, thank you for coming so quickly," Eliza said.

Though Eliza's voice was faint, Katie thought she detected a tremble in it. *This is none of my business*, she thought. *I should hang up.* But she held her breath and listened anyway.

"Would you like tea?" Eliza asked.

"No, Eliza, I don't want tea. What are you doing in that getup? I want to know what was so all-fired important that you called me at work—something I've expressly forbidden you to do."

Katie's stomach lurched as she tried to place the voice. Identification hovered at the edge of her mind. *Who is that?*

"Very well. I shall just blurt it out then. I'm out of money and I must have some to care for my daughter. I need money today or . . ."

"I won't be blackmailed," the man snapped.

A wave of heat swept Katie's face. She heard a door slam, then weeping from Eliza. She wanted to comfort the sobbing young woman. Numb, Katie sat listening to the sobs on the line.

The door slammed again. "Who's there?" Eliza asked in a quavering voice. She gasped, then uttered a noise between a squeak and a cry.

Katie heard a thud, and then the door slammed again. "Eliza?" she whispered. A hiss, like air escaping from a tire, came to her ears. "Are you all right?"

Only silence answered her.

She jerked the cord from the switchboard and broke the connection. Unease twisted her belly. She'd already dispatched the constable to the lighthouse. But what if Eliza was in trouble? Her fingers trembled so much she had trouble slipping the jack back into the switchboard. She muffled her mouthpiece with her hand and asked Nell to come back early. She had to make sure Eliza was all right.

Two

Will watched the physician minister to the two men on the parlor floor. "Will they live?"

The doctor nodded. "The bullets missed anything vital, but they lost a lot of blood. This fellow has a concussion." He indicated the younger man, who was still unconscious. "He nearly drowned, but I think he'll be all right."

The older man groaned and rolled over before vomiting seawater onto the carpet. Will rushed for a cloth and mopped up the mess. *Poor fellow.* He glanced out the window and saw the constable walking toward the lighthouse. "Excuse me a moment, Doctor."

The lawman was on the porch by the time Will exited the house. "Find anything?" Will asked.

Constable Brown shook his head. "No sign of the pirates. Before I came out I called the towns up and down the coast and told them to be on the lookout for the ship. So far, five bodies have washed ashore here. Terrible thing." He nodded toward the door. "Are these men able to answer questions?"

Will shook his head. "They're still barely conscious."

"I'll check in on them at the hospital tomorrow. Now tell me exactly what you saw."

Will relayed his first sight of the pursuing pirates and the actions he'd taken. "It sailed off to the north," he said.

"There's been no piracy in these waters for years. Odd. They were too far away to identify any of them?"

"Much too far."

"Pity." The constable turned to go back to his buggy. "Let me know if you remember anything else."

"Of course." Will watched him whip his horse into a trot, then noticed a figure walking along the water. He was almost upon the lighthouse. Was that Philip? The man waved and Will waved back then strode down to greet his brother.

They met at the base of the cliff to the beach. Will enveloped him in a hug and pulled back when he smelled whiskey on his breath. He quickly hid his dismay. "You're the last man I expected to see today. What are you doing here?"

"Can't I just show up to make sure my big brother is settling well into his new job?" Philip asked, returning the hug, but Will could feel him peering over his shoulder, trying to get a look inside. He was a younger version of Will, right down to the dark curls and even deeper brown eyes, but his build was like their father's while Will was taller and leaner.

Will studied him. His brown tweed suit must have come from Macy's. His raven hair fell over his forehead from under his hat. When had he turned into such a dandy? Will had tried to raise him right, but the lad's course was far from the one Will would have chosen for him. Becoming a private eye. Their father would roll over in his grave.

Philip started for the lighthouse. "I'm famished. Anything to eat in this place?"

Will pressed his lips together, and his arms dropped to his side. He fell into step with his brother. "I have a pot of soup on. It should be ready." He knew better than to ask again why Philip was here. The man never revealed anything until he was ready.

Philip's expression turned sulky, and he stared up at the lighthouse. "When you said you were taking this post, I thought you quite crazy. Now I'm sure of it. There's nothing out here."

"I like it that way."

Philip rolled his eyes. "You'll never make a decent living doing this. Join me in my business. You're observant and astute. You'd be an asset."

"No thanks. I'll be able to study the weather without distraction."

Two horses pulling the ambulance stopped in the road by the lighthouse. Philip stared as two orderlies ran toward the lighthouse. "You rescued the injured sailors?"

Will stopped and turned toward his brother. "You know about this already?"

Philip shrugged. "There was another boat taken about a month ago just north of here. The owner retained me two days ago. He received a tip from a woman here that another ship was in jeopardy. I was heading this way, but see I was too late. Did you watch it happen?"

Trust Philip to be in the right place at the right time. Will finally nodded. "Yes, but I've already told the constable all I know."

Philip's smile was ingratiating. "So, tell your brother too. Recognize anyone?"

"No. They were too far away. I managed to rescue two sailors they threw overboard, but that was all." He stopped as the orderlies came out with a stretcher. They slid the injured man into the back of the ambulance, then went back for the other one.

Philip started toward the ambulance, and Will grabbed his arm. "Where do you think you're going?"

"To question the witness."

Will restrained him. "You will not. Both those men are too befuddled to talk to you anyway. Let them be."

Philip tried to shake off Will's arm, but Will held fast. "You will not take advantage of my position."

"This has nothing to do with you," Philip said, raising his voice. His face reddened. "I'm just doing my job."

Will continued to block his brother. "You can do it tomorrow."

The orderlies appeared with the other man, and Will restrained Philip until the ambulance clattered away with the doctor's buggy trailing behind. "Come inside and eat."

"I want you to take me seriously," Philip said, his voice rising nearly to a shout. "This is my chance to launch my career in the right way. When I get enough money, I can buy my own boat, have a nice house."

"Philip, you have better talents than to spend your life this way. Digging into the lives of criminals. Consorting with unsavory people. It's time to grow up. You're twenty-two. There's still time to go back to school. Papa wanted more for you than this."

Philip waved his hand. "He wanted me to be an engineer. There's not enough money in that. This is the way to make something of myself. You're doing what you want. Why shouldn't I?" He cast a sly glance Will's way. "I suspect the idea of some solitude to study the coastal weather played a part in your decision to put in for this job."

There was no getting through to his brother. Will shrugged. "I might manage to put a balloon or two into the atmosphere in my spare time."

Philip turned to look at the whitecaps rolling in on the tops of the blue waves. "Pretty place to do it."

Will nodded toward the lighthouse. "You want to see inside?"

"What's to see? It's just a lighthouse."

Will bit his tongue. Philip reluctantly followed him to the sentinel on the cliff. The sound of the waves was a soothing murmur. Seagulls cawed overhead and dived toward the flotsam of seaweed the white foam left behind on the sand. In a few hours he would attempt to light the lens and get that foghorn going.

"I don't know anything about maintaining a lighthouse," Will said. He gestured to a wooden bench at the cliff's edge. "I've arranged for a day's instruction though. He'll be here tomorrow."

"I still can't believe you put in for this. What's even more miraculous is that you got it with no experience."

Will sat on the bench. "The man who interviewed me was intrigued with what I knew about weather and tides. I believe he thought the knowledge might help me here."

Philip joined him on the bench. "Indeed. So, Will, what did you see?"

He wouldn't rest until he heard Will's story. Might as well tell him now. Will pointed to the right of their position, out past a point that jutted into the bay. "The ship was taken right out there."

"It was for the gold onboard," Philip said.

Will glanced at him. "How much was it worth?"

"Two hundred thousand dollars."

He whistled. "It would be heavy then. They'd need buckboards to transport it when they're ready to take it off the ship."

Philip nodded. "Or a team of pack animals. So someone here probably had the conveyances ready and waiting to off-load it. Is there any way to a main road without going through town?"

Will shrugged. "I just got here myself. I have no idea of the lay of the land yet." He glanced at his brother. "What of this female informant?"

Philip hesitated. "I don't think she'll talk to me. I hoped you might speak with her."

Will frowned. "I don't understand. You *know* her personally?"

His brother turned his face toward the sea. "I've met her."

Will struggled to keep the exasperation from his voice. "When? How?"

His brother hunched his shoulders but didn't turn to face him. "We had a fling for a while, okay? It's none of your business."

Will's fingers curled into his palms, and he struggled to keep his voice even. "You're forcing me to make it my business." The lad was never going to grow up. And why should he when Will was always there?

Philip turned a pleading gaze on Will. "You surely want to see those butchers brought to justice."

Will's protest died on his lips. He *did* want to catch the barbarians who had done this. "What do you want me to do?"

"Just go see a woman by the name of Eliza Bulmer. Tell her you're investigating the taking of the ship and heard she might know something of it. See what she tells you. Ask her what she knows of Albert Russell. She mentioned the man's involvement."

"Very well. But that's as far as I'm prepared to go. I need to focus on learning how to run this lighthouse."

"Good luck, Will," Philip said, rising from the bench. His gaze was already on the boat down at the wharf. "Call me in a day or two and let me know how it's going."

"You're leaving?"

"I have some other avenues to investigate. I'll be in touch."

Will watched his brother jog down the hill then over to the beach. He stood there until Philip reached the distant quay and mingled with other figures. He turned and stared at the lighthouse, then back at his bicycle.

He'd ride to town and find this Eliza Bulmer.

THREE

BY THE TIME Nell arrived, it was already nearly time for Katie to get off work. Maybe she'd overreacted to what she'd heard. Eliza might have left the house—that's why there had been only silence on the telephone. Katie turned over her headset and exited the building into the last of the day's rays. Addie North was waiting outside for her. The two had been best friends since Addie moved to town a year ago. That friendship had continued even after Addie married John North. They had fallen in love when Addie took a post as governess to his son Edward.

"Something has happened," Katie told her. "Do you mind delaying our dinner for a few minutes?"

Addie's gleaming auburn hair was on her shoulders, though she wore a chapeau. Her green eyes glowed with enthusiasm. "I'm at your disposal for the evening. Is something wrong?"

As she strapped on her skates, Katie told her friend what she had overheard. "I'm sure she's fine, but I want to check on her to ease my mind."

Addie skated alongside Katie. "I would call John to accompany us, but he's outside with Edward. Since we leave tomorrow, he wanted to tire the boy so he's not a whirling dervish onboard the ship."

"I simply want to check on Eliza." She glanced up at her friend. "How is your mother?"

"Driving everyone crazy. Even a badly sprained arm isn't enough to keep her from wanting to putter in the garden."

"Perhaps I can stop in and keep her company for tea one day this week."

"She'd like that."

Out on the sidewalk, Katie paused to let pass the seamstresses hurrying home from the garment factory across the street. Church bells pealed out the time. The scent of bread wafted from the open door of the bakery. "I'm quite sure I'm overreacting." She smiled. "We'll check on Eliza, then go to dinner."

The quickest way to Eliza's house would be down the alley behind the drugstore and over to Ocean Boulevard. When the way cleared, they skated across the street. Lifting her skirts free of the mud puddles from the afternoon rain, she skated down the alley to exit on Redwood Boulevard with Addie on her heels. The houses here were more modest than Katie's home by the sea. Most were single story and the paint was peeling away from the corbels and gingerbread. Two women eyed them as they moved toward the Bulmer house. The kohl on the women's eyes and the smears of red on their lips proclaimed their occupation.

Katie slowed, admitting to herself why she normally avoided this part of town. No one, not even her best friend, knew this part of her history . . . but that wasn't why she was here. She was here to check on Eliza. *Eliza*, she said firmly to herself.

But as they skated on rough brick sidewalks toward Eliza's, Katie slowed. The house was on the corner, the last one before Cannery Row. The modest five-room home with only a covered stoop out front turned its curtained windows as a blank face toward the street. It was in better shape than most.

Katie eyed the seemingly empty building. No shadow of the woman who bore her lingered in the house next to Eliza's. If she walked inside, she wouldn't smell lily of the valley or catch a glimpse of her skirt swishing around the corner. Wherever Florence Muller had landed, she'd never be back here again.

Addie's breath came fast as she kneeled to remove her skates. "What's wrong?" She glanced from Katie to the house.

"Just assessing what to do." Despite her brave words, Katie's limbs still refused to carry her across the street. Florence had been gone from this place for many years. She drew in a breath. "Let's go." She walked briskly to the front door and rang the bell. The bell rang inside, but she heard no steps coming to the door.

"See if it's locked," Addie suggested.

Katie tried the knob, but the door wouldn't open. "Locked." She listened and thought she heard a faint cry from inside. "Did you hear something?"

Addie shook her head. "You're still concerned, aren't you?"

"I think we need to make sure Eliza's all right. Let's get the constable."

"We could call from a neighbor's," Addie suggested. She pointed to the house next door.

Florence's old house. "Not there," Katie said, turning the other direction. She hurried to the dilapidated house around the corner. There was no doorbell, so she rapped on the peeling paint of the door. When a man with a grizzled chin opened the door, she drew back.

"Whatcha want?" he demanded.

"Could you place a call to the constable and ask him to meet Katie Russell next door?" She pointed to the Bulmer residence.

"What's Eliza done now?" the man asked.

"I'm concerned for her safety," Katie said.

He shrugged. "She always lands on her feet."

"If you'd be so kind," Katie said. "Tell the constable we'll await his appearance at Eliza's front door."

"I don't have a telephone." He shut the door in her face.

"Let's go back," she told Addie. They traipsed back to the Bulmer house. Katie tried ringing the bell again and got the same response of silence.

"Maybe she had to go out," Addie said.

"Maybe."

"But you won't be content until you know for sure," Addie went on with a smile. "That's so like you, Katie. Always trying to fix things."

Katie smiled. "It's a curse." She knocked again. Nothing. She sighed. "Let's get the constable."

With the skates dangling from their hands, the women walked along the street back toward downtown. The constable was in his office, but he wore a harried expression. A strong odor of smoke filled the room. Constable Brown was a slender man. He wore a badge on the lapel of his tan suit.

He nodded at the women. "Miss Katie, Mrs. Addie. What brings you here at the dinner hour?"

Katie told him about the call she'd overheard. His brown eyes sharpened as he listened. "I tried ringing the bell but no one came to the door. I—I thought I heard something from inside. A cry."

Brown rose and reached for his bowler. "We'll check it out." He opened the door for the women, and they went to his buggy.

There was just barely room for the three of them. Though Katie prayed Eliza was all right, she realized she would look very foolish if the constable broke in and nothing was wrong. But what if she *was* right?

The buggy stopped in front of the Bulmer house. A bicycle leaned against the side of the house, and the door stood ajar.

"I thought you said the door was locked," the constable said.

"It was." Katie scrambled down from the buggy without waiting for the constable's assistance. She rushed toward the door, but he called her back.

"I will go first, if you please, Miss Katie." He strode past her and entered the house with the women on his heels. He tucked his nightstick under his arm and doffed his hat.

Katie peeked past his shoulder as they stepped into the entry. The stench of mothballs hung in the air. Maybe Eliza had been packing away clothing. She said she was trying on a wedding gown . . . Pausing, she listened. She and Addie exchanged a glance. A faint sound came to her ears. *There.* "Down the hall," she said. Lifting her skirts from the scarred floors, she darted past the constable. The pocket door to the parlor stood open by two feet. She peeked inside.

A man stood with his back to them, looking down at a baby girl lying on the sofa. Katie guessed the child to be about a year old. Brown locks curled around her pudgy cheeks. She was just waking up and was making the nonsense sounds Katie had heard.

The little girl sat up. "Ma-ma?" she asked, glancing around the room. The child didn't seem to be afraid of the man. Katie tore her gaze from the child and realized there was no sign of Eliza. There was also no phone in this room, so the scuffle she overheard did not happen here.

She backed out of the room and held her finger to her mouth. The constable scowled, then shrugged and said nothing to the man. She motioned to the constable and Addie, and they stepped past the open parlor door and across the hall. The hinges creaked as she pushed another door open and stepped into the kitchen.

She spied the telephone on the wall. "The scuffle had to have occurred here," she whispered. Addie nodded. Katie saw only a wood-burning cookstove and a dry sink filled with dirty dishes.

"Why did you not wish me to confront the man?" the constable asked, crossing his arms over his chest.

"I wanted to see if Eliza was all right before you questioned him," she said. "I saw there was no phone in the parlor. She was in this room when I spoke with her last." She stepped deeper into the room. It was empty. No Eliza, no body. A chair lay on its side though, an ominous witness to the struggle she'd overheard. "Eliza?" she whispered. "Are you here?"

"I shall check out back then speak with the man in the parlor." The constable brushed past her to the back door. He opened it and stepped onto the stoop. Katie heard a sound behind her and whirled to see the man standing in the doorway with the baby in his arms. A spreading stain on his shirtsleeve and the stench of urine told her the condition of the diaper resting on his forearm.

The baby rubbed her dark eyes and whined. "Dada," she said.

Katie stared at the man. He had dark eyes. Maybe he was this child's father. "Who are you?" she demanded.

He stepped closer. "I came in when you didn't answer the door. Your child needs attention." He clutched the baby around the waist and held her out to Katie.

She eyed him with suspicion. He had to know she wasn't the baby's mother. "Where's Eliza?"

His dark brows winged up. "Aren't *you* Eliza Bulmer?"

She tried to place his accent. Pennsylvania? The East Coast? She guessed his age to be early thirties. He wasn't the manner of man who normally drew her attention since she preferred blond hair and blue eyes, but she had to admit he was attractive. She was close enough to see the golden flecks in his dark eyes.

"I'm not Eliza, as you well know." She nodded to the baby. "She called you daddy."

His eyes widened. "I just found her in the parlor. I've never seen her before."

The baby clutched at him and chattered "dada, dada," as if to contradict him. He colored and frowned. Urine dripped from the diaper to the linoleum.

"Oh dear, she's quite soaked," Addie said.

"So is my shirt," he said.

Katie backed away from him. The kitchen seemed too small and close with his bulk filling it. "Give me the baby," she said, holding out her arms.

He handed over the child. "I was trying to do that, but you didn't seem to want her."

She wrinkled her nose at the strong odor. "Where are her diapers?"

He shrugged. "How would I know?"

So he was still going to lie. "I think we should fetch the constable. He's out back. Eliza seems to be missing."

"I agree. It's odd she left the child alone."

"I'll get him," Addie said. She stepped out the back door and spoke with the constable. He turned and glanced at the man standing in the kitchen then followed Addie inside.

Katie stared at the man, who returned the favor. His perusal caused her to shift from one foot to the other. "I shall seek a diaper for her while you explain your presence to the constable," she said, reaching for the baby then motioning for Addie to follow.

"I don't trust that man," Addie whispered on the way up the steps.

"Neither do I." Katie found the baby's room at the top of the steps on the right. The room smelled of stale urine. The diapers were in a battered dresser. She snatched a square cloth and a fresh gown then found the bathroom. The little girl popped her thumb in her mouth and regarded Katie with solemn dark brown eyes. As far as Katie was concerned, the eyes told the story. That and the "dada" the little girl had babbled. Katie removed the soggy clothes then washed the baby's red bottom.

"She really needs a full bath," she told Addie. Katie placed the fresh diaper under the wiggling baby then struggled with the pins.

"Here, let me help you," Addie said. She knelt beside them on the rug and managed to pin the diaper in place. It sagged a bit, but at least the little one was clean and dry once Katie slipped on the pink gown.

"I heard something," Addie said softly. "I think the men are outside."

Katie nodded and moved to the door. When she unlocked it and stepped back into the hall, she found the stranger leaning against the wall with his arms folded across his chest. She caught a glimpse of the constable's back as he disappeared into a room down the hall.

"The constable is searching the house," he told her.

She handed the baby to him. "Here's your daughter," she said.

His arms went around the child when she thrust her against his chest. "I told you she's not mine."

"And I don't believe you. Where is Eliza?"

"I just got here. I checked the other rooms but there's no one here."

Katie brushed past him and peered into the other two rooms. They were empty as he said. She found the constable in the third one. "Nothing?" she asked.

Brown shook his head. "Her belongings all seem to be here. I know Eliza. She was trying to break out of the barmaid profession so her daughter wouldn't be ashamed of her when she grew up. She'd been hired as a maid. But she'd never leave Jennie alone." He followed Katie to the hall where Addie stood with the man.

The baby whined and struggled to reach for Katie but she tried to ignore the plaintive sounds. "I think I could use a cup of tea. I'm sure the baby must be hungry."

The man's dark eyes looked her over. "Look, Miss . . ."

"Russell," she said. "Katie Russell. This is my friend, Addie North. You're new in town." He nodded. Since he wasn't offering any information, Katie glanced at the constable. The baby's wails intensified, so she finally took her. The little girl plunked her head on Katie's shoulder.

The dark-eyed man hesitated but didn't drop his gaze. "I'm Will Jesperson. I'm the new lightkeeper."

"It's been unmanned for two months," Brown told Katie. "It's about time we got a new keeper. I met Mr. Jesperson earlier. Which doesn't explain why you're here now, Mr. Jesperson."

The lightkeeper glanced away. "My brother asked me to call on Miss Bulmer."

"And you came in without an invitation?" Brown asked.

"I heard the baby crying."

Katie studied his neat vest and smart hat, tucked under his arm. Most lightkeepers she'd seen dressed more casually. His hair was a mass of closely cropped curls.

He glanced at Katie. "You mentioned tea. Perhaps we could all use a cup."

She led the way down the steps to the entry then back to the kitchen. The constable continued to ask the man questions, but she couldn't hear well enough to determine the words. Addie stepped past her and pumped water into a pan and put it on the stove. Mr. Jesperson glanced around the room then righted the toppled chair. He knew more than he was saying about Eliza's disappearance—she could see it in how he averted his eyes. She jiggled the restless baby in her arms and watched Addie wash some cups.

"I'll make some toast for the baby. I would imagine she's hungry," Addie said.

"I'll help you," Katie said. She passed the baby back to Mr. Jesperson and began to search through the cupboards. Addie had the tea and cut-up toast for the baby ready when the kettle whistled. When Katie carried the steaming cups of tea to the table, she found the tot situated on his knee.

The baby reached for the toast and stuffed a piece in her mouth.

The tea sloshed into the saucer when Katie plunked it in front of Will. "She's much too comfortable with you for you to be a stranger to her."

"I just laid eyes on her for the first time today."

"I agree with Katie," Brown said. "I would like to hear more of why your brother asked you to call on Eliza."

He dropped his gaze. "She's, ah, a friend of my brother's. He wanted me to meet her."

"I don't believe you," Katie said before Brown could answer. The constable frowned and shook his head.

"What are *you* doing here?" Jesperson asked.

She pulled out a chair and sank onto it. "Looking for Eliza." Addie sipped her tea beside her and watched with wide eyes.

"There is something more going on here. Exactly what do you suspect me of?"

"We find you with a baby you claim never to have seen and the mother is nowhere to be found. Anyone would be suspicious."

"You never answered me," he said, staring at Katie. "Why are you here? Are you a friend of Miss Bulmer's?"

She took a sip of tea to avoid answering. Her gaze fell on the telephone. "I came to check out the phone. There was a call I tried to make today that came here accidentally. I'm an operator at Central."

He sighed and rubbed his temple. "Right now, what I want most is to find out where Miss Bulmer is and give her back this baby."

Katie stared at Jesperson. He wasn't telling her the truth.

FOUR

WILL SHIFTED THE baby in his arms and studied the face of the young woman across from him. Though the brim of her wide hat shaded her face, there was no mistaking the suspicion in her eyes and in the face of her companion. The constable, too, though he hid it better than the women. One glance into the child's eyes had made him wonder if she could be his niece. Philip had admitted to a relationship with the child's mother. This was the last thing Will needed.

And what of the young operator's last name? Russell. Philip had mentioned an Albert Russell. Could there be a connection and that was why she was so interested in finding Miss Bulmer?

"Have you any notion of where we might find Miss Bulmer?" he asked. "And for what reason she might have left this child alone?"

Miss Russell picked up her cup of tea then put it back on the table without meeting his gaze. "I don't know."

There was more going on here than Miss Russell admitted.

Will glanced at the baby, who was playing with his watch chain. "Strangely enough, this child seems content to be cared for by strangers."

"Miss Eliza often leaves her in the care of neighbors or friends." The constable's voice was heavy with disapproval. He eyed Katie. "Let's go over what you overheard again."

Miss Russell clasped her hands in front of her, glanced at Will as if she was reluctant to share, and then plunged into her story. "I was on the phone with Eliza and heard what sounded like a scuffle. A man came in and they argued. The man's voice was muffled but something about it was familiar."

"Familiar?" the constable asked.

She shook her head. "I just can't place it." She looked up at him. "Eliza never came back to the phone."

So that was why she'd come. He lifted an eyebrow in her direction. To her credit, at least she flushed, aware that she'd been less than forthcoming. But as he studied Miss Russell's face, he knew she still wasn't telling them everything.

Constable Brown glanced at Will. "And you, sir? What did you see when you arrived on the premises?"

"The door was locked," Miss Russell said.

Will's neck burned. "I, ah, picked the lock."

The constable looked him over, and Will heard Miss Russell gasp. "I heard the baby crying, and when no one answered, I managed to jiggle the lock. She was soaked and hungry. And very much alone."

"Very disquieting," Brown said, frowning at him and then out the window. "I'll see if Miss Eliza has gone back to her old haunts."

"Old haunts?" Will asked.

Brown shrugged. "She plied her trade at the taverns, but in the last couple of months she had been working in a respectable job."

Will gulped and glanced at the baby, who had fallen asleep with her round cheek against his shoulder. He suspected little Jennie might be his brother's child, and this new piece of information about Eliza's morals made him suspect it all the more. "What about this baby? What will you do with her?"

"I would have taken her to the orphanage but it caught fire this afternoon," Brown said. He sighed and lifted a brow. "It's been quite a day."

Will winced. "Was anyone injured?"

Brown shook his head. "The volunteer fire department reacted very quickly and everyone escaped injury."

"Thank the Lord," Miss Russell murmured. She glanced at the baby on Will's shoulder.

"I don't know what I'm going to do about the child," the constable said. "The director of the orphanage is out of town, and we are having difficulty placing the children in temporary homes."

Those eyes. So like Philip's. This baby was likely his responsibility. His grip tightened on the child. "I'll take her," Will said at the same time as Miss Russell.

He wished he could recall the words. What was he thinking? Since he was new to town, finding a woman to care for the baby might be difficult.

Miss Russell batted a strand of hair that had come loose from its pins. "What do you know about caring for a child?" Her tone held a challenge.

The baby smelled sour again. Miss Russell was right. What did he know? Still, he wasn't a man to back away from duty. "Not much. But I can learn."

"Why would you want to care for a baby?" the constable asked.

Will let out a sigh. "She might be my niece."

The constable squinted and took in Will's face. "Your niece, you say? And might your brother have something to do with Miss Bulmer's disappearance?"

"Of course not! Philip has been in the city." Will clamped his mouth shut short of revealing his brother had been in town today. Surely Philip had nothing to do with this situation.

"I don't think a man is the right person to care for a baby girl," Miss Russell said. "I doubt you have any idea how to change a diaper."

He lifted a brow. "How hard can it be?"

"Do you know anything at all about what a baby eats? When she'll need to nap?"

"Do you?" he shot back. They glared at one another, and he realized she wasn't backing down. She was a busybody. Will had seen them before. Spinster women who had nothing else to do but interfere in other folks' business. "Why do *you* want the baby?"

Color rushed to her cheeks. "She needs a place to stay until her mother comes back. You're a stranger to all of us. For all we know, you did away with Eliza then came back for the baby."

The constable took a toothpick from his pocket and stuck it in his mouth. He fixed Will with a stare. "That so, Mr. Jesperson? I must admit you seem to show up wherever there's trouble. You saw the problem with the ship earlier, then you show up here."

"I have never met Miss Bulmer. I came to see her at the request of my brother."

"For what purpose?" Brown asked.

Will suppressed a sigh. He was going to have to tell them everything. "My brother is a private eye. He has been retained to investigate the piracies that have occurred in the past couple of months. When the owner of the *Paradox* spoke with him, he said Miss Bulmer had called with information. My brother asked me to speak with her since she might not be inclined to discuss anything with him, given their past relationship."

The constable's lips tightened. "I won't have him interfering in my investigation. I'm in charge in Mercy Falls."

"He isn't even here. He's back in the city."

"Have him stop by my office when he comes to town," Brown said.

"What about the baby?" Miss Russell asked.

Brown took another chew on his toothpick. "Sorry, Miss Katie, but he seems to have a claim to Jennie. If he's a relative, it's his right to care for her."

Her cheeks turned even redder. "But you don't even know if he's telling the truth! For all we know, he could be a kidnapper. Or worse! We found him here with Eliza gone. Surely that is disquieting, to say the least."

"If it will calm your fears, I can prove I'm the lightkeeper." Will passed the baby over to her then dug his posting duties out of his pocket. He handed the paper to the constable, who skimmed it and handed it back.

"He's got all the right credentials, Miss Katie," Brown said.

"That still doesn't prove he's her uncle!"

"Look at her, Miss Katie." The constable gestured to the baby in her arms. "Don't you see a family resemblance?" He fixed a stare on the lightkeeper. "I'm assigning temporary guardianship to you, and if your brother cares to, he can apply for permanent custody as her father if Eliza doesn't turn up."

Shaking her head, Miss Russell pressed her lips together, then her head came up and she stepped toward the door. "If there's anything I can do to help with the baby, please do let me know. Just toggle the phone for Central and ask for me."

Will watched her and her friend move toward the door with the constable on their heels. He tried to quell the rising panic. She was right. He didn't have the foggiest notion of how to care for a baby. "Wait," he said. "If you could help me figure out what to take to the lighthouse for the baby, I'd be grateful."

She stared at him a moment and then turned toward the stairs. "Let's see what we can find, shall we?"

Will followed Miss Russell's swaying skirt up the steps and prayed he hadn't just made the biggest mistake of his life.

❧

Katie found a small bag in the closet and began to pack some of the tiny gowns she found in a chifforobe. Mr. Jesperson set the baby on the floor and moved to join her. "Let me make it clear I don't trust you," she told him. "Not one bit. Who is going to care for her? You'll have duties to attend to." When he didn't answer her but continued to layer the suitcase with clothing, she wanted to throw something.

The new lightkeeper glanced at the sleeping baby on the floor. "What did you hear on the telephone that made you rush here?"

The impersonal tone in his voice reminded her of the constable's. Dispassionate, analytical. "Who is going to care for that baby?" she asked, ignoring his question. "She needs a bath. The urine will irritate her skin. And she might still be nursing. What will you feed her? She can't live on toast."

To her relief, a touch of uncertainty twisted his mouth and he abandoned his persistent questions. "Perhaps you could give me some advice. I've never cared for a baby before."

"Then why did you insist on taking responsibility?" she asked.

He lifted a brow. "You want to believe it's because I did away with Miss Bulmer, but nothing could be further from the truth, Miss Russell. My brother admitted to a relationship with the woman just this afternoon. Then I arrived here and actually saw the child. She favors my brother a great deal."

"I want to believe you," she said. "Otherwise, I don't know how I can stand back and let you take this darling child."

"I don't see how it's your choice. The constable has already made his decision."

She bristled at the finality of his tone, even though what he said was quite true. "I shall draw a bath for Jennie in the kitchen sink. You can finish the packing."

"I thought we had everything."

"I'd suggest you poke through the kitchen and see if you can discover any pap feeders or a banana bottle. That will tell us what she's been eating. If you find none, you will need to purchase some. Some pap too."

The glance he cast toward the baby held doubt. "Pap feeder? Banana bottle? What do they look like?"

She sighed. "You really are a complete neophyte at this, are you not? Take the suitcase and come along. I shall look myself." She scooped up the little one and carried her down the steps. "Hello there, sweet girl," she said, smoothing the curls back from the baby's face.

Jennie struggled and Katie put her against her shoulder. "Ma-ma?" Jennie asked.

Katie patted the baby's back. "Mama isn't here right now. We're going to have a bath. Do you like your bath?" She reached the dry sink. Addie was on the telephone with her husband, John. Katie stopped the drain and pumped water into it. "Could you bring me some hot water from the stove?" she asked Will.

Mr. Jesperson grabbed the kettle of hot water and poured it into the sink. Katie tested the temp with her hand until it had cooled enough. "That's perfect," she said. She laid Jennie on the counter and stripped the clothes from her tiny body, then plunked her into the water. The child gasped then giggled and began to splash the water. "I shall need a towel and washcloth," she said.

"I'll check the bathroom upstairs." Mr. Jesperson left the kitchen and his footsteps pounded up the stairs.

"I need to head home for a bit to calm John," Addie said. "Edward had another seizure and is calling for me."

"Oh, of course!" Katie said. Addie's stepson had epilepsy, and he was especially clingy to his new mother after a seizure. She smiled good-bye at her friend and rinsed the baby. Already, the stench of urine was fading.

When she first heard the creak behind her, she assumed Mr. Jesperson had returned with the linen items. She flicked a glance behind her and saw a man in a brown tweed suit. A handkerchief covered his face like some kind of bank robber. It took a moment for her confused brain to recognize this man was smaller than Mr. Jesperson and his suit was a different color.

"Get the kid and come with me," the man said, his voice muffled by the cloth covering most of his face. His dark eyes glittered above the red handkerchief.

Katie gasped and stepped between him and the wet baby. She seized a frying pan and whirled to face him. "Get back!" She swiped the air with the frying pan and barely missed the man's head. His hand went to his pocket, and he withdrew a gun that appeared no bigger than a toy. Before she stopped to think, she swung the skillet again and it connected with the man's wrist. The pistol dropped from his fingers and skittered across the floor. The baby jabbered something unintelligible behind her, and Katie glanced back just long enough to assure herself that the baby was still sitting in the water.

The man dived toward the gun, but she threw the skillet at him. It hit him in the head and knocked him to the linoleum. "Mr. Jesperson!" she screamed.

The attacker sprang to his feet and ran for the back door as Mr. Jesperson's footsteps pounded down the stairs. The man left the kitchen door gaping open behind him, and Jesperson skidded into the room.

He glanced toward the baby splashing in the water. "What's wrong?"

"A man," Katie gasped. "That way." She pointed to the open door. "He tried to take Jennie."

Mr. Jesperson dashed through the door. Katie turned back to hang onto the side of the sink. Her knees were wobbly, and her hands shook now that the danger was past. The gun still lay on the linoleum. She normally tended to run rather than fight, and her reaction had surprised her.

Mr. Jesperson came back inside. "He's gone." He picked up the towel and washcloth he'd dropped and laid them on the counter. "What happened? Tell me everything."

Katie recounted everything from the moment she realized the house held an intruder. "There's the gun," she said, pointing it out to him. She dipped the washcloth in the cooling water and with a trembling hand, quickly finished rinsing the baby.

He stooped and picked it up. "A Derringer."

She shuddered and rinsed the soap from Jennie's tender skin. "It's an evil little thing."

He nodded. "It might be small, but it could have killed you. Are you sure he wanted the baby? What did he say?"

"He instructed me to pick up the baby and come with him."

"He might have wanted you."

"I'm quite certain his intent was to take her, and he wanted me to come along to care for her." She lifted the dripping child from the water. Jennie howled until Katie wrapped her in the towel. As she turned around, she spied a pap feeder. A nice one in blue and white. "That's what we were looking for," she said, pointing to it.

"Looks like a gravy bowl," he said.

"It's not." When the baby saw him pick it up, she began to cry and point to it. "I think she's still hungry. Check the cupboard and see if there is any pap formula."

"I have no idea what I'm looking for," he said, pushing aside the blue and white gingham over the shelves.

"Look for Nestlé. That would be the most likely formula," she said.

"I see nothing like that."

"Is there milk in the icebox? I can make it with flour and milk." She began to dress the baby in a white gown.

He peered into the icebox. "Yes, there's milk." He took it out and sniffed it. "Smells okay."

"Here, you take her." She thrust the baby into his arms then took the milk and measured out a pint into a pan. She added a pint of water and a tablespoon of flour and put it on the stove. When the bubbles began to roll, she stirred it and put it in the pap feeder. "I'll feed her as soon as it cools." She nodded toward the high chair by the table. "Make sure you take that with you."

Jennie continued to wail and reach for her, so she took the baby from Mr. Jesperson's awkward grip and tried to soothe her, but the baby refused to be consoled.

Her cries—the cries of a little girl, lost and abandoned—twisted Katie's heart, bringing forth memories she wasn't quite ready to face.

FIVE

THE WIND RUSHED past Katie's ears as she skated home in the twilight. She quite disliked being forced to leave little Jennie in the care of the lightkeeper, but Bart would be waiting for her by the time she got home. She crested Mercy Hill, and then her skates rolled faster down the slope toward the house. The sea foam hurtled toward the shore on the crest of the waves, dark blue in the dim light. The salty scent lifted her mood. She loved living by the ocean.

Gaslight glimmered through the windows and she smelled the pot roast their cook had put in the oven this morning. Katie sat on the bottom step, removed her skates, and then hurried to the front door. The first thing she noticed when she stepped inside the house was the scent of liquor. A pool of liquid ran between broken pieces of glass on the floor. Someone had dropped a bottle of whiskey. Or thrown it.

She dropped her skates in the corner by the bench. "Mama?" she called, her voice quivering. Something was very wrong. Her mother would never allow a liquid to mar her redwood floors. She rushed down the hall to the parlor and found her father bending over her mother, who reclined on the davenport. Bart, a grave expression on his face, stood off to one side with his hands behind his back.

"Mama?" Aware of the accusation in the glare she tossed at her father, she lowered her eyes. He adored Mama. He would never hurt her. "What's happened?"

Her father lifted a brow. "Don't raise your voice, Katie. You'll hurt her head. Someone struck her with a whiskey bottle."

She stepped to her mother's side. Her mother attempted a smile, then a moan issued from her mouth. Katie laid her hand on her mother's forehead. "Did you call the doctor?" she asked her father.

"I did," Bart said, stepping toward her. "He's already come and gone."

She didn't want Bart here. This was a family matter. When he tried to grasp her hand, she stepped away. "What did he say?"

"The doctor assured me Inez will be fine," her father said, his voice trembling. "It appears worse than it is." He stepped back so Katie could kneel at her mother's side.

The maid hurried in with a wet cloth. Katie took it and pressed it to the lump on her mother's forehead. "Who attacked her? A thief?"

Bart cleared his throat. "I came up the porch steps with your father as a man rushed out the door. He had a kerchief around his face and I didn't recognize him. Of course, I hurried inside to check on you and your mother."

Her father nodded. "I found your mother lying on the entry floor with the maid caterwauling over her."

A kerchief. Katie started to ask the color then shut her mouth. How silly to think it might be the same man who attacked her at Eliza's. Her father's voice shook as he went on, and Katie realized he was more upset than he was letting on. Whatever his faults when he was drinking, she knew he loved her mother.

She lifted the cloth from her mother's forehead. "The bleeding has stopped." The doorbell rang.

"That must be the constable. I called him." Her father strode out of the room. His voice floated back as he greeted the lawman at the door.

"Is there anything I can do, Katie?" Bart asked, his voice like velvet.

She shook her head. "You've done so much already."

"I've been waiting nearly forty-five minutes." His voice held reproach.

"I'm sorry. I was held up."

"I wanted to talk to you—"

She shook her head. "I can't think of anything but Mama right now. Please, go on home. We'll discuss this all another day."

He frowned and his eyes searched her face. "Very well," he said stiffly. "It's clear that you'd rather be alone. I'll leave you."

She reached toward him as he stalked toward the hall, then dropped her hand. Her emotions were in too much turmoil to deal with him now.

Her father led Constable Brown into the parlor, glancing back at Bart and then to Katie in dismay.

Katie ignored him and moved away from the davenport to allow the constable to kneel with her mother. She stood by her father with her hands clasped in front of her. Questions hovered on her tongue, but she couldn't ask them if there was a chance her mother would overhear.

"Well now, Mrs. Russell," the constable said. "What's happened here?"

He glanced at Katie. She shook her head, and he said nothing about having seen her earlier.

Katie's mother struggled to sit up then gave up the effort and lay back against the pillow. "Where's Katie?" she asked.

Katie moved back into her mother's line of vision. "I'm right here, Mama."

Fear lurked in her mother's eyes. "Don't go anywhere, darling. That man was looking for you."

Katie put her hand to her throat. "For me?" She shouldn't have ignored her misgivings earlier, but she hadn't wanted to worry her parents. The constable's eyes sharpened. She would have to tell him about the man as soon as possible. It was possibly the same intruder.

Her mother pressed her hand to her forehead and winced. "I heard something in your room and called out, thinking it was you. When you didn't answer, I went to investigate and found that man exiting your bedroom. He ran down the steps when he saw me, and I foolishly chased after him."

Katie's father shook his head. "Very foolhardy, my dear."

"I realize that, Albert," she said, her voice soft. "I didn't stop to think. I caught at his sleeve when we reached the front door. He grabbed the whiskey that had just been delivered and struck me in the head with it. That's all I remember until I found myself lying here. I assume you put me here, my dear?"

Her husband nodded. "You were frightfully pale and had blood all over your face. I feared you were dead." His voice broke.

Katie's mother patted his hand. "I'm fine. You mustn't fret."

"So you have no idea who this man was?" the constable asked.

"Not at all. He wore a brown tweed suit, and his face was hidden with a handkerchief."

Katie gasped and put her hand to her mouth. "It *is* the same man."

Brown looked at her. "Does that mean something to you?"

She nodded. "After you left, a man came in the back door and tried to make me and the baby go with him. He was dressed that way too. Mama, what time was this?"

Her mother raised up. "About an hour ago. What baby, Katie? You're not making any sense."

"Eliza Bulmer's baby." She saw her father jerk and his eyes widen. "Eliza is missing, and the baby was alone in the house."

"How did you happen to find the child?" her father asked. He picked at a piece of lint on his trousers.

There was no easy answer to that question. Not with her mother and the constable listening. "I think I'll fix some tea. Would you care for some, Constable?"

"No, thank you. My wife is keeping supper warm for me, so I'd best hurry home. But Miss Katie, why would someone be looking for you? What have you stuck your nose into now?"

"Perhaps he dislikes telephone operators," she said, forcing a smile. "Eliza is missing, Constable. Maybe she's reluctant to help them and they came back for the baby to . . . encourage her."

Brown pursed his lips. "The argument you overheard. Perhaps it was the same man, and he wants to know what you heard."

"I heard nothing that would tell me who he was."

"He might not know that," the constable said. "I have a man combing the waterfront for Eliza. Until we sort this out, please, Miss Russell, stay in public places, will you? I don't like how reckless this man has already been, trying to get to you." The constable clapped his bowler back onto his head and headed for the door.

Katie left the room before anyone could ask more questions. Even pouring hot water into the teakettle didn't settle her shaking hands. So the man was looking for *her*, not the baby. What could that mean? Her hands shook as she filled the tea caddy with loose tea. She poured hot water from the teakettle on the stove into the teapot then retrieved the cups from the cupboard. Her stomach growled and she felt a little sick. Perhaps a tea biscuit would settle her nerves.

"Katie?" Her father stood in the doorway with his tie askew and his vest unbuttoned. "Do you know more than what you told the constable?"

She turned back to the tea and poured it into her cup. "Do you want tea, Papa?"

He blew out a sigh. "Yes, please." She put sugar in his tea then handed it to him. His gaze probed her face. "Are you ready to tell me?"

She nodded. "I was on the phone with Eliza. A problem with the lines caused her phone to ring when I was calling another customer. She let the phone dangle, and I heard her speaking with a man."

"What man?" his voice trembled.

Something about his voice . . . She stopped and replayed in her head the conversation she'd heard. That's why the man sounded familiar. He sounded like her father. But it couldn't have been. Her father would never betray Mama.

"Katie, you're beginning to alarm me."

She lifted her eyes to his. "It sounded like you, Papa," she said. "Eliza told the man she needed money from him to raise the baby or she would go to his wife and daughter." She licked dry lips. "Is little Jennie your child?"

Tea sloshed over the edge of the cup and into the saucer as he put the cup on the counter. "This is not an appropriate subject to discuss with you, Katherine."

His use of her full name betrayed his agitation even more than his shaking hands. "I have to know, Papa," she whispered. "Another man took Jennie with him because he wondered if the child might be his brother's."

"What man?"

"The new lightkeeper. Will Jesperson."

"I don't know him."

"He arrived in town today."

He stroked his mustache. "He took the child?"

She nodded. "But if this baby belongs to you, we must tell Mama. She will want to do the right thing and bring her here."

He sighed. "Eliza Bulmer is a–a woman of loose morals."

It was true. All of it. She couldn't bear to think of it, but she had to know. "She told you Jennie was your child?"

"I'm not going to discuss it with you, Katie. It's most inappropriate."

She steeled her emotions against his stubborn gaze. "Because you don't want to admit what you've done to Mama? Or because you doubt Eliza's veracity?"

His brows drew together. "This doesn't involve you."

"I've been dragged into it, whether you like it or not. And what about Jennie?"

"If an upstanding man is willing to take responsibility for her parentage, I fail to see why you persist in sticking your nose into this affair. Leave it be." He set down his cup with a rattle and turned to walk out.

"Did you kill Eliza?" she blurted out then put her hand to her mouth.

He stopped and turned to face her. "Is that what you think?" His eyes were hurt. "You know me much too well to jump to such a conclusion. At least I hope you do."

Looking into his familiar face, she couldn't believe she'd actually harbored the notion her father could be a killer. She closed her eyes, thinking back. "I heard you leave. But then the door opened again. There was a frightful thump—what I assume was Eliza, hitting the floor."

Katie opened her eyes again. His face was white, and she knew that he had been there. "Did you tell this to the constable?" he asked.

She nodded. "But not about your voice. I didn't place it until a few moments ago."

"I did not go back," he said, his voice firm. "You must believe me, Katie. I couldn't bear it if you thought I might do something like that. There is no reason to implicate me in this. Please, Katie."

She gave a reluctant nod. "All right, Papa."

Six

THE CHILD'S SOLEMN gaze never left Will's face. He'd already unloaded the buckboard, and he studied the baby sitting on the rug in front of the fireplace. The clock on the mantle chimed eight times, and twilight was giving into night. He'd need to wind the light soon. Philip had better arrive by then to take charge of this little girl.

"A-a, eh-ooh?" she asked. Her index finger pointed for emphasis.

Her expression indicated she was quite sure he knew exactly what she was saying. "Er, I see," he said, feeling like a fool. Was he supposed to understand the string of vowels? "Are you hungry?"

Her small fingers seized the edge of the chair beside her, and she pulled herself up until she stood beside the chair. She sidled around the cushion toward the end table that would support her weight. She glanced at him as if to ask if she was permitted to touch it.

"I think we'd better move you." He lifted her away from the chair and she squawked until he deposited her next to the davenport. Her eyes brightened, and she began to walk the length of it. What did he give a child to play with? And what had he been thinking to take responsibility for her? He'd thought he would insist Philip take charge and grow up, but he had no guarantees his brother would own up to his part in this child's life.

Carriage wheels crunched on gravel outside. Will scooped up Jennie and carried her to the front door in time to see his brother step onto the porch. He carried a glossy black bird on his arm.

"What the devil do you have?" Will demanded, eyeing the bird's yellow wattles.

"A present for you. His name is Paco. He's a mynah."

"I don't need a bird."

"Well, I have no place to put it." Philip eased the bird from his arm onto a nearby table. "And I understand he's quite valuable."

"You've been playing cards again, haven't you?" Will said.

Philip rolled his eyes and shrugged off his coat, hanging it on a peg by the door.

"I thought you intended to pursue this job like a man, Philip. You promised me."

"I am pursuing my job," Philip said, shooting him an aggravated look. "Sometimes that means I must pursue clues where my informants are most likely to be, regardless of whether or not you approve of it."

The mynah screeched and Philip dumped a handful of seeds from his pocket onto the table. The creature picked up one and cracked it. "Step away from the cake!" it screeched.

Will was in no mood for another responsibility. He glared at the bird.

Philip glanced from Will to the baby in his arms, seeming to see her for the very first time. A frown gathered his brows. "Who is *that*?" he asked. The baby wrapped her arm around Will's neck. "Your daughter," Will said, staring hard at him.

Philip took a step back. "I have no inclination to decipher your ramblings, Will. What are you talking about?"

Perhaps he'd been too abrupt. "When did you last see Eliza Bulmer?"

His brother straightened then brushed past Will into the foyer. "Do you have any coffee?"

"In the kitchen." Will followed him down the hall to the kitchen and watched as his brother poured a cup of coffee from the pot simmering on the wood range. "Are you going to answer my question?" The baby squirmed in his arms and he set her down on the rug by the back door. She began to clang together the pot lids he handed her.

"Why this sudden interest in Eliza?"

Will clenched his fists. "Examine this child's eyes and nose and guess what I'm thinking."

Philip set his cup on the table and stared down at the baby. "That child isn't mine—if that's the conclusion you've jumped to."

"Oh no? When did you have this relationship with Eliza?"

James shifted uneasily. "A couple of years ago, I guess. Maybe a little less." His gaze stayed on Jennie. "Lots of people have brown eyes."

Will swept his hand toward the little girl. "Look at the way her hair grows at her hairline. And that cowlick. I believe she's your daughter. Did Eliza ever tell you she was pregnant?"

"I haven't talked to her," Philip said, his tone sullen.

"When did you last speak with her?"

"I received a letter a year ago asking me to call on her, that she had something of importance to tell me."

"Jennie is about a year old."

Philip held his hands out in front of him. "That is very flimsy evidence to try to prove this child is mine, Will. I don't believe it. Why wouldn't she ask for money when she discovered she was pregnant?"

"Maybe she was waiting for you to show up so she could discuss it in person."

"Why don't you just ask Eliza? How did you get this child anyway?"

Will studied his brother's expression. No trace of guilt darkened his eyes or tugged at his mouth. If something had befallen Eliza, Will didn't think Philip was involved. "She's missing. I found the baby alone in the parlor when I stopped by to speak to Miss Bulmer."

"She left a child of this age alone?"

"A chair was overturned in the kitchen. I fear foul play."

Philip picked up his cup and took a sip. "And you thought I had something to do with that? For what purpose?"

"I don't suspect you of harming Miss Bulmer, but I do believe you need to be a man and take responsibility for your child."

"You are not going to foist this baby on me without proof I'm her father!"

Jennie's face crumpled. She dropped the pan lids and began to wail. Will lifted her from the rug and put her against his shoulder. "There, there." He patted her back awkwardly.

The baby wailed louder, and he smelled a distinctly unpleasant aroma wafting from the direction of the diaper that hung heavily from her bottom. "I think you'd better change her, Philip."

"Me? You brought her here. I have no idea how to change a baby and no desire to learn."

Will shifted the squalling child to the other arm. "Do you seriously expect me to believe you don't see the resemblance between this child and yourself?"

Philip thrust out his chin. "She's not mine."

"You don't think she could possibly be yours? That you didn't have relations with the woman?"

Philip's gaze wandered off. "I fail to see how this is any of your business, Will."

"Grow up, Philip. Be a man and take responsibility!" He tried to hand the baby to his brother, but Jennie clung to him and wailed all the more.

"You brought her here. She's your responsibility. Maybe her mother will turn up tomorrow." Philip wheeled and stalked out of the kitchen.

The front door banged a few moments later, and Will stared into the red face of the little girl. His shirtsleeve was soaked in a most unpleasant manner, and the stench from the diaper filled the kitchen. He would have to do this by himself. Cursing himself for failing to consider his brother's temperament, he rushed to the case of baby paraphernalia Miss Russell had packed and extracted a diaper. Holding the baby at arm's length, he went back to the kitchen and found a cloth, which he dampened with warm water from the teakettle sitting on the stove. He laid her on the counter and undid the pins. Flinching at the odor of feces, he cautiously peered inside the soggy scrap of cloth.

And cringed at the mess inside.

How did one go about cleaning up a child when she kept trying to roll over? Keeping one hand on the baby, he rolled up his sleeves and set to work. Fifteen minutes later Jennie was gurgling her nonsense words happily while he was drenched in perspiration and covered with flecks of dark matter he didn't want to think about further.

He had no idea how he was going to survive the contretemps he'd gotten himself into.

❦

The light flashed on the switchboard. Katie's eyes still felt gritty from lack of sleep. Nell would be here by six o'clock and she could go home. She'd hated to leave her mother this morning, but Papa had arranged for another clerk to come in to man the store. He would watch over Mama himself. Katie had called the constable the moment she got to her switchboard, but there had been no sign of Eliza and no clue to the identity of their attacker.

A light flashed on the board. She plugged in the toggle. "Operator."

"Katie Russell?"

The voice echoed strangely in her ear, and Katie glanced at the switchboard to see the location. The skating rink. "This is Katie Russell."

"What did you hear yesterday, Miss Russell?"

Her tongue dried. "Who is this?" She vaguely heard the door bang behind Nell as she came in and removed her hat in preparation for the evening shift.

"You'd better keep your mouth shut, miss. The boss don't take kindly to interference."

She wetted her lips. "What have you done with Eliza?"

Nell's head turned sharply, and she stepped toward Katie. "What's wrong?" she whispered.

Katie shushed her. "That baby needs her mother. Where is Eliza?"

"You don't want to go where she is. If you tell anyone what you heard, you'll join her."

"Why did you try to take Jennie?"

"That doesn't matter. Not now."

The headset clicked in her ear after the ominous words. She tore it from her head and handed it to Nell. "I have to go," she said. If she hurried, maybe whoever had called would still be at the rink.

"Katie, wait, who was that?" Nell called after her.

Katie jammed a pin through her hat and rushed out the door without answering. She didn't take time to strap on her skates but just grabbed them up and ran across the street and down to Hibiscus Street. The gaslight hissed a greeting as she reached the door to the skating rink. From inside she could hear the thump and rumble of skates on hardwood. Pushing inside the door, she glanced around for the telephone. Cigar smoke hung thick in the air. She spotted the telephone on the wall behind the counter.

She stepped to the wooden bar. "Is that the only telephone here?"

The woman behind the counter, a blonde who obviously had rouge on her cheeks, nodded. "Sorry, we don't allow anyone to use it." She popped her chewing gum.

The scent of the Tutti-Frutti gum wafted Katie's way. She'd never seen the woman before. "Did you just come on duty?"

"I've been here for two hours."

It was a man's voice she'd heard. Katie was sure of it. "Has anyone asked to make a call?"

"I told you. We don't allow no one to use it. I'd get in trouble if I let you."

Katie kept her voice low in spite of the noise from the skates. "I don't wish to use it. I want to know who used it fifteen minutes ago."

The young woman popped her gum again and her gaze shifted away. "Told you, no one."

"I'm the operator. A call came from here fifteen minutes ago. It was a man."

The woman picked up a pencil then put it down again. "No ma'am. No calls from here."

"I won't tell your boss, but I have to find out who it was. I know it was from this telephone unless there is another one in the building. Some fellow sweet-talk you into letting him make a call?"

The girl flushed. "It was a short call. There was no harm."

"Did you know him?"

The blonde shook her head. "He was quite the gent though. Dark brown hair and eyes. Tall with nice shoulders and a smile that, well, you understand."

"Of course," Katie said. It sounded like the lightkeeper. "Did you get his name?"

The woman shook her head. "I tried, but he didn't hear me when I asked."

"Is he still here?"

"No, miss. He left just before you arrived."

Katie knew many of the people skating. Perhaps one of her friends could recognize him. "Did anyone else see him behind the counter?"

"I don't think so. I was careful. I blocked him a bit. I didn't want anyone else to ask to use the telephone." The girl looked shamefaced.

"Did the man skate at all?"

The woman nodded her head vigorously. "Oh yes! I wouldn't allow just anyone to place a call."

"Is he still here?"

"Might be," the woman said with a shrug. "Didn't see him leave."

"Do you know what he was wearing?" Katie knelt and strapped on her skates.

"A brown tweed coat and white shirt. Very dapper."

"My thanks." Katie paid her money and skated out onto the floor, shoving aside her fear.

The thunder of the rolling skates was a welcome sound. She scanned the rink and the tables, but there was no tall man in a tweed suit. She rolled around the rink for a few minutes while she assessed who was here. Some were more observant than others. A woman would be most apt to have noticed a handsome man. Katie discounted most women in the rink until she saw Sally, a parlormaid at the North household. Katie lagged at the handrail circling the room until Sally drew parallel.

"Could I speak with you a moment, Sally?" she asked.

"Miss Katie, did I do something?" Sally asked.

"Of course not. I'm hoping you can help me," Katie said. The other woman's troubled face cleared, and they skated off the floor to a backless bench. Once they were seated, she nodded toward the skaters rolling around the floor. "There was a man here earlier. I wondered if you'd noticed him."

The young woman tucked a stray strand of hair back into place. "A man, miss? What did he look like?"

"Very handsome, I hear. Dark brown hair and eyes. A brown tweed coat."

"Oh, I couldn't have missed him! A real dresser, he was. Very dashing. He took me for a spin around the floor and asked me to go to his room. I gave him what for, I'll tell you that. What kind of girl does he think I am?" Sally's voice rose the longer she talked.

Katie paused. "Did you get his name?"

"No, miss."

"You say he asked you to his room. So he's not from Mercy Falls. Did he tell you where he was staying?"

"Oh yes. At the Redwood Inn."

Katie knew the proprietor. She'd have to see if he would tell her anything.

SEVEN

THE BABY SAT on a blanket with some pots and pans to bang on. The sunset cast orange bands onto the undersides of the clouds in a glorious display of God's majesty. Will watched it a few moments then went back to searching for his weather balloon.

Paco, the mynah, meowed from a perch Will had made near the door. The first time the bird had done that, he'd been sure a stray cat had wandered in. Now he was getting used to the bird's strange noises. He eyed the baby. He had to have help. His lightkeeper duties would entail working all night and sleeping during the day. The baby wouldn't sleep all night and all day too. Philip hadn't shown his face after he stormed out, and Will was certain his brother had gone back to the city. Will was too tired to be angry.

He jotted down the description of the sky in his notebook then scanned the horizon for the weather balloon. Was it still afloat? It would ascend to a high altitude, then burst and drop. He was eager to get the readings from the instruments. A flash of white caught his eye and he spotted the burst balloon over on the rocks two hundred yards down the beach. Scooping up the baby, he hurried to the location and set her down, then retrieved the balloon and his instruments. The lamp on the lighthouse would need to be lit shortly, and the night's work of tending the light would begin. He didn't know how he was going to get through it all.

Lanterns wavered along the quay down the beach. Boats were

docking or shoving off. This was a peaceful place, and he missed the city less than he'd imagined he would. Sighing, he picked up Jennie and turned to retrace his steps. When he crested the hill, he saw a shadow move in the twilight down by the road. Squinting, he realized a buggy had pulled up while he was occupied. The man, an older gentleman in his late forties or early fifties, strode toward where he stood. The fellow wore a dark three-piece suit and bowler. His attention was fixed on the glow of lamplight spilling from the front window of the lighthouse, and he hadn't noticed Will yet.

Will dropped his balloon and stepped out of the shadows. "Good evening. May I help you?"

The man jumped then collected himself. "Mr. Jesperson?"

"That's right." Will studied the fellow who hadn't taken his eyes off Jennie. "Something I can do for you?"

"Might we step inside?"

"We may, but I'd like to know who I'm speaking with first."

The man extended his hand. "Albert Russell."

Will barely choked back an exclamation. Albert Russell. The man Philip wanted him to ask Eliza about. "You're related to Miss Katie Russell?"

"My daughter."

"Come in." He led the way to the lighthouse and ushered his guest to the parlor. "Coffee? Tea?"

"Thank you, but no. I can't stay long." Mr. Russell glanced around the room, one of five inside. "Pleasant living quarters. Remote out here, but well appointed."

"Quite." Will was impatient to find out what was on the man's mind. He put a wriggling Jennie on the floor, and she toddled over to grasp at Mr. Russell's pant leg.

The man patted her head awkwardly. "Your daughter?"

"No." Will didn't elaborate. He was sure Miss Nosy Operator had filled her father in on the situation from last night. "How can I help you, sir?"

The man glanced at the baby then back to Will. "I'll be honest with you, Mr. Jesperson. I'm looking for one of my possessions that I'd left at Miss Bulmer's. It is no longer at her premises. I thought perhaps you picked it up with the belongings you brought here for the baby."

"I brought nothing but diapers and clothing." Will knew guilt when he saw it. "You had a relationship with Miss Bulmer?"

The man flushed. "That is hardly your concern."

Was this why his daughter had offered to take Jennie—because she was aware of the affair? Will glanced at the baby, who seemed quite comfortable in Mr. Russell's presence. Of course, Jennie didn't seem to fear strangers. The man's brown eyes were the same color too. But he didn't have the cowlick like Jennie's. That resemblance was to Philip instead.

It wouldn't hurt to ask though. "Is Jennie your child?"

"No, she is not," the man said, his voice rising. "Did my daughter tell you that?"

"No. How are you so certain Jennie is not your child?"

"The woman was hardly faithful to any one man. And the chit looks nothing like me." Mr. Russell waved his hand in a dismissive gesture. "I realize my eyes are brown, but hers are shaped differently. Nothing about her resembles me or Eliza, so she must look like her father."

"Dad-dad," Jennie chanted, banging on the man's knee with her small fist.

Will raised a brow. "She seems to know you."

Mr. Russell removed the child from his side and straightened. "Of course she does. However, that does not mean that I sired her."

She promptly began to wail. Will scooped her up. "So what item are you looking for?"

"It was a pocket watch. Engraved with my name on the back. My mother purchased it for me on my twenty-fifth birthday, and I'm quite loathe to part with it."

"I found nothing like that. You're sure it's not at her house?"

Mr. Russell shook his head. "I searched the house before I came out here. It's not there." He rose. "Thank you for your time. I'll be off now."

Will walked the man to the door and shut it behind him. "Now what was that all about?" he asked the baby.

⤳✦⤲

The Redwood Inn was in a part of town that had once been fashionable but now bore the marks of neglect. It was still respectable, but only just. The hotel was ornate and massive but its glory days were twenty years in the past. Time had taken its toll on the corbels and ginger-bread trim, which had lost much of their paint. Katie skated to the picket fence gate. Darkness had fallen but the glow of gaslight pushed back the shadows with a warm yellow light. She removed her skates and walked up the porch. The bell tinkled on the door when she pushed inside.

Mr. Wilson was polishing the wooden counter when she entered. "Miss Katie," he said. "What brings you here so late?" He glanced at the grandfather clock in the corner as it chimed the time, eight o'clock. He used to stop by to play pinochle with her father, and he never failed to bring her a stick of peppermint. But it had been some years since he had done that.

A high shelf circled the room. Birds and animals of every kind stared down on her. Mr. Wilson was a taxidermist as well and he took every opportunity to display his handiwork. She shuddered and averted her eyes. "I need some information, Mr. Wilson." She joined him at the counter. The registry lay right in front of her but she had trouble read-ing it upside down. Besides, she didn't know the man's name.

"What's that, Miss Katie?"

"Do you have any new guests here right now? A man, in particular. Dark hair and eyes. Youngish, maybe midtwenties. Snappy dresser."

The man bared his teeth in a grin that showed a silver-capped tooth. "You scouting for a beau, Miss Katie? I thought you and Mr. Bart were cozying up."

Heat flamed in Katie's cheeks. "Of course not, Mr. Wilson. This inquiry has nothing to do with any romantic feelings. Is the man here?"

"No ma'am, but I think I know who you mean. He picked up his things a few minutes ago and left to catch the packet to the city."

"What was his name?"

"Joe Smith." The proprietor smiled again. "A false name, I'm quite certain, but I don't pry into the business of my customers."

"Did he say why he was in town?"

"I didn't ask. That would be taken for nosiness." He gave her a pointed look.

"Thank you, Mr. Wilson. Have a good evening." She retraced her steps to the gate by the sidewalk and put her skates back on. It would be useless to go to the dock. The last packet for San Francisco would have departed by the time she could get there.

She skated slowly back toward her house. As she reached the edge of town, she stopped to adjust her right skate and saw her father's buggy turn from the road to the lighthouse. Why had he been out there? She was tempted to go find out. Pausing at the lane that led to her house, she decided she couldn't bear not knowing. She skated down the concrete road to the lighthouse. When the road turned to macadam, she removed her skates and walked the rest of the way.

She heard the foghorn before she saw the lighthouse. Her breath came fast by the time she saw the light blinking its warning. As she began the climb up the hillside to the edifice atop it, she heard the wail of the baby. "That man," she muttered. She quickened her step and reached the front door. The crying wasn't coming from inside the house but from around the other side, near the cliff. Was Mr. Jesperson harming the child? Her hands crept into fists, and she flew around the corner of the house to confront him.

Mr. Jesperson had Jennie against his chest and he was walking back and forth across the grass. The faint refrain of "The Old Rugged Cross" lifted on the wind, and Katie stopped short. He was *singing* to her? A lump formed in her throat. Maybe he wasn't such a bad sort. Her father had never sung to her, but he was kind and indulgent most of the time. She didn't know why she was allowing such dark suspicions to sway her emotions this way.

The baby's cries faded then stopped. The little girl's head stayed down on Mr. Jesperson's shoulder, but he continued to hum and pat the tiny back. Such a small baby on such a big shoulder. He was even more attractive when he was showing such tenderness to a child. Her earlier misgivings assaulted her. Could he really be the baby's father and not his brother as he'd claimed?

Before she could examine the thought further, he turned and spotted her in the moonlight. Wariness replaced his placid expression. She managed a smile. "Is she asleep?"

"Finally. Let me put her down."

He carried Jennie to the door. Katie followed him into the house, where he laid the baby in a crib in the parlor.

"There's no bedroom for her?"

He shot her a quick glance. "I'm supposed to stay in the light tower all night, but there is no way I can do that and watch her too. I moved her crib in here so I can nap on the sofa between trimming the wicks."

"You look tired," she said, observing the circles under his eyes.

"I was unable to sleep today after being up all night." He covered the baby with a blanket then patted her back when she stirred. "Why are you here?"

"I wanted to find out why my father was here."

He turned, and his brown eyes crinkled with his smile. "Just can't stand it, can you, Miss Nosy Operator?"

Heat rushed to her cheeks. "I shouldn't have come." She turned toward the door.

"At least now I know why you wanted to take charge of Jennie," he said.

She turned back to face him. His expression warned her of the meaning of his words. "He admitted his involvement with Eliza?"

"In so many words. He was looking for a pocket watch he left at her house. Did you see such an item?"

"No." She knew the watch of which he spoke.

"I assume he fears if it's found he'll be a suspect in Miss Bulmer's disappearance."

"He had nothing to do with it," she said quickly. She wished she was as convinced as she sounded. "I'm sorry to trouble you. I'll be on my way."

"I quite dislike you traveling back to town alone in the dark," he said. "Why don't you take my horse? You can bring it back tomorrow. After the attack on you in the kitchen yesterday, I'm unwilling to see you in harm's way."

She nodded. "I appreciate your thoughtfulness, Mr. Jesperson. I shall return your horse tomorrow."

"He's in the barn at the base of the hill. The saddle is in the shed. Do you need assistance?"

"No, I'm comfortable around horses."

He glanced at the baby. "I wish I could say the same about Jennie. Do you know of a reliable woman I could hire to help care for her?"

"I'll think on it," she said. "Thank you again for the loan of your horse." She was eager to get away from his probing, curious eyes. She escaped the lighthouse, saddled the horse, and galloped for town.

EIGHT

KATIE BOLTED UPRIGHT at the pounding on the front door. Her father hadn't been home when she arrived last night. He'd probably been out drinking. Or trying to cover his tracks with Eliza. After rubbing her mother's forehead with peppermint oil to help her migraine, Katie had fallen into bed after midnight. She glanced at the clock on the mantel. Only six a.m. Who could be rousing them so early?

The maid's soft voice murmured down the hall, then Constable Brown's voice echoed in the foyer. "I must speak with Mrs. Russell," he said.

Katie leaped from the bed and grabbed her dressing gown then shoved her feet into slippers. She fumbled for the doorknob and nearly fell over her kitten, Nubbins, who entangled himself around her ankles. After extricating herself from the cat, she stumbled into the hallway and rushed down the stairs to find the constable pacing the redwood floors.

"Ah, Miss Katie, I must speak with your mother."

Katie tightened the sash on her gown. "What's wrong, Constable? Mama went to bed with a migraine and I don't wish to disturb her if we can avoid it."

The constable was pale, and he had dark circles under his eyes as if he'd been up all night. "I'm afraid it can't be helped. Please call your mother."

Katie gulped at his serious expression. Was that compassion she glimpsed? "Very well. Get Mama," she told the maid.

Her mother's voice spoke from behind her. "I'm here, Katie. What is the commotion?"

"Come into the parlor, Mrs. Russell," the constable said, his voice grave.

Her mother took Katie's hand in a fierce grip. The women obeyed the constable's directive and sank onto the gray horsehair sofa at his gesture. Her mother leaned her head against the doily that covered the back of the sofa. Katie didn't let go of her hand. Whatever was coming was bad, very bad.

Brown cleared his throat. "Mrs. Russell, I regret to inform you that your husband was discovered in the pond at the base of Mercy Falls this morning at four o'clock."

She squeezed her mother's fingers. "No," Katie whispered. "Is he—dead?" Hysteria bubbled in her throat.

"No, but he's gravely ill. I had him transported to the hospital."

"Was it a–a suicide attempt?" The falls was notorious for attracting the despondent.

"It appears so."

Suicide. All the doubts crashed over her head again. It made him appear guilty of Eliza's disappearance. This was her fault. She should never have let him know she'd overheard.

Katie's mother had still not spoken. She sat motionless and without expression. "Mama?" Katie choked out.

"I believe I shall go back to bed," her mother said in a clear voice. "This migraine is quite unmanageable."

Katie fought to keep her tears at bay, to be calm for her mother. She and the constable exchanged a long look. She slipped her arm around her mother's shoulders. "Mama, did you hear what Constable Brown said? Papa tried to do away with himself."

Her mother clapped her hands to her ears. "I don't want to hear anything more from you, Katie," she said, her voice shrill. Hysteria was in the last note of Katie's name. Her mother's eyes went wild. "Your father would never do such a thing. Never! What would our friends say?"

"I think we should call the doctor," Katie mouthed to the constable.

He nodded. "In the hall or the kitchen?"

"The kitchen."

He slipped out of the room while she hugged her mother. "He'll be all right." But would he? The constable's manner had been most grave. What if her father died? Her mother would never survive the trauma. Her parents had always been so close . . . or at least that was what she'd thought until she learned of Eliza's involvement.

Her parents. Today had brought back too much of the past, before they'd taken her in. She preferred not to remember all that pain.

Brown stepped back into the room. "He's on his way."

"What happened? How was he found?"

He shrugged. "An early morning hunter discovered him half in the water and dragged him all the way out. He has a bad cut on his head."

"Will he live?"

His expression turned grimmer. "The doctor is examining him. He's unconscious. Does your father have any enemies? The break-in yesterday, Miss Eliza's disappearance, the attack on you. Might they be connected?"

She glanced at her mother. "I'd like to wait until my mother is under the doctor's care before we discuss this further."

"Of course." His keen gaze probed her face. "Do you fear his suicide attempt is connected with Miss Eliza's disappearance?"

"I–It's possible," she choked out. The doorbell rang. "That must be Dr. Lambertson. Could you get it? I don't wish to leave Mama alone."

"Certainly."

Katie's tongue was as dry as sand. Her eyes burned, and her throat convulsed with the effort to hold back the sobs building there. How much should she tell the constable? How could he find what had happened to Eliza if she wasn't honest with him? Of course, her father was not responsible for Eliza's disappearance, but if she kept anything from the constable, she wouldn't be doing the right thing. When the doctor turned to tend to her mother, she slipped down the hall and beckoned to the constable to follow her.

"Miss Katie, what are you hiding from me?" The constable's voice was gruff but kind.

She bit her lip. Her father had begged her to stay quiet, but what if he hadn't tried to kill himself? "I realized why the man's voice on the phone was so familiar," she told him. "It was my father who argued with Eliza."

He took out a cigar and struck a match. "I see," he said, drawing in a puff. "You feared I would assume your father was involved in her disappearance if you told me the truth?"

"I didn't realize it was his voice at first. I just knew it sounded familiar." She sent him a pleading glance. "Truly, Constable, I wasn't hiding it from you. I realized it after we talked."

"So you think your father came back and disposed of her?"

"No!" She wetted her lips. "I think someone else came in. In fact, what if Papa didn't try to do away with himself? What if that man attacked him?"

"What would be the motive? I suspect Miss Eliza was blackmailing him." His voice was heavy with disapproval.

"I asked my father if he was Jennie's father. He denied it and I believe him." She knew her tone lacked conviction and put more force into it. "Papa's a good man. He wouldn't hurt anyone."

"Not even when he's drinking?"

Heat raked her face. "Not even then."

"When did you see him last? Did he seem despondent?"

She hesitated. "I glimpsed him on his way back from the lighthouse last night."

"Why was he there?"

"Mr. Jesperson told me he was looking for a pocket watch he left at Eliza's. He thought perhaps Mr. Jesperson had picked it up with Jennie's things."

"Why would it matter?"

"His name was on it. I'm sure he didn't want his relationship to become common knowledge. There's something else you need to know, Constable. I received a threatening telephone call last night just before I left work."

"Did you recognize the voice?"

She shook her head. "But the call came from the skating rink. I rushed there to see if I could perhaps catch the perpetrator, but he'd left for the Redwood Inn. When I went there, I was informed he'd left town. According to Mr. Wilson, the man called himself Joe Smith. A fake name, of course."

Brown puffed on his cigar. "Miss Katie, you need to let me do the investigating here. You're going to get yourself in trouble. I told you— you need to watch yourself."

"I'm sorry, Constable. You're quite right."

He continued to study her. "So that is why you offered to take Miss Eliza's child. You suspected little Jennie was your sister."

She opened her mouth to say she didn't consciously know why she'd wanted the child, but before she got out the words, she saw a shadow move.

Her mother spoke from the doorway. "Child? What are you saying, Katie? That your father had another child?"

Katie didn't want to face her mother's accusing stare, but she forced herself to wheel and look at her mother's stricken face. "I'm not sure, Mama. We have no real way of knowing now."

"I'll leave you to deal with her for now," the constable said. "We will talk more tomorrow." His voice held a note of warning.

Her mother grabbed the door frame for support, and the doctor seized her arm to steady her. "I've administered laudanum," he said. "She needs to go to bed."

"I'll see she gets there." Katie took her mother's hand.

Her mother jerked her fingers away. "Not until you tell me what you're whispering about out here. I shall speak to your father about this. He'll be most distressed at your accusations." There was a wildness in her blue eyes, and her mouth pulled to one side.

Katie pitched her voice to a soothing tone. "Let's talk about it tomorrow. You're about to fall down."

"The laudanum will let her sleep," Dr. Lambertson said. "Let me help you get her to bed."

With Katie on one side of her mother and the doctor on the other, they managed to get her to the high bedstead before she collapsed. "Will she remember any of this when she awakens?" Katie asked.

"I hope her head is clear after resting a few hours," the doctor said. "But it's been a hard blow to her mind. I'll check in on her later in the morning. Stay with her until then."

He took his leave, and Katie arranged for the groom to take Mr. Jesperson's horse back to him. She dragged her pillow and quilt to the floor by her mother's bed. Nubbins followed Katie into the soft folds of the bedding. The kitten curled up on Katie's chest and closed his eyes, but Katie watched her mother's chest fall and rise. She prayed for a way to open out of this confusion.

⚜

The sugar failed to cover the bitterness of the tea. Katie took another sip, hoping the beverage would sharpen her mind. The grit in her eyes reminded her of the tears she'd cried most of the morning. And the reason for them. She watched the sun illuminate her sleeping mother's pale face on the pillow. If only she would awaken with the light of sanity in her eyes after sleeping for a few hours. Katie set her tea on the bedside table.

When the blue orbs focused on Katie's face, her silent prayer was answered. Her mother sat up and reached for Katie's hand. "Have you been here all along, darling? What time is it?"

Katie hung onto her mother's cold fingers. "I didn't want to leave you. It's ten. How are you feeling?"

Her mother's eyes filled. "Your father wanted to leave us, didn't he? I can't fathom it."

"We don't know that for sure, Mama. Someone broke in here and attacked you. What if that same person hurt Papa?" She'd rather believe that than that her accusations had driven her father over the edge of sanity.

Her mother clutched Katie's hand. "Don't think this is your fault, darling. I didn't want to worry you, but your father's business is in trouble. I fear that was why he jumped off the falls, regardless of what this business with Miss Bulmer might lead us to believe."

Katie shook her head. The haberdashery had always seemed indestructible, bustling with customers. They had a good life, one of comfort and respect. "You mean in danger of bankruptcy?" The very thought filled Katie with horror. The shame of it all would destroy Mama. She'd grown up with the best of everything.

Her mother twisted a lock of loose hair around her finger. "He told me two weeks ago. The bank had turned down his request for a loan on the business, and this house is mortgaged for the maximum amount."

Katie tried to absorb the dreadful meaning. "We shall have to move?"

"We may have no choice." Tears flooded her mother's eyes, and she glanced around the lavishly appointed bedroom.

Katie followed her gaze. Damask curtains hung at the windows. The fine blue rug had been imported from Persia. The bed linens were of the finest silk.

Her mother's lips trembled. "My father built this house, and I was born here. I don't know how I shall bear this."

"I–I have my job," Katie said. When her mother's face didn't change, Katie realized how ridiculous that sounded. Her meager earnings would never support this household. The servants, the upkeep. Not even with additional hours.

"We could sell the haberdashery, I suppose," her mother muttered. "Perhaps it is worth something. It is the only shop in town. Surely someone would like to own it."

"When Papa recovers, he'll know what to do." Her father always had a plan. And he *would* recover. "I shall go to the hospital and check on him this morning. Perhaps I can discuss the situation with our solicitor tomorrow," Katie said.

"The thought of it gives me a sour stomach," her mother said, leaning back against the pillow. She focused her gaze on Katie. "Bart Foster is still pressing his suit, is he not?"

Katie heard the hope in her mother's voice and could see where this was going. "Yes, he is. I . . . but I don't know him well yet, Mama. I have not thought of marriage."

Spots of color came to her mother's face, and her grip tightened. "I've groomed you for a respectable marriage, my dear. You're twenty-five, past time for marriage. You have no better prospects."

Katie nodded, but acid burned the back of her throat. Bart was handsome enough, but her pulse didn't flutter when he took her hand or paid her a compliment. But did that matter when she'd always been expected to make a suitable alliance? She couldn't bear to see her parents spending the rest of their days in a hot flat over the garment factory. Not if it was within Katie's power to attend to the matter.

Her mother glanced away. "Bart has approached your father about a partnership at the haberdashery. An infusion of new stock and new energy would save it."

Their maid, Lois, appeared in the doorway. "Miss Katie, Mr. Foster is here. He heard about your papa."

Katie tried to ignore the hope in her mother's face. "Bart is here? Show him into the parlor, please." Katie pushed her loose hair away from her face. Though she'd dressed, she hadn't taken time to put up her hair or wash her face.

Pink rushed to her mother's cheeks. "Put on your blue dress and pinch some color into your cheek. And leave your hair down. I know it's not proper, but your curls are very fetching. Men are quite fond of seeing a woman's hair down."

Heat ran up Katie's neck. "Under the circumstances, I thought this gray one most appropriate. I'm sure he's here to offer his assistance, Mama. Besides, I couldn't marry without a suitable engagement. A year at least."

"You *must*, Katie," her mother said, flinging back the covers. She staggered from the bed and gripped Katie's shoulders. Her eyes held a feverish glint. "It's the only answer. You're attracted to him anyway. He holds so much power and wealth."

Katie tried to twist away, but her mother held her firmly. "But what if he finds out who I really am?" If people knew she wasn't really Inez Russell's daughter, would her friends all desert her?

"How could he possibly find out? My dear sister knows better than to show her face here after all these years."

"She might hear of my marriage and come back to demand money." The idea had plagued Katie most of her life. She never wanted to see the woman who had abandoned her again.

"Just let her try!" Katie's mother stepped back and dropped her hands to her sides.

"I wouldn't want to humiliate Bart." Or to face such disgrace herself.

Her mother's face softened. "I've often wished we could wipe away the memories you have of your early years with Florence. I did the best I could to salve your wounds with love."

"You've been a wonderful mother," Katie choked out. She hated to talk about Florence. The memories still made her ache.

Her mother made a shooing motion. "Make yourself presentable, my dear. Your future husband awaits."

Katie made herself smile back into her mother's serene face. "Yes, Mama, the blue dress." She hurried to her room and changed into her new dress then raked her fingers through her curls so they lay on her shoulders in casual abandon. Tucking a hanky into the sleeve of her dress, she descended the stairs and stepped into the parlor where she found Bart Foster standing with his hands clasped behind him as he stared into the garden. Sunshine gleamed on his carefully combed blond hair.

His appearance never failed to remind her of his status in the community. His navy suit had been tailored in the city, and he stopped to have his shoes shined every morning. His grandfather had been a Mercy Falls's founder, and every unmarried woman in town cast longing gazes his direction. She should be thrilled he gave her more than a passing glance. And of course, she was. As his wife, the specters of her past couldn't harm her. She could hold her head high.

He turned and spied her standing in the doorway. "My dear Katie, I came as soon as I heard." He crossed the Persian rug and took Katie's hand in his.

She returned the strong pressure of his fingers. "I'm so glad for your help and strength, Bart," she said. Though they'd been on first names for two months now, she still relished the way the syllable rolled off her tongue. The admiration in his blue eyes never failed to lift her spirits, though today the warmth of his gaze only raised her mood slightly above the floor.

Keeping her hand in his possession, he led her to the sofa. "How is your mother?"

"She's . . . resting," Katie said. Her mother would be mortified if Bart became aware of how she'd fallen apart this morning at the news.

He squeezed her fingers. "What is your father's condition?"

"I don't know yet. I'm going to check on him shortly."

"I would be glad to accompany you."

"Thank you, Bart, but I have several errands to run as well. I wouldn't want to take up so much of your time. I'm sure your father expects you at the sawmill."

"I have some meetings later this morning." He pressed her hands far longer than was appropriate. "Telephone the office if there is anything I can do."

"I shall do that."

His gaze lingered in her hair. "You look quite lovely today."

The heat of his glance made her want to wind her hair into a French roll and cover it with a chapeau. "Thank you." Her mother's advice had been right. She only wished the touch of his hand would make her feel something beyond . . . invaded.

He gave her fingers a final squeeze. "I should go and let you get to your errands." He paused as though to give her time to object.

She knew she should offer Bart refreshment, but she wanted to find out about her father. To confront him and see if he'd really tried to do away with himself. It was so difficult to have to shoulder the burden to try to make sure everyone was taken care of. She knew she had to figure out a way to meet everyone else's expectations.

She rose and smiled down at him. "Thank you for stopping by, Bart. You're a good man." He smiled his pleasure, and she ushered him out then leaned against the door and closed her eyes. Mama would expect a full report.

NINE

THE BABY'S HOWL awakened Will. He'd been dreaming he was in a hot air balloon floating along the clouds with his barometer. He opened scratchy eyes and got up. The clock on the mantel struck ten thirty. He'd slept since dawn when he'd extinguished the lighthouse lamp, and most fortunately, so had Jennie.

"Are you hungry, honey?" he asked. "Want some bread and jam?"

She gave him a toothy smile and reached up. "Ree," she said.

Did she just try to say *hungry?* He scooped her up. She'd wormed her way into his heart so quickly. In the kitchen, he deposited her in the high chair Katie had suggested he bring from the Bulmer residence, then spread a slice of bread with butter and jam. He cut it into pieces and placed it in front of her.

She rammed a piece into her mouth. "Umm, umm," she mouthed around her food.

Cute the way she did that when she ate. He prepared some oatmeal for himself, and when she reached for it, he fed her a few spoonfuls. After breakfast he cleaned her up, changed her diaper, and carried her back to the parlor where he put her on the floor with some wooden blocks. Too bad Philip wasn't here to bond with his baby girl. She was quite charming. He glanced out the window and saw a horse and rider at the bottom of the hill. Constable Brown dismounted and trekked up the hillside toward the lighthouse.

Will sighed and went to open the door. "Good morning, Constable Brown. What brings you out here?"

"I wish to speak with you, Mr. Jesperson."

"You're looking a little tired. Busy night keeping the peace?" Will asked, stepping aside to allow the constable to enter.

"Bad night," the constable said.

Will led him to the parlor. "Have a seat."

Brown sank onto the sofa. "I don't suppose you have any coffee?"

"I do." Will went to get a cup for the man, and when he came back, he found the constable dangling his closed pocketknife in front of the baby's rapt face. "I don't think that's the best thing for her to play with," he said.

"She can't get it open. It's much too difficult."

Will retrieved it from Jennie anyway and distracted her with the pan lids before she could wail. "So what's the problem, Constable?"

"Albert Russell was found half-drowned at Mercy Falls last night."

Will put down his cup of coffee on the marble-topped table beside him. "What happened?"

"Attempted suicide, I suspect."

"He'll be all right?"

The constable hesitated. "He was still unconscious this morning when I checked at the hospital. The doctor isn't sure if he will recover."

"I'm sorry." He was too. He thought of Miss Katie and the pain she must be going through. Suicide. Did it have anything to do with Miss Bulmer and her call suggesting Philip investigate Russell? "How does that correspond to your visit here?"

"Miss Katie mentioned her father came to see you yesterday. Looking for a pocket watch."

Will nodded. "He was here just a few minutes."

"Did he seem upset? Distraught?"

"Not suicidal, by any means. He asked if I'd seen the watch, and I told him I had only taken baby items from Miss Bulmer's house."

Brown took out a cigar. "Did he seem upset that it was missing?"

"He did not seemed pleased. Look, Constable, I find it difficult to believe the man tried to kill himself. Especially in light of Miss Bulmer's disappearance and the attack on Miss Russell."

Brown rolled the cigar in his fingers and nodded. "There is that. I was about to mention it to you. I spoke with the owner of The Redwood Inn. He described the man as in his midtwenties with dark hair and brown eyes. A nice dresser."

An image of his brother flashed through Will's mind, but he pushed the thought away. Philip would never threaten Miss Russell. Besides, he'd gone back to the city. Hadn't he?

Brown took a gulp of his coffee then set it on the table beside him. "Where is your brother, Mr. Jesperson?"

The man was no fool. Will might have implicated Philip in this mess by admitting he suspected Jennie was Philip's daughter. Will kept his expression impassive. "He's in San Francisco. Investigating the missing ship, as I mentioned."

Brown took out a notebook. "What's the name of his agency and where can I find him?"

Will told him and watched while the constable wrote it down. "If you suspect Philip of involvement in this, you're mistaken, Constable."

"Of course, of course." Brown put his notebook away and rose. "I shall be in touch."

"Constable, while I have you here—" Will began.

The man turned with a questioning expression. "Is there another problem?"

"Not a problem, necessarily. I wondered if you'd heard anything else about that missing ship."

"We found some more bodies floating in the bay. Barbarians, that's what those pirates are."

"Any clues to solving that case?"

"It's as dead as the squid I saw on the beach. I've combed the roads and coastline for clues, but they've vanished." Brown raised his brows. "Now see here . . . why don't you leave the investigating to me?"

Philip had told him that local law enforcement tended to be proprietary about their investigations. "You're quite right. In the worry about Miss Bulmer, I forgot something my brother told me. I mentioned he'd asked me to speak with her. There was a man she thought might be involved in the taking of *Dalton's Fortune*."

"The ship that was taken a month ago," the constable said. "Who was the man?"

"Albert Russell."

Light dawned in Brown's eyes. "Perhaps his daughter is not as far off as I'd thought. She wondered if he might have been attacked."

"Or he was involved and would rather kill himself than go to jail."

"True." Brown put on his bowler. "Thank you for your time, Mr. Jesperson. Our discussion was most interesting."

Miss Bulmer had said to check out Albert Russell. Was it only revenge or had the man truly been involved?

❦

Katie tiptoed into the room. She still trembled from seeing her father's still form, settled under a crisp, white sheet. His chest had barely moved up and down and he hadn't opened his eyes, though she'd called his name and held his hand until the nurses had shooed her out.

The light from the open curtains illuminated her mother's blotchy, aging skin. She was beautiful to Katie, though. What other woman would have taken her in and loved her so completely? Katie went to the window and struggled to release the heavy drapes from the tiebacks.

"I'm awake."

Katie turned at the sound of her mother's voice. "I was going to let you sleep."

Her mother plumped the pillows and sat up. "I can't hide in bed forever. How did it go, darling?"

"Very well. Bart was solicitous and offered to escort me to the hospital, but I declined his offer. I went to check on Papa and then to see about the state of his affairs."

Her mother sat up. "How was he?"

Better for her mother to realize how serious his injury was. "Unconscious. The doctor is doing what he can."

Her mother swallowed hard. "He's strong. I believe he will be fine. I must go to him." She struggled to sit up.

Katie pressed her back against the pillow. "Not yet. The nurses told me we must stay away and not tax his strength."

"They'll not keep me from my husband's side. You must help me to dress and go to him." Her mother gripped Katie's hand. "You're so competent, my dear. I don't know what I'd do without you. Now tell me about Bart."

The springs groaned as Katie sat on the edge of her mother's bed. "I–I don't really love Bart, Mama. Am I even ready for marriage?"

Her mother patted her hand. "Love will come in time, dear girl. This modern-day obsession with love is ridiculous. Respect is what you need for a marriage to flourish. You respect him, do you not?"

"Oh yes. He's a good man. Honorable."

"And wealthy. There will be no problems he can't handle with his family's money and influence behind him." She put her hand on her forehead. "My head aches quite dreadfully."

Katie positioned herself to massage her mother's head. The weight of responsibility pressed her down. What would it be like to choose a man who seemed somewhat . . . unsuitable? Mr. Jesperson's brown eyes flashed through her memory, but she told herself not to be ridiculous. He was the last man on earth her mother would accept. A lightkeeper earned a bare pittance. There would be no more pretty dresses and slippers, no more baubles and perfume, let alone a chance for her parents to keep their home and servants. Such things were only important to Katie because they ensured that the people she admired would never know the squalor from which she'd come. A woman had to think of future children and caring for her mother. That was how things were done. Inez had made that clear.

Her mother's smile faded. She seemed to gather herself. "Katie, did I dream it or did you say your father had a . . . another child?"

Katie paused in her ministrations. "Oh Mama, I'd hoped you wouldn't remember."

"Tell me what you know."

Unable to watch the pain in her mother's eyes, Katie plucked at the sheet. "I was at the switchboard. I overheard Papa talking to Eliza Bulmer. She said her child was his responsibility."

"Did you ask your father about it?"

"I did. He admitted to a relationship with Eliza but didn't believe Jennie was his child." She dared a peek at her mother and found the older woman stone-faced.

Her mother shrugged. "Please don't harbor any pity for me, dear girl. Men find it quite impossible to be faithful. This is something you shall discover one day."

"Never," Katie said under her breath.

Her mother smiled. "You're young and idealistic. I was quite happy to run the household and let your father take his pleasure elsewhere. It relieved me of the duty."

Duty? There was much about the love relationship Katie didn't understand. "The Bible says a man is to love his wife as his own flesh. Surely it's not too much to ask that my husband would want only me." She'd read the Song of Solomon and longed to find true love for herself.

"Sometimes you're such a child, Katie." Her mother closed her eyes and pressed her fingers to the bridge of her nose. "Where is this baby? I must see it for myself."

"She's with the new lightkeeper out at Mercy Point. Mr. Jesperson."

"How old is she? And why does he have her?"

"I think she is about a year old. He seems to think she might be his brother's child."

"But you're not convinced."

Katie shook her head. "No, Mama. Not after what I overheard on the phone."

"Does she look like your father?"

"She has dark eyes, but then, so does the new lightkeeper. I would assume his brother does as well."

"Oh dear. Such a conundrum. We must get to the bottom of it. But secretly. Tell no one your suspicions. Bring the child to me and let me have a look at her. I'm quite sure I shall be able to tell." Tears hung on her mother's lashes. "This is too much for me to bear. You must fix it somehow, Katie."

Katie bit back the question, *how?*, and nodded. "I'll go out and check on her. It's the least we should do."

"I want to see her."

"I can't do that. What if someone sees me bring her here?" That was assuming Mr. Jesperson even allowed her to take Jennie.

"You are well known for your acts of charity, my dear. Our neighbors will think you are doing one more good deed."

"And if you determine she is Papa's daughter?"

Her mother fell back against the pillow. "It's too much for me to think through. Let's take one step at a time, shall we?" She plucked at the covers. "Your priority must be to make a suitable marriage. How close is Bart to declaring himself?"

"I have so little experience with men, Mama."

"Has he held your hand with obvious reluctance to release it?"

Katie nodded. "He did that today."

"Has he kissed you?"

Katie's cheeks burned. "Of course not, Mama!"

Her mother's bark of laughter came. "My dear, there is nothing wrong with allowing the man you want to marry to kiss you. Once you're sure his intentions are honorable, of course. Bart has not hidden his open admiration for you. He's been pleased to show you around town, and I suspect he will invite you to come to dinner at his home with his parents very soon."

"He may slow down the relationship now," Katie said. "Now that . . . well, Papa."

Her mother's gaze narrowed. "Is that what you'd like?"

Katie forced a smile. "I'm just upset, Mama. So much has happened in the last twenty-four hours."

Katie saw the fear drain from her mother's eyes. "I like Bart very much. He'll be a good husband and a good father." She swung her legs out of bed. "Now help me dress. I must tend to your papa."

TEN

KATIE STOOD LOOKING at the man in the bed. The murmur of voices from nurses tending to others in the ward faded as she prayed for her father to live. His eyes were closed, and his skin was nearly the color of the sheets. What would they do if he died? She touched his hand. "Papa?" she whispered. "I've brought Mama to see you."

There was no response. Not even a flutter of his lids. She glanced at her mother seated on the other side of the bed then turned her attention back to her father. The bruise on his forehead was huge and mottled. There were a few cuts on his face, and she saw a lump on the back of his head poking up through his thin hair. Could someone have struck him and thrown him over the falls? She knew she was grasping at straws.

Her mother leaned closer. "Albert? You must wake up now." There was no response. "Leave us, Katie. I'll stay with him. Go see about that child."

Katie hesitated then pressed a kiss on his cold cheek and hurried out of the hospital. Out on the sidewalk she strapped on her skates and skated toward the bank. Before she reached it, she saw a familiar horse and buggy. *Addie.* Her friend was certainly on her way to Katie's house. Katie waved, and John guided the horse to the side of the street. He helped his wife alight, and the two young women flew into each other's arms.

Katie clung to Addie while John and his son, Edward, stood to the side of the road. Addie's dog, Gideon, pressed his nose against Katie's leg as if to comfort her. The dog was well known for being able to sense distress.

"Katie, I'm so sorry," Addie whispered. "How is your father? Did you just come from the hospital?"

Katie nodded. "He's still unconscious. I–I'm not sure he'll live, Addie."

Addie pressed her hand. "God is in control. When I pray, I feel he is telling me not to worry. That your father will be all right. Be strong."

"Let me buy you some lunch," John said. He stood in front of the café and opened the door, gesturing inside.

Katie followed him and his family into the café. A waitress seated them at a corner table. They ordered the special roast beef plate. Gideon lay at Katie's feet.

John sipped his coffee. "If there is anything we can do to help, you have only to tell us, Katie." Six-year-old Edward tugged at his sleeve and whispered in his father's ear. "Ah, we'll be right back. Edward needs to visit the men's room." He took the hand of his son, and the two went toward the back of the café. Gideon got up and followed them.

"How are you really doing?" Addie asked.

"I'm frightened. Something more than we realize is going on." Katie told her friend about her father's visit to the lighthouse in search of his pocket watch and about the threatening phone call she received.

"So you think your father might not have tried to kill himself?" Addie asked. "That whoever is responsible for Eliza's disappearance tried to harm him? I quite dislike bringing this up, Katie. But what if your father suspected? What if he was worried he would be accused and chose to end his life rather than face the dishonor?"

Katie sipped her tea. "I have considered that, and you could be right." But it still felt wrong to her. There was something more, something she was missing.

"How is your mother this morning?"

"Better. Bart's call lifted her spirits considerably."

"So Bart came to call already," Addie observed after a short silence. "I wondered if he would come immediately. He seems quite taken with you."

"Mama wants me to marry him," she said. "We–We are in financial straits. My father's business is on the verge of bankruptcy. A favorable marriage is our only hope of keeping this estate. It would destroy Mama to lose it. She was born here."

Addie leaned forward. "Oh Katie, don't let such a thing sway your decision. Real love is worth waiting on."

"Mama says the most important thing in a marriage is respect."

"Of course I respect John, but I love him too. More and more I have come to believe that the most important thing is to know that God has a plan for your life. We do well to listen and obey that plan."

"I know you're right, but how do you *know*?"

"Jehovah-Shalom," Addie said. "God, our peace. I see you're unsettled about Bart. That tells me right there that he isn't the right man. When we follow in the way God has laid out for us, we have peace."

"I'm not sure I've ever experienced true peace," Katie said.

"It's because it's hard for you to let go of control," her friend said. "You think you have to manage everything. Learn to turn loose of things, Katie. God really does know what he's doing."

"That's hard to see right now."

Addie reached over and patted her hand. "Does your mother know about Eliza?"

Katie nodded. "I tried to keep it from her, but she overheard me tell the constable."

"Have you heard how little Jennie is doing?"

"I saw her last night at the lighthouse. Mr. Jesperson seems to be very good with her. He was singing to her when I arrived." Katie smiled at the memory. It had so warmed her heart.

Addie stared at her. "Why are you smiling so strangely? Are you attracted to the lightkeeper?"

Katie wiped the smile from her face. "Of course not. I know nothing about him."

"I knew nothing about John either, but I was drawn to him from the moment we met. Sometimes it happens that way."

"Not in this case," Katie said with enough emphasis she hoped would convince her friend. She glanced at the dog trotting back toward them on Edward's heels. "I do believe Gideon exercises peace."

Addie laughed. "Nothing ruffles that dog. If we could all be so even tempered." She glanced back at Katie. "Don't change the subject, my dear. I saw Mr. Jesperson. He's quite handsome."

"I like blond men," Katie said. "The lightkeeper appears almost dangerous. Such dark eyes."

"I think he is a strong man. Protective. You saw the way he took charge of the baby. What woman wouldn't respond to that?"

"Me," Katie said. "You must put him out of your head. I know nothing about the man and what I do know, I rather dislike. He's much too overbearing."

She almost believed it until she remembered the way she'd heard him singing to the baby. It was most endearing.

❦

Katie sat in the third pew with her mother. The minister gave a final prayer, and the worshipers began to stand in their pews and greet one another. Several hurried over to ask about her father. She shook their hands as they assured her they were praying for him. He'd regained consciousness but was still incoherent. She looked past her mother to where Bart stood with his parents. Good people. Good friends.

But would they be so kind if they knew the truth?

She shook the unpleasant thought away. They would never find out. She escorted her mother outside toward their buggy. Live oaks shaded the green expanse of the yard. Buggies and a few automobiles lined the road. Mr. Jesperson held Jennie facing forward in his arms as he strode across the lawn toward her. Katie glanced toward her mother. Good, she was occupied with a group of ladies. Katie moved to intercept him. This was not the time to allow her mother to inspect the child. Not in front of all their friends.

"Mr. Jesperson," she said. "How surprising to see you."

He took the hand she offered. "I make a practice of being in God's house on Sunday."

Her heart gave an unwelcome flutter at the touch of his warm fingers. What was the matter with her? Bart was just across the yard with his parents. It was most unseemly for her to even notice the broad span of gray wool on Mr. Jesperson's chest or the curl in his dark brown hair. "I hope you will understand when I say, please don't make yourself known to my mother. She's in no condition to deal with Jennie's presence."

"I wouldn't dream of it," he said.

The baby reached for her. Katie took the child and kissed her soft curls. She'd always wanted a baby sister. The child smelled clean and fresh as though she'd just been bathed. "You seem to be having no trouble caring for her. She is quite content."

"I wish I could say the same for myself. I must find someone to help me." He scanned the crowd with a hopeful expression. "Is there anyone here you might recommend?"

Katie opened her mouth to tell him she had no idea who he might hire when Addie joined them. "You remember Mr. Jesperson, don't you, Addie?" Katie said.

Addie offered her hand. "Of course. And little Jennie too."

Katie ignored the sidelong glance her friend slid her way. She noticed the way Jespserson's sharp gaze scanned the crowd as though he were looking for someone. Probably still on the hunt for a nanny for the child.

He held out his arms for Jennie, who pointedly turned her head and clung to Katie's neck. "Na, na," she said, shaking her head for emphasis.

The child's small hands clutched at Katie's neck, and a warm sensation settled in the pit of Katie's stomach. It felt good to be so wanted. She kissed the soft cheek nestled so close and inhaled the scent of the toddler. What a blessing it would be to care for this little one every day.

"Katie, introduce me to your friend."

Katie turned to see her mother standing behind her. "Mama," she faltered. How did she get out of this? An awkward pause ensued.

Her mother extended her hand. "I'm Inez Russell. You must be Mr. Jesperson."

Katie should have known better than to try to hide anything from her mother. "This is Jennie, Mama." She turned the baby around to face her mother.

"Hello, sweet pea," her mother cooed to the baby. "Aren't you a little bright-eyed girl?" Jennie reached for the older woman and grabbed at a ribbon on her hat. "Will you let me hold you?" The baby held out her arms and Katie transferred her. Her mother's gaze roamed Jennie's face. "Her eyes are quite dark. Much like yours, Mr. Jesperson."

And Papa's. Katie didn't say it but she saw the fear in her mother's eyes. She wanted to point out the way the baby's hairline differed from her father's and how Jennie's eyes varied too. But she held her tongue. Her mother liked to come to her own conclusions without coercion.

Jennie reached for Mr. Jesperson and he took her. She laid her head on his shoulder and began to hum to herself. After a moment, she lifted her head and squawked at the man.

"She's tired and wants me to sing to her," he said, his voice apologetic. "I should take her home."

Katie found it impossible to hide her smile. The baby had the man wrapped around her little finger.

"I would welcome a call from you in a few days," Katie's mother said. "There is much to discuss."

Katie's smile faded. Her mother obviously thought she saw some resemblance between the baby and her ailing husband.

"I should be most pleased to speak with you," Will said, his eyes flicking between Katie and her mother, clearly understanding the direction of Inez's thoughts. "Do understand, though, that you have not yet met my brother. If you were to see him, you would know there is no doubt about this child's parentage." He nodded to Katie and Addie. "Good day, ladies. I'm sure I'll see you again quite soon. If you hear of a dependable woman looking for a live-in position as nanny, please send her to me."

ELEVEN

WILL OPENED ONE scratchy eye at about eleven o'clock in the morning. Jennie slept in the crook of his arm. She'd howled the whole night long, and he'd hauled her up and down the lighthouse steps as he tended to the light. They'd fallen into bed at dawn, but even then she'd been restless next to him and hot enough to make his forehead break out in a sweat.

Hot. Wait a moment. Was she ill? He touched her skin and found it dry and very warm. Holding her against him was like nestling up to the hot coals in a fireplace. She coughed and the harsh bark made him sit up and stare at her. Spots of red dotted her pudgy cheeks. He scooped her up and leaped from the bed. While he had no notion of where to find the doctor, someone in town could direct him. He rushed down the steps to the front door and yanked it open to come face-to-face with Miss Russell's fist poised to land on the door.

Her eyes matched the color of the sea foaming at the foot of the cliffs. What would you call the shape of her face—heart-shaped? The high cheekbones were pink. So were the full lips above her narrow chin. The lilac dress and wide-brimmed hat she wore were in the latest fashion, and she clutched her bag in her gloved hands as she stared up at him. She looked every bit as beautiful as she had at church yesterday.

She dropped her hand. "Mr. Jesperson. You were going out?"

Before he could answer, the baby let out a wail loud enough to call Poseidon from the depths of the ocean. He shifted Jennie to his other arm. "Could you direct me to the doctor?"

Miss Russell peered into the baby's face. "She's flushed."

"I think she has a fever." He handed the baby to the woman with a sense of relief, then stretched out the cramp in his arm muscle.

Miss Russell put her hand on Jennie's forehead. "A high fever. We must get it down right away. Run some tepid water in the sink."

He sprang to do her bidding. Had he done something wrong? Perhaps this was all his fault. Another person might have recognized the child's condition last night by her inability to settle. After pumping water from the hand pump into the dry sink, he poured in enough hot water from the kettle on the stove to bring the temperature to lukewarm.

Miss Russell crooned to the wailing baby then tested the water. "Perfect." She laid Jennie on top of the cabinet and quickly stripped her clothing off. The tiny girl screeched when Miss Russell eased her into the sink. "I know, sweetheart," she said.

She splashed water along the baby's skin for what seemed an eternity. Will wanted to clap his palms over his ears so he didn't have to listen to the child's cries. "I'll get a towel," he said. He rushed up the steps to the bathroom and found a stack of towels in the corner cupboard by the claw-foot tub. By the time he got back downstairs, the baby's wails had tapered off to an occasional hiccup.

He opened the towel between his hands, and Miss Russell lifted the dripping wet baby from the water and deposited her into the folds of the terry cloth. He wrapped the edges around Jennie, and Miss Russell cuddled her against her chest. The baby's eyes closed.

"She seems better," he said.

"For now. We should let the doctor examine her to ensure she doesn't have something like diphtheria." She quickly dressed the sleeping child and lifted her to her shoulder.

"I'll get the buggy ready. You'll have to direct me. I don't know where to find the doctor."

She followed him into the entry. He paused and glanced down at her. "How did you happen to come by this morning?"

"It can wait," she said.

He studied her face and noticed the dark circles under her eyes. "Is something wrong?"

She sighed. "My mother wants to see Jennie again. She's always one to do her duty."

"I'm certain she's my niece. When you meet my brother, you'll be convinced as well." He stepped onto the porch. A buggy was parked outside. "Could we take your buggy?"

"Certainly."

He took Jennie and noticed she wasn't as hot. Once he helped Miss Russell into the buggy, he handed the baby up to her then climbed in himself. "Why is your mother so willing to believe Jennie is your father's child?"

She glanced at the baby sleeping on her shoulder. "I think she knows I believe it."

"And why are you so sure?"

She bit her lip and looked away. "I overheard Eliza demand money from him. For what other reason could she have been black-mailing him?"

His pulse quickened. He could think of something else. Maybe Miss Bulmer wanted money to stay quiet about the taking of the ship. But perhaps he was wrong about Philip being the father. His gaze fell on Jennie's swirl of a cowlick. Just like his brother's. His doubt ebbed.

"My brother is investigating the taking of the *Paradox*."

"Yes, you called me about it," she said.

He raised a brow. "You were the operator I spoke to?"

She nodded. "I don't understand why you bring that up now. We are discussing Jennie's parentage."

He slapped the reins against the horse's back, and the buggy began to move. "You asked why else Miss Bulmer might be blackmailing your father."

Horror filled her eyes, and she whipped her head from side to side. "My father had nothing to do with the ship. Besides, Eliza disappeared only a short time later."

"Another ship was taken a month ago. My brother said Miss Bulmer had suggested a man in town was involved. Albert Russell. There is no other Albert Russell in town, is there?"

"No. But what you're suggesting is impossible. I know my father. He would never do such a thing."

He heard the quaver in her voice. "I'm sorry. I did not mean to upset you."

She arranged her skirt on the seat. "If your aspersions on my father's name are meant to deter me from my duty to Jennie, you have failed. You can't possibly want to care for a baby!"

He turned the horse's head from the county road to the main street to town. "It has most certainly complicated my life. But sometimes duty demands we do the inconvenient."

The woman gave him a severe glance. "A baby is more than a duty."

He urged the horse forward. "Indeed she has already crept into my heart. But isn't duty part of why you're here?"

Her bonnet hid her face. "I love children. I already care about her. She would not be hard for me to love."

"Nor for me. She's an engaging little mite." The sea air blew his hair over his eyes, and he realized he'd forgotten to grab his hat. "Can we agree we both want what is best for Jennie?"

"Of course."

He glanced at the wind blowing wisps of shiny hair across her cheeks. He didn't want to be enemies with this woman.

TWELVE

KATIE DIDN'T LIKE the child's lethargy. Her initial goal to let her mother get another peek at the baby had evaporated the moment she saw the child. "Can you go a little faster? We need to get her to the doctor," she said again.

The towering redwoods cast a shadow over the macadam road, and the damp odor of the ferns growing along the banks added to the sense of isolation. What did she know of this man? She still suspected he had something to do with Eliza's disappearance. The buckboard reached the edge of town. Church bells rang twelve times. The scent of fudge from the candy shop lingered on the breeze.

She glanced at the telephone office. Under normal circumstances she would be at work, but she'd taken a few days off since her father's . . . accident. She directed Will to the doctor's office, the downstairs rooms of a brownstone on the corner of Mercy and Main.

He parked the buggy then jumped down and took the baby from her before assisting her from the conveyance. She glanced toward the doctor's office. People jammed the waiting room and spilled out the front door. Katie stopped and put her hand on Mr. Jesperson's muscled arm.

"What's wrong?" he asked.

"I'm not sure," she said. The voices from the waiting patients held panic and fear. "I don't know if we should take the baby into that crowd."

"Let me see what's going on." He thrust the baby into her arms.

She rested her head on Jennie's soft hair. The child did seem to be better. Her little body didn't radiate heat, and her brown eyes were more alert. Her nose was running now. Perhaps Katie had overreacted. It might only be a cold.

The little one grasped a lock of her hair in her fingers. "Um?" the baby said, pointing to an oak on the tree lawn.

"Tree," Katie said. She patted down Jennie's cowlick. A woman whose back had been to the street turned, and when Katie caught a glimpse of her face, something kicked in her chest. It couldn't be Florence. Too many years had passed, and the woman's memory was too dim. Still, there was something about how she stood with one hand on her hip that sent a shock of recognition vibrating along Katie's spine.

She tried to sort through the vague memories in her head. This woman's dull hair and lackluster complexion didn't match the vibrant woman she still dreamed of. But it had been twenty years since she'd seen her. Was it possible? She rejected the thought, but her gaze still lingered on the woman who stood talking to a man in the doorway.

Mr. Jesperson walked back to where she stood jostling the baby, who squirmed to be put down. He stopped four feet from them and blocked her path to the door. "We're not going in there."

"What's wrong?"

"Smallpox." He stared down at the baby. His eyes opened a bit wider. "She looks better."

"I think her fever has broken." She noticed the panic spreading among the waiting crowd. "All those people fear they have smallpox?"

He nodded. "I don't want to run the risk of spreading it to you and Jennie. I'll take the buckboard home so I can bathe, and then I'll return for you. Is there somewhere you can take Jennie to avoid any contamination?"

"My father's haberdashery shop," she said, pointing to a brownstone down the street. "I'll wait for you there. His assistant would have closed it for lunch, but I have a key. I want to telephone home and check on my mother to see if she has any news of my father." She glanced at the baby. "Her nose is running a little so I think it's just a cold."

"Let's hope it stays that way," he said, his mouth grim. He stepped past her to the buckboard. "I'll be back as quickly as I can." He leaped into the buckboard, took the reins, and then urged the horse into a canter down the street the way they'd come.

She glanced toward the doctor's office again, but the woman who had caught her attention was gone. Maybe she'd made it inside. Quite silly to be so taken with a stranger. Katie shifted Jennie to the other arm then hurried down the brick sidewalk to Russell's Haberdashery. After she dug her key from her bag, she stepped into the empty shop. The smell of the store was a familiar one: wool, pipe and cigar tobacco, and the spicy scent of cologne combined in a very masculine aroma— one she'd always associated with her father. Her throat closed, and she breathed the odor of her childhood.

What would happen to the store? Her mother said it was nearly bankrupt, and the realization that her life might be changing forever swept over her. Though people were kind, she saw the questions in their eyes, the censure. They all wondered why her father would try to kill himself.

The baby had fallen asleep, so Katie balanced her in the crook of her arm and went to the telephone hanging on the wall. She rang through to Central and asked for her home. When the maid answered the phone, Katie asked for her mother.

"I'm sorry, Miss Katie, but your mama took sick right after you left," Lois said. "High fever, hurtin' all over, vomiting. Even breaking out in spots." Her voice quivered. "The doctor been by. He said i–it was smallpox. We're already quarantined."

Dear God, no! "Take every precaution. I'll be there as soon as I can."

"No, Miss Katie. Your mama would have my hide if I let you come into a sick house. You go stay with a friend. Maybe Mr. Foster would take you in. I'll take care of your mama."

"I want to care for her," Katie said. "I'll be fine."

"If your mama was to lose you, she would go crazy. You listen to what I say now, miss."

Rather than arguing with Lois, Katie rang off. The baby's nose was running freely now, and her skin was cool and dry. Katie prayed the baby hadn't been exposed to the pox. They'd have to stay at the shop. Her father had collected some old suits to give to the poor, and she found the box of them in the back and made a bed on the floor for Jennie by the front counter, then covered the suits with a clean sheet she found in a cupboard. The child rolled to her side when Katie laid her down.

Driven by a compulsion she couldn't explain, Katie wandered the shop. She remembered the days before the drink had gotten control of her father. The joy on his face when she skated in to see him after school. The Saturdays when she helped by stocking shelves and hanging jackets and pants. Little by little, everything changed. She could always tell when he'd had a shot of whiskey. His reddened eyes would narrow when he saw her. Instead of smiling, he would bark orders at her. She still didn't understand why she was made to pay for her mother's sins. The months when he didn't drink would gradually wipe away the pain, and she'd think it would never come again. It always did though. Always.

She stepped into the back room. Wooden counters and a sewing machine for alterations sat as though waiting for the tailor. If the store closed, what would happen to the people her father employed? It would be hard to find work with the depression. She touched the smooth, cool surface of the Singer sewing machine. Soon dust would gather on its surface. Wandering along the shelves and counters, she remembered the days when workers crammed the place. Those days would never come again. Now garment factories churned out ready-to-wear. Her gaze fell on the shelves that hid the safe. What if her father had more money than they knew of? It might help them weather the stormy days ahead. She knew the combination.

She dug her glasses out of her bag and perched them on her nose before shoving away the stacks of wool and cotton to reveal the safe. Her hand touched the dial. It had been years since she had opened it. The safe refused to unlock on the first try. She ran through the sequence again and it popped open. She pushed the door as far as it would go and peered inside. Stacks of paper lay inside along with a money pouch. Hope surged until she picked up the pouch and found it too light. Sure enough, it was empty. She dropped it onto a shelf and lifted out the papers in the back of the safe. She glanced through them. Contracts, invoices, and receipts were all she found.

She stopped at a note that read: *Ship will dock an hour early. Have men waiting.*

The second directly under it read: *Operation perfectly executed. Booty more than expected. Will transmit location tomorrow.*

Booty? Her throat closed. Mr. Jesperson thought her father was involved in the piracy of the ships. She couldn't bear to admit to herself that he might be right.

THIRTEEN

WITH HIS SKIN raw from scrubbing as hard as he could in the hot, soapy water of the bath, Will dressed then washed down everything he'd touched. With a twinge of regret, he tossed a match to the clothing he'd thrown into the fire pit outside and dashed back to the horse and buckboard. An hour had passed since he left Miss Russell in town with the baby and he wanted to get them as far away from the pestilence as possible. He urged the horse to a trot.

Bluebirds sang from the berry bushes along the side of the road, and he watched the clouds building in the west over the water as the buckboard bounced along the rough road. With Miss Bulmer missing, he wasn't sure where to look for the next link. But it wasn't his problem. His brother could handle his own case. He had enough to handle.

He scanned the hillside, blanketed with some kind of blue wildflowers. Pretty place, this northern coast, but a little more tame than he was used to. He normally strode city streets and dodged clanging streetcars and rearing horses. This was exactly what he had been longing for.

As he looked around, he noticed two men atop a hill in a cypress grove. One man wore dungarees and a floppy hat. The other appeared to be a businessman dressed in a suit and bowler. They hadn't seen him yet. He reined in the horse in the shadow of a large tree and watched them a moment. Taken at a casual glance, there was no real reason for his unease. A landowner might have been giving direction to one of his hands, but something about the way the men talked seemed furtive. That alone made Will's senses go to alert. He wished he were close enough to overhear. He watched the man in the bowler point out to sea, toward where the point jutted into the bay.

Where the pirates had overrun the ship.

He told himself not to jump to conclusions. There could be any number of reasons to gesture to the point. He watched the suited man count out paper money and hand it to the worker. The man in dungarees tipped his straw hat then walked off. The businessman saw Will and scowled before he turned and strode away.

When both men were out of sight, Will started back toward town. He took out a notepad and jotted down descriptions of the men and of the incident. It was probably nothing, but he wanted the criminals brought to justice after seeing what they had done to the sailors. If these men had anything to do with it, he didn't want to miss any details to report to his brother.

He reached Mercy Falls and saw that the streets were deserted. Blockades declaring quarantines closed several roads, and he saw more signs on doors. There was no problem finding a spot to park the buckboard outside Russell's Haberdashery. Most businesses were open but had few clients.

There was a CLOSED sign in the window of the haberdashery. He turned the knob and found the door unlocked. The bell jingled when he stepped into the shop. Jennie stirred from a makeshift bed on the floor then turned her head and went back to sleep. Rather than calling for Miss Russell, Will walked through the store to the back room where he found the woman peering into a safe.

"Are you all right, Miss Russell?" he asked.

She jumped and turned at the sound of his voice. He caught a glimpse of her blue eyes behind her glasses before she snatched off the spectacles. "You startled me." She shut the door to the safe and locked it. "I believe Jennie is still sleeping."

"She is. She barely stirred when I came in." He watched her thrust a paper into her bag along with her glasses. It was none of his business. He followed her toward the front of the store. "Do you know who lives out by the lighthouse? I saw a fellow in a tweed suit and bowler talking to another man in that cypress grove. The one atop the hill with all those wildflowers?"

She stopped and turned to face him with a puzzled frown on her face. "No one lives there. It's part of a conservatory area. The only people I've seen there are gardeners."

"One might have been a gardener. The other was clearly not."

Her expression sharpened to keen interest. "Can you describe him?"

He grinned. "You really *do* like to be kept up on everything, don't you?" When pink touched her cheeks, he held up his hand before she could answer. "Please don't think I'm being critical. I can see you're the one I should bring any questions to."

"What kinds of questions? And why would you care, Mr. Jesperson? It hardly concerns you. The constable won't take kindly to interference."

"He wouldn't care for your involvement either," he pointed out, hiding another smile when she blushed again. The current trend of simpering beauties who were only interested in parties and fripperies made her intelligence rather appealing. Though she barely reached his chest in height, he'd begun to admire the way she barreled through any problem in front of her.

Whimpering noises came through the doorway. "The baby is awake," she said, turning on her heel.

He followed her swishing skirt into the storefront. Jennie had crawled from her makeshift bed and sat in the middle of the floor, rubbing her eyes and working up to a wail. Miss Russell scooped her up and nestled her close. "There, there," she said.

The baby quieted, staring at Will with inquisitive eyes. She waved an index finger his way. "Eh, eh?" Jennie said with a question at the end of her nonsensical syllables.

"That's Mr. Jesperson," Miss Russell said.

"You think she's really asking who I am?" he asked.

"Of course. She's very smart. You can see it in her eyes."

Will let the baby grip his finger. "Uncle Will," he said, touching his chest with his other hand. "I'm Uncle Will. I think I am anyway."

"She needs her diaper changed." Miss Russell pressed her lips together then plopped the baby back on the bedding and dug in the satchel for a fresh square of flannel.

He watched while she removed the sodden diaper that hung loosely around the baby's waist. She finished changing the baby and allowed Jennie to stand then toddle over to explore the base of the coatrack. Miss Russell stepped to the window and peered into the empty street.

"No one is moving about much," he told her. "I saw quarantine signs on some houses as I passed. I should get Jennie out of the threat of contamination."

Her cheeks were pale when she turned back to face him. "Yes, indeed!"

"Did you reach your mother?"

"I talked to our maid. Mama was too ill to come to the phone."

"Ill?" he asked. "Not smallpox?"

She bit her lip and nodded. "So the doctor said. Our maid forbade me to come home and said she would care for my mother, but my place is with her. I only waited so you could take Jennie. I didn't want to expose her."

"If she's been quarantined already, you won't be allowed to enter the home."

"Oh dear. I hadn't thought of that," she said. Her gaze wandered to the baby, who had managed to pull herself up on the coat stand. "Perhaps I could sneak in."

"And then what? You'd be sick, too, unable to get out and wondering what was happening on the outside."

"My mother needs me."

"I have a feeling you'd be a most impatient nurse," he said.

Her black lashes lowered to her cheeks as if to mask her feelings. "You don't even know me."

But somehow he did. "I know more than you think. You like to know what's going on and that indicates you like control. You abhor the unexpected. You can't *make* your mother get well any sooner by hovering over her." Her lids raised to reveal eyes bluer than any he'd ever seen. Like a summer sky just before dusk. A frown crouched between her eyes, and she turned her gaze away. He could tell his assessment had been spot on. And she didn't like it.

"Addie and John left today for their trip to Europe. I should telephone Addie's mother and see if I can stay there. I'll do that now." She went to the telephone and rang Central, then asked for the Carrington residence.

He listened to her instruct the operator to call her friend's home. From what he gathered from the conversation on this end, the Norths, Lady Carrington's daughter and son-in-law, had left town just before the disease had broken out, and several servants had already fallen ill at their residence. Jennie crawled to him and pulled herself up on his pants leg. She studied him with alert eyes and lifted her arms.

"You want me to pick you up?" He lifted her as Miss Russell rang off. "I would assume staying at the Norths' is not an option?"

"There is illness at the big house," she said. "And Lady Carrington has no spare room in her tiny cottage. Besides, I'm still quite determined to sneak home and care for Mama."

The phone rang and she jumped. "No one knows I'm here but Lady Carrington." She picked up the earpiece and held it to her ear. "This is Katie," she said into the mouthpiece. "Oh, Mr. Daniels, Nell must have told you where I am." She listened a moment. "I see. I'll have to get back to you. I'm going to try to get home." She listened, and her expression fell. "Oh, I see. Very well. Once I arrange for lodging, I'll call you back." She rang off and turned toward him with a frown on her face.

"Is something wrong?" he asked.

"That was Mr. Daniels, owner of the Mercy Falls Telephone Company. With the illness raging through town, he doesn't want to run the risk of having no operators. He was going to arrange to have a switchboard brought to my house, but he's informed me that roadblocks are set up to enforce the quarantine. He doesn't believe I'll be able to get home. Once I find a place to stay, he'll make arrangements for a switchboard, and I can work from there instead of going into the telephone building."

"Any idea where you could stay?" Will had an idea that just might work.

"I have other friends. The Fosters would be happy to have me, but they would be most disapproving of having a switchboard set up in their home."

There was plenty of room at the lighthouse. He'd barely gotten any sleep this morning. Caring for the child while he worked every night hadn't been a good situation either. He could use some help with the baby, but he didn't like admitting he felt inadequate to the task ahead of him. He could hardly ask her to stay at the lighthouse without a chaperone, though. There did not seem to be a respectable answer to the dilemma here.

"You're frowning," she said. "Is something else wrong?"

"I'm quite exhausted," he admitted. "After being up all night, a lightkeeper must sleep for a few hours after dawn. Caring for a sick baby has made that difficult. An ideal solution would be for you to stay at the lighthouse, away from the pestilence, and help with Jennie. There is adequate room for the switchboard as well."

She blushed again. "Without a chaperone? That's hardly suitable, Mr. Jesperson."

"That's a problem," he agreed. "One I'm not sure how to solve."

She said nothing for a long moment. "I have an idea," she said finally. "Lady Carrington is alone at her cottage. Her nurse fell ill and has not come in to work, and Mr. Carrington left this morning on a business trip before he realized she would be left alone. The housekeeper was unsure what to do to help. I could ask Lady Carrington to chaperone. Then I could help her and care for the baby as well."

"What's wrong with Lady Carrington?"

"She is recovering from a fall she took on her horse two weeks ago. Her right arm was sprained, and she needs some assistance in dressing and preparing meals. Very light work."

"She has no family to help her?"

"Her sister Clara lives in town but she went with the Norths' to help care for Edward on the trip."

This young woman was a take-charge sort. He had to admire that. She didn't wait for his answer but went to the telephone and rang up Central again, repeating her request to be connected to the Carrington residence. He listened to her persuasive tones as she talked to the woman on the other end of the line. He had no doubt she could talk a seaman into buying a house in the desert.

She hung up the earpiece. "It's all settled. We shall stop to pick her up on our way out of town. Addie left a few things there I can borrow to wear. I do dislike not caring for my mother though."

"You have no choice," he said.

"There is always a choice," she said.

He smiled. "You can't control everything, Miss Russell."

She thrust out her small, pointed chin. "I can try. In fact, before I agree to this for sure, I want to try to get home."

Fourteen

The baby played with the buttons on Mr. Jesperson's jacket. Katie kept her gaze on the passing scenery of coastal redwoods and hillsides covered in wildflowers. What was going on at home? Not knowing how her mother was doing moment by moment was difficult to deal with. It grated at her, not to be where she was needed most. She'd tried to see her father but had been turned away from the hospital, and then they'd tried three different avenues to get home and she'd been turned back at every one.

She stole a glance at him from under her lashes. The way he'd put his finger on her need for control unsettled her. He looked down at Jennie and smiled. The love in his gaze left a warm sensation in the pit of her stomach. Not many men would take on a burden like little Jennie so readily. She stole a second glance. She didn't want to notice his wide shoulders or the unruly black hair that spilled from under his hat and curled at his collar. She needed the security of a stable future. Like she would have with Bart.

"Lady Carrington lives at the end of this lane," she said, pointing to a narrow opening between neatly trimmed rhododendrons.

"Not with the Norths?"

She shook her head. "The cottage is just a summer home for them. Lord Carrington has an estate in England."

He guided the horse into the drive. The Carrington cottage came into view. Framed by the overhanging limbs of redwood and hemlock, the quaint cottage had been freshly painted with a coat of cheery yellow with white trim. A small porch held two rocking chairs. It was only a one-bedroom, as different from Lord Carrington's castle in England as possible. Once the horse stopped in front of the home, Katie handed Jennie to Mr. Jesperson and clambered down without waiting for assistance. Being in Mr. Jesperson's company had her every nerve tingling with awareness. Holding her skirts in the blustery wind, she hurried up the steps to the front door.

The door opened and Addie's mother peeked out. "There you are, Katie. I'm so worried about your mother. Have you heard how she is?" She adjusted the sling on her arm then stepped out to give Katie a quick hug.

"She was too ill to come to the phone, but our maid seemed confident she would be all right."

"I'm sure you're most distressed. Come in, child. There are some things of Addie's in the chest that should keep you for a few days."

Lady Carrington turned a brilliant smile in the man's direction. "Your baby has your eyes."

The baby squirmed to be let down, but he shifted her to his other shoulder. "I found her abandoned at Miss Bulmer's residence," he said. "But I believe she is my niece."

Lady Carrington's smile faded. "Oh dear me, I hope I haven't offended."

"Certainly not," he said. "Thank you for agreeing to stay with us at the lighthouse. Quite frankly, I find myself out of my element."

His confession of misgivings endeared him a bit to Katie. She'd thought his confidence knew no bounds, and from what she'd witnessed, he was most competent. "I shall collect a few things."

She left them on the porch and stepped into the cottage. The trunk of clothing was in the bedroom, and she selected several items and layered them in a bag Lady Carrington had evidently left out for her use. Daily laundry might be necessary for a few days, but this situation would be resolved as soon as the epidemic passed. By then she might have figured out her father's involvement in the ship incident.

When she returned to the porch, she found Lady Carrington holding Jennie in her lap on the swing while the lightkeeper loaded the buggy with bags. Mr. Jesperson took her bag and his hand grazed hers. Her skin felt warm from the contact, and her cheeks responded with heat as well. He retrieved Jennie and strode back to the buggy with Lady Carrington on his heels. Though he offered a hand, Katie clambered into the buckboard by herself, then settled Jennie on her lap when he handed the baby to her. He helped Lady Carrington into the buggy. Katie was glad Lady Carrington was between them.

Once they were on the road, the baby relaxed against her in sleep and grew heavy, but Katie welcomed the child's warmth in the chilly wind that whistled through the redwoods. Fingers of fog crept out of the woods and along the ground and sank into the low spots along the road. The buckboard rounded the last curve, and the craggy coastline lay before them. Whitecaps raced to touch the land then ebbed away, leaving behind kelp and seaweed whose odor mingled with that of the salt. Katie filled her lungs with the salty scent. A dim light shone through the fog from the lighthouse perched on the hillside. There were no neighbors. Maybe this wasn't a grand idea when she knew so little about Mr. Jesperson. And Katie had dragged Lady Carrington in on it as well.

Mr. Jesperson stared at the lighthouse. "I didn't leave a gaslight on," he said. "I wonder if Philip is there?" He flicked the whip above the horse's ears, and the animal broke into a trot. "I must get to the lighthouse and start the foghorn. This fog rolling in will soon be as thick as gravy."

As the horse cantered up the lane to the lighthouse, a bundle of white on a black rock down by the water caught Katie's attention. "What's that?" she asked, pointing. She squinted to see through the fog.

"I'm not sure. Wait here and I'll check it out." He stopped the buggy and leaped to the ground.

Katie wasn't about to wait behind. She passed the sleeping baby to Lady Carrington, who cradled her awkwardly in one arm, then followed him. The wind whipped Katie's skirts and she had to grab them to stay modest. The slope was slick with moisture from the fog, but she managed to reach him when he was halfway down to the white rags. Rocks rattled down the slope and she called out to him.

"Just couldn't handle not knowing what was happening?" He grinned and held out his hand to help her down the hillside.

She hated to be laughed at but she reluctantly accepted his assistance. The loose rocks demanded she cling to his warm fingers, and together, they sidled down the slope. As they neared the pile of white cloth, she stopped but still clutched his hand. Her gaze traveled to the heap of fabric on the sand. Swaths of white from the wedding dress lay matted on the rocks. She gasped and clutched his hand more tightly.

"Miss Russell, what is it?"

"It's Eliza . . . she was wearing a wedding dress . . . the last time I spoke with her." She let out a strangled cry and turned to press her face against the comforting warmth of Mr. Jesperson's wool jacket.

❧

Will cradled Katie against his chest. He wasn't used to holding a woman. Her hair smelled like some kind of flowers, and her bonnet brushed his chin. When she stepped away, he had to force himself to drop his arms. "Are you sure this dress belongs to Miss Bulmer?"

She brushed the tears from her face. "I–I don't know. Not for sure. But she's missing, and she was wearing a wedding dress the last time I spoke with her."

"Does the constable know this?'

She shook her head. "I didn't mention it to him. It didn't seem relevant."

He glanced up the hillside to the older woman standing at the front stoop. "I'll tend to this matter," he said. "If you would be so kind as to get our little group settled, I'll make sure there's no . . ."

"Body," she finished for him. The moisture in her blue eyes made them as luminous as the sea. "Poor Eliza." Her gaze went back to the dress on the rocks. "And poor Jennie."

He hadn't stopped to think of what Miss Bulmer's possible death would mean for the child. Now what did he do about her? His brother was going to have to bear some responsibility. "I'll help you up the slope. Could you call the constable? And if my brother is there, ask him to join me, if you would be so kind."

She nodded. He assisted her along the slick rocks to the top of the hill then retreated back to the yards of fabric. He studied the tides and the wind then noticed a small island offshore looming out of the wisps of fog. Gauging the distance and the force of the waves, he wondered if Eliza had been dumped on the island and the tide had carried her dress here. He didn't disturb the dress, but he squatted beside it and looked around in the dim light. The buttons up the back were broken or torn off. He walked quite a ways up the beach but saw nothing more.

He needed to poke around the island. After all, there was no assurance the constable himself wasn't involved in the piracy. It wasn't uncommon for a man sworn to uphold the law to be found breaking it. Footsteps crunched on the sand, and he turned to see his brother striding toward him.

"You found Eliza?" Philip's voice was hushed.

"We found a wedding dress," Will corrected. "Miss Russell said that when she spoke last with Miss Bulmer, the woman mentioned she was trying one on." His brother stepped closer, and Will noticed the way he blinked his eyes. "You cared about her."

"Of course I cared about her," Philip snapped. "I'm not a cad." He stared at the heap of bedraggled white on the sand then glanced out at the waves. "The tide is coming in."

Will pointed at the island. "I was thinking about looking out there for her body. She might have been dumped on the island."

"She was murdered, of course," Philip said. "She'd hardly go swimming in such attire."

"You think it was because of her involvement in the taking of *Dalton's Fortune*?" Will asked.

"I suspect so. Her tip to my client indicated she was involved. The company president sent me a telegram to let me know he'd received a ransom demand for the *Paradox*. He got back *Dalton's Fortune*."

"So they haven't sunk the ship."

"Unless it's a ruse to get more money." Philip nodded toward the island. "Let's go search."

"We should wait for the constable," Will said.

His brother snorted. "You know how inept local law enforcement is. Why do you think the shipping company hired me?" He set off down the beach, heading toward the pier. Will followed him. A skiff was tied up on a mooring at the end of the pier. They stepped over a smelly heap of kelp just before the pier and walked the length of the boards to the boat.

Will steadied the boat as Philip climbed into it then stepped in himself. The boat rocked in the waves and he nearly tipped, but he regained his balance and untied the rope. Philip settled onto the seat at the bow, so Will shrugged and took the seat with the oars. Putting his back into the work, he rowed out past the breakers and angled the skiff toward the small island teeming with gulls and frigate birds. Twilight was coming on fast in the low fog, and he realized he should have started the foghorn before he left. They would have to scout the island fast and get back to shore to tend to his duties.

Philip jumped out of the boat with a splash and dragged the

dinghy to the rocks. "It shouldn't take long to walk the perimeter. You go that way and I'll go this way," he said, gesturing to Will's left.

Will nodded and picked his way across the driftwood and flotsam. He found no sign of Miss Bulmer, but he did spy a large footprint that had been partially erased by the surf. The heel imprint was the only clear mark. A man who rolled over on his shoe. Not much to identify but it was enough to indicate someone might have dropped her here. He patted the sand and shoved back the vegetation in search of the missing body. Though he didn't truly expect to find Eliza so easily, he was still disappointed when he came up empty-handed.

He stood and brushed the sand from his hands. If he didn't get moving, the twilight and fog would make it impossible to see the shore. His foot struck something as continued around the island. The gleam of yellow caused a hitch in his lungs. A pocket watch lay partially buried in the sand. He picked it up and rolled it in his fingers. It was imprinted. He squinted to make out the letters: Albert Russell. His gut said it was too much of a coincidence to ignore.

With the watch safely in his pocket, he headed toward the dinghy. Something rustled in the thin, scrubby foliage nearby. Before he had time to consider if it was the wind or an animal, he was struck hard in the back. The heavy weight of his attacker bore him to the ground and pressed his face into wet mud and decaying vegetation.

Will fought back, driving his elbow into the gut of the man atop him. Air hissed through the attacker's mouth as the two fought silently in the fog that swirled along the shrubs and weeds. The man held a knife aloft, and Will got a glimpse of a skull on the shank of it. He managed to get his knee up then kicked out. The man rolled off him and Will leaped to his feet. His adversary did the same and Will stood poised to jump back into the battle. To his surprise, the thug turned and ran off. Will gave chase, but an exposed tree limb tripped him up and he hurtled back to the mud. He was unhurt except for a scrape on his cheek, but the man had disappeared.

Will bounded to his feet. "Philip!" he shouted. "Watch out!" He rushed back toward the dinghy. When his brother didn't answer, he picked up his pace and reached where the boat lay beached. There was no sign of Philip. Darkness had fully descended. Will shouted for him again, and this time he heard a groan. He moved toward it and nearly tripped over his brother's legs.

Philip groaned again. He muttered something unintelligible. Will touched his brother's face and his fingers came away sticky. Blood poured from a huge knot on Philip's head. "You're going to be all right, Philip."

Between the fog and the starless night, he couldn't see his hand in front of his face. Would they have to spend the night in the cold and damp? There'd be little opportunity for rest with the likelihood of an enemy lurking, and Philip needed to be warm, dry, and possibly under a doctor's care. Without being able to see the shore, he might as easily row for the open sea as for the lighthouse, her lamps still dark. A pang of guilt ran through him. Fine lightkeeper he was turning out to be.

Then he heard a wonderful sound: the foghorn brayed from off to his right. The deep tone was the sweetest sound he'd ever heard. He managed to get his brother into the dinghy, then shoved it into the water. He put his palms to the oars and rowed toward the sound, rolling through the dark.

FIFTEEN

THE FOGHORN TOLLED its warning in the dark. Tendrils of mist snaked around Katie's ankles and distorted what little she could see in the wash of the light from the lantern she held in her hand. Will should have been back by now. She caught herself thinking of him by his first name. When did that happen?

She swung the lamp back and forth, though she knew it was futile. The lighthouse behind her now blessedly threw out more light, but was it even penetrating the fog more than a few hundred feet? With the constable's help she'd managed to wind the light. Lady Carrington was keeping an eye on Jennie, but there was still no sound of oars in the water or the slap of water on a dinghy. If she hadn't glanced at the pier just before twilight, she would never even have known they'd taken the boat out to sea. Irritating men.

The constable joined her. "I fear he's lost his bearings. Where did you say they went?"

"I'm not sure. I went to call you, and when I came back out, I saw them rowing a small skiff out to sea. There's a tiny island out there. Perhaps he went there."

"Why would they head there?"

"He didn't reveal his plans to me," she said, unable to keep the displeasure from her voice.

"It's getting quite late. I need to get back to town. When he arrives, would you telephone me, please?"

She stared at him. "Aren't you going to search for them? They might be in distress." Her main concern was for the lightkeeper, but the thought of being alone in the dark frightened her as well. Someone might have killed Eliza, and that person could still be lurking about.

The constable took out a cigar. "Miss Katie, it's far too late to attempt a rescue. The fog will clear in the morning. If he hasn't returned by then, I'll commence a search." Brown turned to depart.

She extended her hand toward him. "That might be too late!" She shivered, wishing it didn't matter to her that Will had been foolish enough to go out on the sea in these conditions.

"They are grown men. They'll have to take their chances on their own foolishness," the constable called over his shoulder. "Butting into my investigation and all. Now see that you aren't foolish too. Get to the lighthouse and lock it up tight until morning."

His trim figure vanished in the fog. Katie strained to see out past the mist, but it swallowed up even the sound of the waves lapping at the shore. The eerie silence unnerved her. The foghorn bellowed again, and she jumped at the sudden blast of noise. Maybe she should go down to the shore and wave her light. She picked her way down the beach through the seaweed-strewn rocks. If they came to shore down that way, they might not see the lighthouse. Even now, it was dim behind her.

Katie's shoes slid on the slimy stuff, and she teetered on the edge of a steep drop-off. The lantern fell from her hand and shattered on the granite shards. What little light she'd had blinked out as she pinwheeled her arms and tried to maintain her balance. Her right hand caught the sharp edge of a rock and she steadied herself before managing to climb down to the sand.

When she stood on trembling knees by the water, she drew in a shaky breath and blew it out. The sound of the foghorn rolled through the mist again. When it ended, she cupped her hands to her mouth. "Will!" she shrieked. "Can you hear me?"

No voice answered her. She stepped closer to water, taking comfort in the rhythmic sound of it, lapping on the sand. She started to shout again then heard something odd. Was that a moan or the wind? A wave washed over her shoes, and she gasped as the frigid water touched her skin. A grinding sound came to her ears. Was it a boat scraping on the rocks? If only she could see. She strained to hear. There it came again. Something bumping on the rocks.

"Will!" she screamed again.

"Katie!" Will's voice held relief and something else. She moved in the direction of his voice. Shivers raced down her spine at the way the sound seemed to echo around her, out of nowhere. This fog was disorienting.

Waves soaked the hem of her dress, and she lifted it from the strands of kelp floating on the foam. The sound seemed close, about six feet away, though she could still see nothing and wished she had the lantern. "Will?"

"Here!" he called. "We're stuck on these rocks . . ."

She waded farther into the cold water. The sand fell away under her feet, and her head went under the water. Her wet skirts weighed her down and salty water filled her nose and mouth. Her toe touched something solid and she pushed off with all her might. Her head broke through the waves and she gasped in air. The salt burned her eyes and nose. Panic closed her throat as her sodden skirts threatened to drag her down again. She flayed about, trying to stay afloat.

Strong fingers closed over hers and the next moment she was lying on the bottom of the dinghy breathing in the oily scent of pitch. She coughed up salty water then gagged at the taste.

Big hands smoothed her hair back from her face. "You're all right. I've got you," Will said. "Cough it up."

She coughed again then sat up. "I thought you were dead."

"We might have been if you hadn't started the foghorn."

He hadn't let go of her hand yet, and she found herself wanting to cling to him. Which would never do.

❧

Will rolled the watch around in his pocket. The fireplace radiated warmth to his frozen limbs. The gray chair was quite comfortable, and he could go to sleep right here if he allowed himself.

"What did the fellow look like?" Philip asked, his voice weak but intent.

Will struggled to remember something about the man who had jumped them.

"He was heavy, and he had hard hands."

Philip touched the goose egg on his temple and winced. "That's not much to go on."

"Well, you were there too! What'd *you* see?" Will rubbed his head.

Katie came into the parlor with a box in her hand. She'd been remarkable. Fearless, as she'd leaped to his aid. If not for her clear thinking in starting the foghorn, things might have turned out very different.

She bit her lip as she approached his brother, who was lying on the sofa. "I found a first aid kit under the sink in the kitchen. I'm not very good at this."

She placed the box on the table beside Philip and lifted the lid. His brother was quiet as she tended to his cuts. Will read dislike in the rigidness of her shoulders as she dabbed antiseptic on Philip's skin. The glare she shot at him delighted Will, but he stuffed that happiness down deep until he had a chance to examine just why he didn't want Miss Russell to be impressed with his younger brother's good looks. She washed his wound then dabbed iodine on the cut and positioned a bandage around his head.

She turned toward Will. "Now you."

"I'm fine," he said.

"There's a small cut on your cheek and one on your hand. It's best to tend to them now."

She knelt beside him and dabbed iodine on the minor injuries. With her this close, he could smell the sea on her skin. Tendrils of wet hair had escaped her pins, and a long curl brushed his cheek. He resisted the urge to entwine it around his finger. She put a plaster on the cut and stepped back and turned. He watched her replace everything in the box.

"You look quite fetching in glasses," he said softly.

She colored and whipped them from her face, sticking them in the pocket of the apron she wore over her dress. "There is some acetylsalicylic acid powder in here. Does your head pain you?" she asked Philip.

"I don't want anything like that, but I wouldn't refuse coffee."

"There is some in the kitchen, in the cupboard by the sink," Will said. When she nodded and exited the room, he found himself watching her swaying skirts.

He glanced at the pocket watch. She needed to know about it. Philip was nodding off again, so Will rose and padded out to the kitchen. He found her measuring coffee into the pot on the stove. "There is something you should see."

One perfectly shaped brow arched. "Another problem?"

When he opened his extended hand, the watch lay in his palm, inscription up. The color drained from her face. She picked it up. "Papa's watch. Where did you find it?"

"On the island just before I was attacked." He watched the knowledge come into her face—the idea that her father might have had something to do with throwing Miss Bulmer into the sea.

Those blue eyes slammed shut then opened again, blazing with pain. "I don't believe my father would harm anyone."

"He did show up here looking for this watch," Will reminded her.

"That means nothing." She turned her back on him and went back to preparing the coffee.

He watched her stiff back and knew she wouldn't say another word. Retracing his steps, he found his brother sitting up again with his head in his hands. "How are you feeling?" Will asked.

Philip lifted his head. "Like I was just beat up."

"Did you see who attacked *you*?"

"No. One minute I was walking the shore, and the next second my face was in the sand." Philip cradled his head. "At least this will get me off the hook with the constable."

"I'm not so sure about that," Will said. "He was already suspicious of your whereabouts the night Eliza disappeared."

Color rushed to Philip's face. "If you hadn't offered to take the child, he wouldn't have known anything about me."

"A Jesperson doesn't run from his duty," Will said.

"I'm not that child's father, Will!"

"You can't be sure, can you?" Will was suddenly weary of his brother's constant excuses. "You refuse to take responsibility for anything, Philip. Nothing is ever your fault. You will take Jennie home with you and own up to your situation." The very thought of losing the baby made him cringe, but it was right that she should be with her father.

His brother bolted from the sofa. "I will do no such thing!"

Before Will answered, Miss Russell stepped back into the parlor with a tray of coffee in her hands. She glanced from Will to his brother with wide eyes.

She set the tray on a table. "I couldn't help but overhear. You don't believe Jennie is your daughter?"

"I do not," Philip said emphatically.

"There is the possibility that she is my sister," she said.

Philip shot Will an enraged glare. "I see. Does my brother know of your suspicion?"

"Of course. We argued over who should take charge of Jennie."

"I see." Philip's mouth grew more pinched. "You've been unable to convince my brother of that fact?"

Will barely suppressed the urge to roll his eyes. "Jennie's appearance convinced me, along with your admission of a relationship with the woman." Miss Russell's cheeks turned pink, and he realized how inappropriate their conversation was. "I apologize for the indelicacy of this discussion, Miss Russell. Please forgive me."

She handed over a cup of coffee without speaking. "I don't believe any of us know for sure who Jennie's father is," she said, narrowing her eyes at Philip. "But don't you feel some responsibility since you don't know for certain?"

He scowled. "She's not my child."

"You're quite positive?"

Philip hesitated, but that was all it took for Miss Russell to set her coffee on the table and cross her arms across her chest. "What about Eliza? Did you harm her?"

"Of course not!" Philip scowled at her. "I think your father did away with her." He rubbed his head. "For all I know, he's the one who attacked me on the island."

"Don't be ridiculous. He's in the hospital."

"Are you sure?" Philip's voice was taunting. "Why don't we place a call and see?"

"He's not even conscious," she said.

"Or he's playing possum," Philip shot back.

"I'm not going to stay here and listen to your hideous innuendoes." She marched off and the stomp of her footsteps on the stairs echoed back.

"She's quite the spitfire," Philip said. He took a sip of coffee and grimaced. "Too strong." He put it on the table.

Will took a cautious gulp and shuddered. "You were goading her."

"I suppose I'd best stay around," Philip said, with a sly glance at Will.

Will scowled, though he knew his brother was baiting him. "If you have plans to court Miss Russell, that's not acceptable."

"Don't tell me a woman has finally caught your eye." Philip's grin was cheeky.

"Don't try to change the subject. We were discussing your duty to Jennie," Will snapped.

Philip splayed out his hands. "I had nothing to do with the baby or Eliza's possible murder. I'm only here to find those ships and the missing money."

Will sighed. Philip's constant denials were beginning to sway him. "You had a relationship with the woman."

"So did a lot of men."

"I'd like to believe you. But Jennie looks a lot like you, Philip. Even has your cowlick. And those eyes are shaped like yours."

"Babies all look alike," Philip said. He took another gulp of coffee. "If I thought for a moment she was my child, I'd admit it and take responsibility for her."

Will stifled a scoff and decided not to remind his brother of the many times he'd left Will to smooth ruffled feathers, broken promises, and missed appointments. The boy was so unreliable. No, not a boy. Man. It was time Will recognized that his brother was a grown man. He needed to let Philip endure the consequences for his actions. Even if it was the hardest thing he'd ever had to do.

He walked toward the stairs. "You'll sleep on the sofa so you're near Jennie. If she wakes up in the night, you can care for her. I'll be tending the light."

"Lady Carrington already has her."

"I'll get her. She's our responsibility until we get this figured out."

"I know nothing about babies! Besides, I have a date tonight."

"Cancel it! I don't know anything about children either. But we're both going to have to learn. Jennie is not Miss Russell's charge. She is ours."

"Russell!" Philip said. "Is her father Albert Russell?"

"He is."

"He tried to kill himself. Maybe he knew I was on to him. He must know something about the two ships being taken. If only you'd been able to talk to Eliza before she went missing."

Did his brother ever think of other people? "Forgive me for not getting *your* job done the way *you* wished."

"Eliza's the one who knows what's happened here," Philip said. "I can feel it in my gut."

"The baby is what is important here, not your investigation. Jennie's *mother*—not your *informant*—is missing, probably dead. Doesn't that mean anything to you?"

"Of course it does," Philip said, his voice sulky. "But I must solve the case to get paid."

"There are more important things than your career. I hope you'll figure that out sooner rather than later." As Will led the way up the staircase, he despaired of ever seeing his brother grow into a man.

What made him think he could raise a little girl when he'd failed so miserably with his brother?

Sixteen

What was that squawking? Katie opened a bleary eye. Lady Carrington slept beside her. The two women had shared a bed, and Katie had been so concerned about disturbing the older woman that she'd lain awake, struggling to not move. Their bed had been comfortable but hardly the luxury they were both used to. A simple yellow and green quilt covered the mattress on the iron bedstead, and a rag rug was the only thing to warm their feet. The curtains were frayed and worn but clean. They'd obviously been left here by the previous lightkeeper and his family.

The sound came again. She swung her legs out of bed. The other woman didn't move. Katie belted her robe around her and tiptoed to the door. She snatched her glasses from the dresser beside it. Light slanted through the curtains. She should have been up already, seeing to the baby. She opened the door and stepped into the hall in her bare feet.

A voice barked, "Step away from the cake!"

The harsh tone made her shiver. She was tempted to flee back to the safety of her bedroom—after all, a killer was still on the loose—but curiosity won out and she eased down the steps. It sounded like the man was in the kitchen. If he was talking about cake, that would make sense. She scurried along the painted wood floors to the door to the kitchen. It was closed. No more sound came from the other side of it. Her hand grasped the cold ceramic knob, and she gave it a twist and a shove until the door opened a crack. She peered inside as the grating voice repeated its command.

She saw no one in the small room. Pushing the door open further, she stepped past the icebox and glanced around, seeing it with fresh eyes in the bright wash of daylight. No one here. The simple wooden counter held a dry sink. Curtains covered the shelves under the counter. There was a wood range that took up most of one side of the kitchen. The floor was green-and-gray linoleum, in good condition, and everything was clean. Her gaze swept the room.

Something moved at the table. It took a moment for her to realize a giant bird stared back at her from its perch on the back of a chair. Newspaper lined the floor under the perch. The black avian stretched its neck then picked up a nut from the table and cracked it open.

"Step away from the cake!" The bird sidled a few steps toward her.

"It's a bird," she breathed. She moved nearer to the table and held out her hand.

"I wouldn't do that if I were you," Will said from the doorway. He was dressed in a white shirt, open at the collar and slightly wrinkled, over gray slacks. His hair was wind-tossed. He brushed past her and held out his hand. The bird stepped delicately onto his wrist. "He doesn't like strangers, and he's apt to nip you."

She snatched her hand back. "He's beautiful." The bird preened as if he heard her. The light glistened on his wings. Her fingers itched to stroke him. "What is he?"

"A mynah. He talks."

"I heard him. How long have you had him?"

"A few days. Ever since Philip got tired of taking care of him." Will carried the mynah to the back door and out onto the stoop where he put him on a perch.

She followed him. "Was he out here last night? I didn't see him. And won't he fly away?"

"He was in a covered cage in my bedroom last night. His wings are clipped. He's a homebody too. Likes being waited on hand and foot."

"A typical man."

He grinned. "A suffragette, are you? Marching in the Easter Day parade?"

She tipped up her chin. "And if I were?"

One dark brow lifted and his generous mouth twitched. "I'd say you've got courage. The vote for women is long overdue."

His stance surprised her, but she just nodded and kept her attention on the bird. "He keeps saying that about the cake. Whatever does it mean?"

"I haven't the least notion. It's rather annoying." He dusted the nuts from his hand and moved back to the kitchen.

Katie followed after a backward glance at the parrot. She wanted to just sit and watch the bird. "How is Jennie this morning?"

"Still sleeping."

"And your brother?"

"Doing the same. He refused to get up with her."

"You're sure she is his daughter?"

"I'm reasonably certain."

She wanted to turn from the way his dark eyes probed hers. He was much too intimate in his ways.

"We must decide what is to be done with Jennie," he said. "My brother appears unready to accept responsibility."

"My mother would like to spend a little more time with her."

"Do you think she might be your half sister?"

"It will be difficult to ascertain the truth," she admitted, stopping momentarily in the doorway to the parlor. "Unless my father regains consciousness." She bit her lip. "What I heard was very incriminatory."

"I took the liberty of calling to check on your father this morning. No change in his condition. He's still unconscious. I was informed again that no one could visit until the smallpox epidemic was past."

She winced at the news. "Thank you." A knock on the door sounded, and she realized she was in her nightgown and robe.

"I'll get it," Will said, exiting the kitchen.

Hardly respectable to be talking with the devilishly handsome Will Jesperson in her nightwear. She started to follow him but the telephone on the wall rang. She snatched the earpiece from the hook and spoke into the mouthpiece. "Mercy Falls Lighthouse."

"The constable hasn't been by to see me, so I think you've been a good girl," the man on the other end said. "See that you keep your mouth shut. I can get to your father in the hospital with no problem. You wouldn't like how I could hurt your mother."

The voice was the man who had called from the skating rink. "What do you want?" she whispered.

"Just to remind you to stay quiet about anything you heard Eliza say."

There was a click in her ear. "I don't know anything," she said, but there was no one on the other end. She toggled the switch to summon the operator.

"Operator," Nell's voice said.

"Nell, where did that call come from that you just put through?"

"How are you, Katie?" Nell asked. "I wish we could go back to the office. I don't like working from home."

"Things will be back to normal soon. About that call. Where did it come from?"

"The shipping office down at the dock. Is something wrong?"

It would be useless to go down there. "The man didn't identify himself. I just wondered. See you soon, Nell." Katie hung the earpiece on the hook then rushed from the kitchen and up the stairs to the bedroom.

Lady Carrington still slept as Katie dressed and poked hairpins into her coil of curls with shaking hands. The menace in the man's voice terrified her, but of course her parents were safe. Orderlies wouldn't let the man near her father, and her mother was protected by the servants. Though they'd been little help when that man attacked her with the whiskey bottle. She would just call and make sure everything was all right when she went back downstairs.

She removed her glasses and tucked them into her pocket. When she went back downstairs, she heard the low murmur of male voices in the parlor. She sidled past to the kitchen and had Nell ring her mother. After the maid assured her all was well, she checked in at the hospital. Her father's condition was unchanged. Relieved, she stepped out of the kitchen and entered the parlor. She found Bart seated by the fireplace with a cup of coffee in his hands. Why did her heart sink when she wanted so much to love him?

He put down the cup and bolted to his feet. Dressed in a light gray sack coat, he oozed wealth and status. "Katie, I apologize for such an early call. I phoned your house and your mother said you'd been forced to come here to avoid the sickness in town. My home is completely free of the disease. You should have called me." His voice held reproof, as did his stern expression.

She stepped into the room and forced a smile. "That's very kind of you, Bart. My boss asked me to arrange to set up the switchboard where I was lodging. I couldn't presume upon your mother in such a fashion."

His smile faltered. "I'm sure she wouldn't have minded," he said, but his tone lacked conviction.

"Mr. Jesperson was in need of a nanny for the child, and I was in need of a temporary home. After fetching dear Lady Carrington as a chaperone, it seemed an equitable arrangement."

"Mr. Foster tells me the two of you have an understanding," Will said, his tone frosty. His dark brows were drawn together. "I can well fathom his trepidation at your temporary residence here."

Bart nodded. "We have plenty of room, Katie. I'd be happy to take you back to the house."

Katie's spine stiffened. "Thank you, Bart, but as I said, Lady Carrington is here too. I wouldn't want to impose with extra guests. I've also already arranged for the switchboard to be delivered here and it should be arriving momentarily. You'll see—it will all be over soon and everything will be set back to rights."

Bart's mouth pulled downward, but he took her rejection with reasonable grace. "Yes, well, I also stopped by to bring you up-to-date on the status in the town. The constable and Dr. Lambertson moved quickly to quarantine any possible cases of smallpox. They feel the cases will drop off soon if everyone stays calm and remains at home as much as possible."

"Good news," she said. "Is there any idea where this disease came from?"

He nodded. "A ship brought it in. It's been quarantined at its mooring up in Oregon."

"Your family is all well? You know my mother has come down with the disease and everyone was at church. They could have been infected."

"The doctor says a patient is only contagious when they have a fever and the pustules break out. Your mother was perfectly fine at church, was she not?"

"Yes, she was fine until yesterday."

"So perhaps you will escape as well."

Katie hadn't stopped to think about the possibility of having contracted the disease—or of passing it on to the baby and everyone else in the house. She prayed none of them would get sick. And that her stay at the lighthouse might be God's leading—that she could discover what had happened to make her father want to kill himself.

❧

Will kept busy for the next few days. After getting up around one o'clock every afternoon, he cleaned the windows on the lighthouse, touched up paint on the tower, organized his equipment, and avoided the pretty Miss Russell as best he could. It was easy enough—he took over the duty of watching Jennie about the time she needed to sit down at the switchboard or Mrs. Carrington needed a rest.

He saw little of his brother. Philip was presumably out looking for the missing ship, commandeered by the pirates, but seemed to spend more of his time talking to men at the quay every day.

As far as Will knew, Philip had found no real leads until the day he asked Will to accompany him along the coast. An informant had told Philip he'd seen a ship pass that way. Will had awakened at eleven and his duties were done, so he agreed. Katie was on the switchboard in a corner of the parlor. He doubted she would notice or question the fact he was gone. And Lady Carrington and Jennie seemed to have made for a special relationship, content to be together for hours at a time.

The temperature hovered near sixty-two degrees, and there wasn't a cloud in the sky as he guided the buckboard down a muddy lane that was more potholes than road. Philip had been told this narrow path led to the section of coastline where the ship had last been spotted.

Philip readjusted his grip so as to not get unseated. "This is complete wilderness."

"It will be difficult to find the ship if they went upriver some-where," Will said. He pulled the buckboard to a stop. The mare tossed her head and snorted then leaned down to munch a patch of grass. He tossed the reins around a shrub as he got down, then walked out to a spit of land that poked into the sea. The whitecaps foamed against the rocks and left the tang of salt in the air. Seagulls squawked overhead.

Philip joined him and the two stood staring out at the rugged coast lined with redwood and hemlock. The sea breeze nearly took Will's hat, and he grabbed at it before it careened off the cliff. "Looks like nothing has ever happened out here," he said. "Peaceful and serene."

Philip wrinkled his nose. "Rotting kelp." He pointed at the

steaming piles of tangled kelp on the rocks below them as the gulls pecked through the mess for bugs.

Will ignored the smell. He stared out past the breakers to where the shoreline curved in and out again, then he looked back to the woods again. No one lived out here but bears and hawks. If they intended to press further into this area, they'd have to do it on foot or horseback. He buttoned his jacket against the stiff wind. "You ready to go back? Nothing is out here."

Philip shook his head. "Not yet. As far as I know, no one has probed this area very well." They walked along the coast as far as they could but found nothing. "It's pure wilderness," he said. He turned and set off along the rocky beach.

Will shrugged, his attention on the interesting cloud formation overhead. "Because there's nothing to see."

"Perhaps." Philip turned and climbed up a small cliff that blocked the way.

Will followed, reaching for one handhold after another. As soon as he got home, he'd look for the weather balloons he'd released this morning. On the other side of the cliff, he settled in to watch the tides. They had walked for nearly an hour.

"Philip, are we going to walk all the way to Oregon?" He kicked a stone into the air. It pinged off the rocks as it fell toward the water. Instead of a splash, he heard it *clank* against something. He dropped to his knees and peered over the side. A ledge projected out from the face of the escarpment, ten feet below. Something glinted on it. From his position, it appeared to be the ring from an old harness.

"What is it?" Philip asked, backtracking to his brother.

"Perhaps nothing." Will couldn't let it go though. He grabbed a tree root sticking from the ground and slipped over the side.

"What are you doing?"

"Going to see what's down there." Will lowered himself until his feet dangled three feet from the ledge. He took a deep breath and let go, praying the ledge wouldn't collapse. He slid down the rock face, then fell to his knees on the ledge. It held. Dusting himself off, he got up and glanced around. Vegetation blocked the cliff wall but he thought he glimpsed a hole in the rocks. He shoved aside a hedge nettle to reveal a cave. The opening was about three feet in diameter.

"What's down there?" Philip called.

"A cave. Wish I had a lantern." Will tried to see further into the space, but the sun only illuminated the first two feet. He thought he saw something glitter inside. Maybe mica catching the sunlight. He knew he should grab his brother's hand and get out, but an inner compulsion made him press farther into the cave. He had to put his hands on dried gull dung to squeeze through, but they would wash.

He waited a moment for his eyes to adjust. The dank space smelled of dirt, mold, and sea salt. From what he could see, the walls opened out from the mouth of the cave another three feet on either side. The space was fairly good sized, and the ceiling rose overhead to about nine feet tall. He could crawl inside and stand up, but his efforts would be useless without a lantern.

"You coming up?"

"In a minute," he called to his brother. He peered toward where he'd seen a shimmer. Was that a chest? He crawled in a little farther until he could run his fingers over a leather chest bound in brass. The metal must have been what he saw gleaming in the sunlight. The thing was padlocked, so he couldn't open it. It was about one foot by two. Small, but when he tried to lift it, he found it heavy. Panting, he dragged it toward the opening and out into the open air.

"Everything okay?" Philip called down.

"I found something. A chest. We're going to need a rope to get it up. There's one back in the buckboard."

"A chest?" Philip's voice sharpened. "I'll come down."

"No! Then we'll both be stuck here. We need that rope."

"It will take me two hours to walk there and return!" Displeasure coated Philip's words.

Will craned his neck to stare up into his brother's face. "Hurry. Perhaps I can pick the lock while I'm waiting."

Philip glanced out to sea. "I don't like leaving you here alone. Why don't you come with me? The chest will be safe enough."

"Seems foolhardy to leave something that might be a valuable clue. Whoever stashed it here might come back."

Philip's brow creased. "And do you have a weapon if he does?"

"No."

"Here, catch." Philip brandished a pistol.

Will caught it and stuffed it in his waistband. "I'll be fine. Hurry!"

"Watch yourself. I shall be back as soon as possible."

Philip's face disappeared from above. It sounded as though Philip was moving fast. They'd meandered their way here, so perhaps his brother would return in less than two hours. Will glanced at the sun that was nearly overhead. His stomach growled, but there would be no lunch for him. That, too, was back at the buckboard.

He picked up a rock to try to knock off the padlock, but before he brought it down, he heard a rustling from the opposite direction of where they'd left the buckboard. The sounds of male voices drifted toward him.

He shoved the chest back into the cave then scrambled inside with it. Moments later a rope dangled in front of the opening. Someone was coming down.

SEVENTEEN

"OPERATOR," KATIE SAID. She chatted a moment with Mrs. Silvers and found out most people were beginning to recover from smallpox and there had been no new cases, though the existing cases would be contagious until the scabs dropped off. Another couple of weeks and the town would likely be totally clear of the scourge. She connected the woman's call to her daughter-in-law. Once she heard the other woman pick up, she saw the lamp light for another call. It was Mr. Gleason calling the bank. No chitchatting with him.

There was a lull when the switchboard remained dark, then Katie's shift was over. She checked in with Nell to make sure the other woman was ready to go at her remote location, then removed her headset and stretched. Working away from the office had proven to be rather enjoyable. There had been no problems so far.

Lady Carrington came in, chasing the toddler, and gave Katie a weary look. Jennie reached for her.

"You want to go outside?" Katie scooped her up and smiled at Lady Carrington. "I have her. You go and rest." Lady Carrington gave her no argument and they went out the back door, stepping past the bird.

Paco gave her a baleful look and shifted on his perch. "Step away from cake!" he screeched.

Jennie flinched and hid her face against Katie's shoulder. "There is no cake," Katie muttered. Though it sounded good, she wasn't in the mood for baking. Truth be told, she was an atrocious cook. Her mother had tried to teach her, but Katie's mind always drifted out the window to the city streets and what she was missing.

Jennie craned her neck to watch the birds soaring overhead as Katie strolled the beach. The sea breeze tugged at the tendrils of hair that had escaped her pins, and she pushed them back from her face with an impatient hand. The blue of the sea reflected the brilliant sky overhead. The whitecaps were like frosting on the tops of the waves. She shook her head at her constant thoughts of cake. Silly bird. She stopped to stand Jennie on the beach. The baby stooped and grabbed a fistful of sand and started to cram it into her mouth until Katie stopped her. The sun struck Katie's face and she realized she hadn't seized her hat.

Katie let Jennie hang onto her finger as the baby toddled along the shore of the water. Her giggles mingled with the sound of the surf and soothed Katie's jitters. All morning long she hadn't been able to raise anyone at her house. All was well, she told herself—her father was holding his own and surely her mother was fine. But then, why wouldn't Lois pick up?

A movement caught her eye, and she noticed a female figure approaching from the road. She wore a white lingerie dress that swayed around her slim figure. The broad brim of her hat shaded the woman's face. The parasol she carried blocked the view even more, but something about the way she walked seemed familiar to Katie. The buggy in which she'd arrived was at the steps to the lighthouse.

Katie smiled as the woman stopped a few feet away. "May I help you?"

The woman lifted her head, but her hand still shaded her face. "I'm looking for Katie Russell."

Katie stepped nearer. "I'm Katie. Have we met?"

The woman dropped her hand, and the sun pierced the shadows thrown by her hat. "Don't you know me, darling?"

Every muscle tensed. The seashell Katie had found fell from her hand. Her heart rebounded against her chest wall, and she struggled to breathe. No, it couldn't be. She wouldn't let it be true. She squeezed shut her eyes and drew in a deep breath. When she opened them again, the mirage was still before her. As solid as the ground under her feet. It was no ghost, no figment of her imagination. Was that powder on the woman's face? And blush. She concentrated on the shocking makeup rather than on what she longed to deny.

The woman in front of her was Florence. The woman who bore her.

The moisture dried on Katie's tongue. She continued to stare at the woman smiling back at her. The years had not been kind to Florence. Katie couldn't think of her as her mother. Inez Russell was her mother.

"Cat got your tongue?" Florence stepped nearer. She touched a gloved finger to Katie's cheek. "I would think you would be over-joyed to see your mama."

Katie flinched then attempted to harness her racing thoughts. "What are you doing here?" she managed past her closed throat. She scooped up the baby for comfort.

"You don't seem glad to see me." Florence's pert smile faded, and she tugged on one glove. Her blue eyes, so like Katie's own, narrowed, and she gave the parasol on her shoulder a spin.

"I—I'm shocked," Katie said. "I never thought I'd see you again." She glanced back at the house. All she could do was pray Lady Carrington didn't happen to look outside. Katie had to get rid of this woman. Quickly, before anyone saw them together. "Did you go by my parents' house?"

Florence's brows drew together even more. "When I reached town, I stopped to buy some headache powder but quickly left the doctor's office when I learned of the smallpox making its rounds. When I inquired about the Russells, I was told you were out here. You are the one I came to see anyway, not my treacherous sister."

"Did you go see Papa?"

"I was denied entrance until the smallpox is past, but the doctor said he was improving. I slipped down the hall when no one was looking and peeked into his room though. He's gotten quite old, hasn't he?"

Katie said nothing. Most likely the woman had no idea she'd aged as well. It was as though a giant hand squeezed Katie's soul. She wanted to wail and cry, but more than anything else, she wanted not to have to look into this woman's face. "I think you'd better go. There's nothing for you here."

"You're the only reason I'm here."

"We severed all ties years ago."

The way the woman pressed her lips together accentuated the lines around her mouth. "You mean Albert severed them. I want to weave them together again."

Weave them together again? There weren't even ruins left of that original foundation. "I have no interest in a relationship with you," Katie said. "You abandoned me to go off with your boyfriend. Is that supposed to be forgotten now?"

Florence grimaced. "I just went out for a little fun! I was coming back. You had to go running to Albert. Of all people." Her voice was thick with disgust and she rolled her eyes.

"I was five years old! Much too young to be left alone at night. I was frightened." Katie still remembered the terror of the night with a strange man knocking on the door in search of her mother. "That man you'd been with the night before. Harold something. He came by after you'd gone out. I—I didn't like the way he looked at me." She shuddered.

"He wouldn't have hurt you," Florence said with a hard smile. "But I know you were young. I forgive you."

Katie clutched the baby to her chest. *She forgives me?* Her stomach roiled with nausea. "Why are you here? You were always too busy dancing and going to parties to even notice me. I have a new life. If you care about me at all, you'll leave before anyone finds out."

"Finds out what?"

She bit her lip. "That you're my mother," Katie finally whispered.

Florence stared. "You mean people think the Russells are your real parents? How is that possible?"

Katie hunched her shoulders, wishing she didn't have to broach the subject at all. "You were only in town for a week in that boarding-house. You were going by a different name. My father had just moved here and Mama was still packing up in San Francisco. She arrived the morning after Papa took me in."

"So everyone assumed you were their daughter," Florence said slowly.

"I *am* their daughter. In every way that matters," Katie said, her voice fierce. "If you're here for money, Papa doesn't have any."

Florence laughed. "Do you truly expect me to believe that, Katie? I'm not stupid. The Russells are wealthy. My dear sister is rolling in money. There is no reason she shouldn't share with me since I gave her my own flesh and blood." She glanced toward the house. "Aren't you going to offer me some tea?"

"No. I want you to leave, forever. My life is fine without you. I have a mother. I don't need another." Katie raised her voice. "Please, can't you just leave me alone?"

Florence's mouth grew pinched. She stared at Katie with a specula-tive gleam in her eyes. "How much will you give me to go away?"

Katie took a step back. "I have no money."

"Then you'd better get some." Florence twirled her parasol again and turned back toward the buggy. "Move quickly, Katie. Or I will tell everyone your mother is a vaudeville dancer and a lady of the night."

The woman sauntered away and left Katie staring after her with her hand to her throat. This couldn't happen—not now.

⌘

Staring at the rope dangling in front of the cave opening, Will tried to decide what to do. It was dark in here. He could move to the back and try to hide. Observing what was going on might be more profitable. And prudent. But if the man climbing down here had a lantern, he might be discovered, and the idea of being caught, hiding out, grated at him.

He heard the men talking topside. The one with a gruffer voice said, "We need to get this stowed and ready. The next ship will be here in two days. Once we get the plunder from it, we can get out of here."

The pirates. They were planning another theft.

The rope in front of him swayed, and the tip of a boot appeared. Will didn't have long to make up his mind. He stood and stepped to the back of the cave. As soon as he moved away from the opening, it was too dark to see. He held his hands out in front of him and groped along the rough rock walls. Shuffling across the uneven floor, he walked about fifteen feet before he came to the back of the space. He crouched and swept his hands around to try to find something to shield him from view. There was nothing. He stood and faced the light at the front of the cave. He withdrew the pistol tucked into his waistband.

A figure blocked the light in the cave's opening. The man stooped and peered into the cave. Will knew him right away—the worker who'd been talking to the businessman on the hillside. When the fellow stepped into the cave, Will saw he had no lantern attached to his waist.

The man moved to Will's left, toward where the chest had been stashed. Will realized he hadn't gotten the chest back into the place where it had resided. It sat two feet further from the opening and was not shoved against the wall. The fellow crouched and moved his hands along the rock wall. Will heard a clatter and something scrape. Then a tiny light flared, and he saw a lantern and matches in the man's hand.

Will crouched down and pressed back against the rocks behind him. If he stood still, perhaps the man wouldn't examine the rest of the cave. The wick caught flame, and the lantern's warm yellow glow pushed back the shadows in the cave to two feet in front of Will. He remained just barely covered by the dark. As the light probed the other corners of the space, he saw the outline of the cave better. It widened to about eight feet and went back into the hillside fifteen feet or so.

The fellow set the lantern down and crouched in front of the chest. Will could only pray the pirate didn't remember exactly where he'd placed it last. A click echoed against the cave walls and the man lifted the lid on the box. Will sidled to the right so he could see better. His boot scraped a loose rock. He froze when the fellow stopped and lifted his head. The man reached toward his waist, and Will caught the gleam of a gun in the lamplight. His fingers tightened on his own gun, but before the fellow withdrew his weapon, another man called down from atop the cliff.

"Chesterson, are you about done? I need to get back." The accomplice's voice was cultured.

"Almost," the workman shouted. "Give me a minute." The man tipped his head and listened with his hand still on the butt of his gun. Will didn't move. "Lousy rats," the man muttered. He knelt in front of the chest again and withdrew a stack of ledgers. He laid a compass and other instruments on the rocky floor. A metal lockbox came out next.

Will couldn't let the evidence get away. He brought up his pistol. The man pulled out a burlap sack then put the lockbox into it before tightening the top and turning back to the rope dangling outside the opening. Will relaxed a bit when he realized the man intended only to take a small portion of the contents of the chest. Could he apprehend the perpetrators? If he let them leave, Will might not be able to discover their identity. But if he stopped them now, Philip might never find the ship itself. Uncertain how to proceed, Will took another step and a rock rattled.

The man whipped out his gun and turned toward him. "Don't move!" he barked.

Will had the advantage because he could see the man and the guy couldn't see him. "Drop it! I've got a gun on you," he said. Will's finger tightened on the trigger, but rather than dropping his gun, Chesterton fired. Something struck Will on the left side of his head, and his vision blurred. He struggled to stay conscious, to depress the trigger on his pistol, but he was dizzy. The next thing he knew, he was falling. His hand struck a rock and the gun clattered across the rock floor. Then a cold metal barrel dug into his forehead.

"If you move, I'll kill you," the man said. He dragged Will roughly to his feet.

Will's head throbbed, and a wave of nausea struck him. The man half-dragged him toward the front of the cave. Philip's pistol was somewhere behind them and of no help to him. He had no strength to fight the man's rough handling. In the shaft of sunlight streaming into the mouth of the cave, Will saw the hard glint in the fellow's eyes, the cruel twist of his mouth. This was no gardener but a thug dressed as one.

"We've got a problem," the man shouted up to his partner. "There's a snoop in here."

"What?" The accomplice's voice was faint, as though he'd moved away from the edge. When he spoke again, he was louder. "Did you shoot him?"

"Yeah, I nicked his head. What should I do with him?"

There was silence for a long moment. Will felt his strength beginning to return. If he could ward off action for a few more minutes, he might be able to get out of this.

"Kill him," the man above said. "We leave no witnesses."

"We should make it look like an accident," Chesterton said, "so no one comes looking for us. Maybe tie him up here and let him die on his own, then come back and take off the ropes?"

"He'll stink up the cave. Besides, that's too risky. He might get away," the voice said from above.

There was another pause. Then the man's hand tightened. He hauled Will out of the cave opening. Will's muscles tightened in preparation for a fight. He wasn't going down without a struggle. Before the other man from above spoke, the thug's grip on Will's arm turned painful. Will had no time to realize what was happening. He went sailing off the ledge where they stood. He plummeted toward the waves crashing on the rocks fifty feet below. His arms pinwheeled out, and he bit back a shout.

Time seemed to slow as he fell over the cliff face. If he struck the rocks, he was a dead man. He barely had time to pray before the water rose to meet him. A wave took him under and battered him against the rocks. Something struck his forehead. Saltwater filled his mouth. His lungs burned with the need to breathe. He couldn't see, couldn't tell where he was or how to escape the roiling ocean.

Pain shot up his arm when a wave rolled him into another rock. The waves tossed him until he lost all sense of time. He made it to the surface, took a lungful of air, but then was hit by another five-foot wave, which drove him down again. He was barely able to stay conscious.

His arms flailed as he grasped for something to cling to. His hands scraped a rock and a fingernail tore from his forefinger, but he barely felt it. His head came up and he drew in a breath before the sea took him under again. His backside scraped sand on the bottom, and then the current shot him to the surface again, suddenly twenty feet out. When his head next broke the surface, he found himself rolling out to sea in the grip of an undertow. He weakly tried to swim to shore, but the strong current carried him farther away. His arms came up but were puny weapons against the power of the sea.

He would never make it to shore.

EIGHTEEN

KATIE CHEWED HER scone but it was like choking down sand. The sun shone through the window into the parlor, but its cheery presence wasn't enough to lift her from the gloom that had encased her since Florence had confronted her hours ago. What was she going to do? If the good folks of Mercy Falls found out her real heritage, any respect she'd managed to earn for herself would be gone. No one would take kindly to being deceived for all these years.

Jennie played at her feet, and Katie didn't smile when the baby giggled at her. She felt like crying instead.

"Katie, dear, is something wrong?"

Katie glanced at Lady Carrington. Her green eyes were filled love and concern. Katie managed a smile. "I'm not hungry. I didn't sleep well last night." She took a sip of her tea.

"I saw you speaking with a woman earlier. You haven't been yourself since. Who was she, my dear?"

The tea scalded Katie's tongue and she choked. Setting down the cup, she searched for some way to avoid Lady Carrington's question. She smelled the stew on the stove. "Does the stew need to be stirred?"

Lady Carrington sniffed the air. "I think perhaps you're right. I shall be right back." She put her tea on the table and rose.

Katie leaned against the back of the sofa and let out the breath she'd been holding. Her head throbbed and she still felt sick. Of all the things she'd tried to control over the years, this was the one she'd always known would become a wildfire if any wind blew on the spark.

She longed to speak to Mama. First to be sure she was truly making a recovery and then to ask for advice. But no, she couldn't tell her of Florence's demand. Not now when she was so sick. Papa was no help either. He was still incoherent. It was Katie's duty to protect her mother, to smooth the rough road ahead. If she had the money, she'd gladly give it to Florence to make her disappear, but as far as she knew, there was little money for them to even live on.

She rubbed her forehead and got up. A shout came from outside, and she went to the front door to see what was causing the commotion. The buckboard was parked at the foot of the hill below the lighthouse. Philip ran up the slope toward the house.

He shouted again. "I need help!"

Her pulse picked up speed. She threw open the door and stepped out onto the porch. "What is it?"

He reached her. "Something's happened to Will!"

A brief vision of Will's dark smiling eyes flashed through her mind. He had to be all right. "He's been hurt?"

Philip stood panting and red-faced from his run up the slope. "We found a chest in a cave. He sent me to the buckboard to get a rope to haul it up. When I got back, he was gone. The gun I'd given him was lying on the cave floor, and I found blood by the opening to the cave. A piece of his shirt was caught on the ledge hanging out over the ocean. As if—as if he went over the side."

"And the chest?"

"It was still there."

She tried to place this cave of which he spoke. "Are you saying the cave was in a rock face overhanging the sea?"

He nodded. "Just south of here, down Hanging Rock Road. We walked about an hour beyond the end of the road down the beach.

He had to have a rope or someone to help in order to get up with the chest."

"Could he have climbed down?"

"No way. It's a fifty-foot drop."

"You fear he—he fell?" She covered her mouth in horror and wanted to close her eyes against the mental picture of Will's broken body on the rocks.

Philip went even whiter. "He wouldn't have left of his own free will. He was waiting for my return with the rope, and he would have been stranded on the ledge without help."

She didn't want to believe anything could harm that strong man. "I'll come with you. We must call the constable. Get a search party."

"I'll have Lady Carrington call the constable. You and I will go by boat to search for him. If he fell into the sea, perhaps he needs our assistance." She could only pray he was still alive. Anyone diving into the sea was more likely to hit rock than water.

She stepped back inside and told the older woman what had happened.

Lady Carrington promised to call the constable. "Take my yacht. It's moored down at the dock."

"Thank you so much!" Katie returned to find Philip gazing out to sea. "What is it?"

"I'm not sure," he said. "I thought I saw something out there."

"I saw binoculars in the well house," she said. "I'll fetch them." She rushed around the side of the house and threw open the wooden door to the building that housed the pump for the well. A pair of binoculars hung on the wall by the door. She grabbed them and stepped back outside. The currents could have carried Will close to the lighthouse from where Philip had told her they'd been. She handed the binoculars to Philip. He trained them on a spot just to the left of the lighthouse. She prayed for Will as his brother scanned the waves.

Philip lowered the binoculars. "It's just driftwood," he said, his voice sharp with disappointment.

"Let's take the binoculars with us. If you suspect he's adrift, we'll need them. The constable will be searching the land," she said. "Lady Carrington has a small yacht moored nearby."

He stared at her. "You can sail?"

"A bit."

"I'm an expert seaman," he said.

He led her down the stone steps to the road and down to the pier where the boat floated. Under less stressful circumstances, she would have delighted in exploring the hold and expansive deck. She stepped into the boat as he held it steady. He hopped in with her and grabbed the rigging on the small craft. The sails flapped then billowed with air. Once the rope was loosened from the piling, the wind caught the canvas and the boat picked up speed. She moved to the bow and brought the binoculars to her eyes. Finding a man in this vast sea would be as difficult as finding an unbroken seashell on the rocks.

She put down the binoculars. "So you believe the pirates who took the ship stashed that chest? And that they found Will, I mean Mr. Jesperson, at the cave, that they—disposed of him?"

Philip paled. "I hope not, but the evidence—" He broke off, his voice choked.

She shielded her eyes with her hand and stared out at the rippling waves, hoping to see Will's hailing wave. The thought that he had been harmed made her shudder.

Philip steered the boat with obvious expertise. "I think we should keep it about a hundred yards offshore," he called above the flapping of the canvas and the rush of the wind.

"There's a riptide that runs along here," she said. "I've heard it said that the current hugs the shoreline only about fifty yards out. Perhaps we should go in a little closer."

He nodded and moved the rudder. The boat veered toward shore.

Katie looked through the binoculars again. She saw an albatross float-ing atop the waves, several pieces of driftwood but no man in the whitecaps. "How far is this cave?" she asked.

"We're a ways out yet," Philip said.

"How long since you left him?"

"About three hours. If he'd gone over the side just before I got back, that would have been about two hours ago."

She prayed that God would buoy him up and keep him safe until they found him. Spending that kind of time in fifty-degree water would be deadly.

Philip pointed. "There is where we left the buckboard."

"Then we should be seeing him if he is in the water." She redoubled her efforts to find anything in the sea. "Will!" she screamed over the sound of the wind and waves.

Her eyes ached from the brilliance of the sun bouncing on the water. A gull flew up with a startled squawk. She moved the binoculars to that direction. At first she saw nothing but whitecaps and moved on.

A flutter of something made her return her gaze. "I see something!" A white face appeared then vanished in the water again. "It's a man!" She pointed in the direction, twenty feet closer to shore. Will clung to a piece of driftwood. One hand waved weakly, then the movement made him lose his grip on the log. He made a grab at it but it floated away.

His head went under the water and she screamed. "He's drowning!"

"Take the rudder!" Philip yelled to her when they were ten feet from Will.

She moved back to where Philip was shucking his shoes and jacket. She steadied the rudder as he tossed the anchor overboard. The boat slowed as the weight took hold.

"Haul down the sails!" He dove overboard and with swift strokes, aimed toward Will.

Praying frantically, Katie raced to the mast and yanked down the sails. By the time she returned to the railing, Philip had reached the spot where they'd last seen his brother. He floated and glanced around. Katie saw a dark head break through the waves behind him. "There! He's there!"

Philip turned around and grabbed him by the collar. Katie grabbed a life preserver and tossed it at the two men when she was sure Philip had seized hold of Will. Philip snatched at it with his other hand and missed. The preserver floated on past. She pulled it back to the boat and hefted it again as Philip fought to keep his brother's head above the water. This time it landed nearer the two, and she nearly shouted with victory when she saw Philip grab hold of it and slip it over Will's head. Philip towed his brother toward the craft.

She rushed to the stern and grabbed Will's arm as the back of the boat slewed in the water. Panting, she helped Philip get Will into the craft then held out her hand to assist Philip, but he shook his head.

He waved off her help and grabbed the side of the boat. "Tend to Will," he gasped. He treaded water, gasping for oxygen.

Katie turned to Will, who was lying on his stomach on the deck. She pressed her fingers to his neck. Nothing. Panicking, she slid her fingers to another spot and tried again. There. A slight pulse pumped against her fingertips. But he wasn't breathing. She pressed on his back until seawater spewed from his mouth and nose, but she still saw no signs of his lungs filling with air.

"Please, God, let him breathe," she whispered. She rolled him over and wiped his face with her skirt. A shadow loomed over her, and she realized Philip had managed to get aboard.

"He's not breathing," she said, trying to keep her voice calm. She tipped his head back and pinched his nose closed. She'd only watched a demonstration about this technique and had never tried it, but she couldn't stand by and let Will die.

Running over the steps she remembered, she checked to make sure his airways were clear then pressed her lips to his and began the kiss of life. His lips were cold and tasted of seawater. She tried not to believe she ministered to a dead man. When he didn't respond, she pushed on his chest and tried again. Nothing.

"Breathe, breathe," she begged. Her eyes burned, and her throat ached with holding in her emotion. She shook him and screamed into his face. "Don't you die, Will Jesperson!"

He had to live. She couldn't bear it if he died. She pushed his chest then filled her lungs again and blew oxygen into his mouth. Were his lips a bit warmer? She was nearly afraid to hope. She drew in another deep breath and leaned down.

He coughed, and she rolled him onto his side. Water ran from the corner of his mouth. His eyes opened and she nearly cried with relief.

"Where's your hat?" he asked through a strangled voice before he closed his eyes again.

Katie let out a laugh of surprise and then sank back on her heels and gave in to her tears.

NINETEEN

WILL WANTED TO feel those warm lips on his again. The ones that had called him from a deep, cold place. He shuddered as the cold sank further into his bones. He'd been sure he was dead. There was little he remembered other than an eternity of fighting the cold and the waves until he'd given up all hope of surviving. Then he'd felt warmth and passion, a call he couldn't resist. Katie. He opened his eyes and watched the beautiful woman who had saved his life weeping beside him.

Katie must have seen his involuntary movement because she glanced at his brother.

"Where do you think we could find a blanket?" she asked, wiping her face.

When she moved to follow his brother, Will grabbed her hand. She turned back toward him with her blue eyes wide.

"You kissed me," he said. "Somehow it made me want to come back."

Color rushed to her cheeks but she held his gaze. "It wasn't a kiss. I was putting air into your lungs."

He clutched her hand more tightly. "Your mouth was warm. I was cold—so cold." An explosion of shivers shook him. He wanted to pull her down to him and wrap his arms around her, bask in her warmth.

She put her hand on his forehead. "Your brother is looking for a blanket in the hold. We'll head for shore and the doctor shortly."

His eyes strayed to the strands of gleaming brown hair that the wind had released from its pins. He'd never seen a more beautiful sight. "You don't have your hat," he said.

Though she smiled, the anxiety still stayed in her blue eyes. "So you said. I rushed out with Philip to try to find you and quite forgot it."

A lady never went out without her hat. He could see a smattering of freckles across her nose and a pink tinge already on her forehead. Miss Katie Russell was no typical lady, only concerned with propriety and decorum. He'd never known a woman to put herself out in such a way for another. He struggled to sit up then bit back a groan. His chest burned when he tried to pull in a deeper breath. His head throbbed and his skin felt as though it had been stripped away.

She placed a warm hand on his chest. "Lie still. I don't want you to further harm yourself."

He put his cold hand atop hers. "What is the saying . . . when someone saves your life, it belongs to them?"

She flushed a deeper pink. "Anyone would have done the same."

When she tried to withdraw her hand, he kept it pressed to the place over his heart. "I don't think so. You're a remarkable woman, Miss Russell."

"It's Katie," she said. "You can call me Katie."

He nodded. "With something like this between us, I think first names are in order. In fact, I thought I heard you call me by name when I was in the water."

Sparks of awareness pulsed between them. Will told himself it was because she'd given him the kiss of life, but he suspected it was more than that.

His brother returned with a wool blanket in his hand. He tucked it around Will. It smelled musty but the warmth it offered was all Will cared about. "Thanks," he said. Shudders wracked him again.

Philip crouched beside him. "What happened?"

When her gaze sharpened with interest, Will struggled to sit up again, and this time, with Philip's help, he made it. He leaned against the side of the boat and Katie helped him wrap the blanket all around him.

"I was about to bust open the lock on the chest when a rope fell to the ledge. Our pirate friends."

"What makes you say it was them?" Philip asked.

"Before they knew I was in the cave, I saw one open the chest. Where else would ship equipment come from? I saw a logbook, compass, other instruments. I'd wager it's from the missing ship."

"Why hide that stuff? They could send it to the bottom of the sea with the ship."

Will rubbed his aching head. "It was one of several chests. I guess they took them all in case there were valuables. They'd want to know what they had in their possession before they ransom it back to the shipping company."

"Was it the men you saw on the hillside?" Katie asked. "The ones you questioned me about?"

He nodded. "And they are planning something else."

Philip winched up the anchor. "Why do you think they have something planned?"

"I heard them say something about a ship bound with money coming in two days."

"Did they name the ship?" Katie asked.

Will shook his head.

"Bet we can figure it out," Philip said.

She glanced at his brother. "What a thrilling life you must lead as a detective! I think I should like to help you find the pirates."

"The Pinkertons' reputation lately has made all detectives appear that they're accepting bribes and hobnobbing with criminals," Will said. "You'd lose your precious respectability."

She turned away and studied her hands. "What makes you think I care a fig about respectability?"

"You're quite eager to take on any and every responsibility that looks your way. That usually denotes a strong streak of respectability."

"I could say the same about you."

"That's true," Philip put in. "Case in point: taking charge of the little girl when she's not even mine."

"What is the truth about Jennie's heritage?" she asked. "We really must sort that out. Quite soon."

"See, there you go again. You can't help but take charge." Will moved his head and winced.

"Can we save this conversation until he's doing better?" Philip asked.

Will glanced at his brother. "I'll be all right."

Her sunburned skin turned even pinker as she glanced back and forth between the brothers. "We can't let this situation continue. That poor child deserves better. We need to get her settled."

"I thought once we found her mother we'd ferret out the truth," Philip said. "Finding her mother's killer is the goal now. That may be the only way we figure out Eliza's involvement in all of this and who fathered Jennie. But I can't do it alone." Philip shot a quick glance Will's way.

Will sighed and lifted a hand up to his head. It was aching. "I'll do what I can, but remember, I have another job as well. I must perform the duties I'm being paid for."

Katie glanced from Philip to Will and back again. "Surely you two don't still suspect my father."

Will opened his mouth to mention the pocket watch at home on his dresser then closed it again. No sense stirring up a painful subject. The truth would come out sooner or later.

"His suicide attempt indicates guilt," Philip said, jerking on the tack so hard the boat veered toward the shore. He righted course.

Will smothered a sigh. While he didn't believe Philip had anything to do with Miss Bulmer's death, he hated to think what Katie's father's potential guilt might do to her.

She turned to him. "I'm going to help you get to the bottom of this. My father had nothing to do with Eliza's murder, and I'm going to prove it!"

"You're not an investigator."

"Neither are you." Her eyes glowed. "And I know everyone in town. And nearly everything that has gone on in this community for years."

❧

Katie's face felt tight and dry. She stared at the apparition in the mirror. A red-faced horror stared back at her. If her mother could see her now, she'd be *tsking* and shaking her head as she exclaimed about the fact that Katie had gone out without a hat or parasol. Whatever had she been thinking yesterday? Bart was coming to take her to lunch at his home this morning. She could only imagine what his parents would think when they saw her.

She touched her red, roughened cheeks. There was no way to hide the damage. She finished her hair, but no adjusting of her hat covered the sunburn on her face. Sighing, she removed her glasses and tucked them away, then closed the bedroom door behind her and proceeded down the steps. Bart would be here any moment. She should have telephoned him this morning and canceled the plans. When she reached the foyer, Will was exiting the parlor with Jennie in his arms. He was still pale and his head was bandaged.

The baby smiled and reached for her. Her small teeth gleamed in her smile. Katie took the baby then had to rescue a feather the child grabbed from her hat. "Has she eaten lunch?"

"I fed her." His gaze probed under her hat at her sunburn. "Does it hurt?"

"A little." She nuzzled the baby's soft cheek. "How are you feeling?"

"I'll live." He paused and studied her face as she adjusted her hat to shade it better. "You could wear your glasses. They would hide part of your face." His voice was full of amusement.

"I think not," she said.

"You look quite fetching in them. Rather intelligent. I like intelligence in a woman."

Her hot face flamed still hotter. Was he mocking her? She couldn't tell if he was serious or not. She heard steps on the front porch then saw Bart's familiar bowler through the door window. "I must go."

She handed the baby to him and turned toward the door, but not so fast that she missed the frown that gathered in his forehead. There was a skip in her pulse. He couldn't be jealous, could he? A smile lit her face when she opened the door. The delight faded when she saw Bart's eyes widen at his first glimpse of her.

"Is that a sunburn?" he asked.

She opened the door and stepped out onto the porch to escape Will's amusement. "It is, indeed. I got a little too much sun yesterday."

He couldn't seem to look away from her face. "You lost your chapeau?"

She turned her face away and took his arm. "I went boating yesterday."

"Ah, the wind blew it off." He picked up her gloved hand and patted it. "Most unfortunate."

Some perverse impulse made her tell him the truth. "Not really. I quite forgot to take it."

He stumbled on the grass. "It is of no matter. You look lovely."

His gallant words made her wince. A woman never forgot her hat. It just wasn't done. He was bound to wonder what could have caused her to behave in such an unseemly way. And now to show up to his house with a sunburn. She blinked her eyes as they blurred. It was most uncharacteristic of her. Her mother would be appalled too.

She said nothing more as Bart helped her into the carriage then climbed in after her. The coachman urged the matched horses away from the sea toward town. She stayed on her side of the seat. If she'd been at home instead of the lighthouse, she might have dared to purchase a bit of powder to cover the evidence on her cheeks.

"Mother is delighted you're coming," Bart said. He reached over to take her hand again.

She checked the impulse to pull away, but she smiled at him and left her fingers clasped in his. With Florence demanding money, it was even more imperative that Katie marry. It was growing more difficult to fight her attraction to Will, but now she had Florence to contend with. She could not allow things to spin out of control.

The carriage stopped at the grand porch attached to the three-story stone manor. She'd skated past it many times and had longed to see inside. Now she would have the opportunity. Bart helped her down and escorted her up the wide steps. A doorman opened the double doors for her, and she stepped into a foyer so elegant she nearly gasped. The walls were papered in silk and the wood floors gleamed. Though her own home was beautiful, this was in the very latest style and lavish beyond comprehension. She needed to act as though she were used to this kind of luxury.

Holding her head high, she stepped onto a thick, plush runner. Bart led her into a grand drawing room with so many expensive items it was all she could do not to stare. Though the curtains were held back with ties, the room was a bit dark, which suited Katie fine. It would make it more difficult to see her sunburn.

Mrs. Foster smiled from her seat on a pink velvet sofa. "Katie, my dear, I'm so pleased you could join us. You sit right here by me." She patted the space beside her.

Katie dropped her hand from Bart's arm and went to join his mother. "I'm honored at your invitation, Mrs. Foster. You have a lovely home." Bart's mother was lovely too. Though she had to be in her fifties, her skin was still smooth and unlined. Long black lashes fringed her brown eyes.

Mrs. Foster beamed. "I picked out everything myself. Mr. Foster wanted me to hire a designer from the city, but I wanted our home to reflect my tastes, not someone else's. If you like, take off your chapeau, dear. Make yourself comfortable. We want to be like family."

Katie untied the strings of her bonnet. If she kept a bright smile on her face, perhaps the other woman wouldn't notice. She removed her hat and smoothed her hair a bit. "Luncheon smells delicious."

"Cook is preparing lamb," Mrs. Foster said. Her eyes widened when she glanced at Katie, but she quickly recovered. "Are you too warm?"

"No, I—I got a bit too much sun yesterday."

"She went boating," Bart said. He dropped into a chair across from them and crossed one leg over the other. "And the wind took her hat."

Katie started to frown at his lie but forced herself not to react. He had every right to be ashamed of her appearance.

"The sun can be quite brutal," his mother said, her gaze still lingering on Katie's cheeks. "I have something that might bleach those freckles out again. Let me fetch it for you." She rose and hurried from the room.

Katie kept her smile fixed in place though she wanted to burst into tears.

TWENTY

WHEN WILL SAW the constable dismount in front of the light-house, he knew what he'd come for. It was the last thing Will needed. He'd already been muttering under his breath and throwing things ever since Katie had gone off with her dandy.

When Will had gotten back last night, the constable had been there but Will hadn't been up to answering questions. He had hoped to have longer than overnight before the constable returned, demanding answers. The man was bound to order them to get out of his investigation.

He put down the polishing cloth and climbed down the ladder from his perch atop the lighthouse. His muscles screamed at the indignity after the beating they'd endured yesterday in the sea.

"Constable Brown," he said in greeting when the men met outside the front door of the lighthouse.

"Morning, Mr. Jesperson." The constable took out his cigar and struck a match. He puffed and a curl of smoke drifted Will's way. "You look a tad better than last night. I trust a good night's sleep has cleared your mind enough to answer some questions." He gestured to a bench overlooking the crashing waves.

Will nodded. The men settled on the bench. Gulls cawed overhead and swooped low to snatch crabs on the rocks below the lighthouse.

Brown gestured with his pipe at the bandage on Will's forehead. "Ready to tell me the full story now?"

"I fell off a cliff."

"I know there is more to it than that." Brown puffed on his pipe. "Care to explain why you were investigating instead of getting a message to me? I've found nothing to indicate that our pirates are still in the area. If there's evidence to the contrary, I should be the first to know of it."

"Sorry, Constable. I was hardly out for a leisurely sail," he said, gesturing toward his head. "One of our pirates threw me off that cliff." Will launched into what had happened the day before as the constable's cigar smoke curled around his head.

Brown lifted a brow. "Sounds like a tall tale to me. Are you pulling my leg? Pirates hiding a chest in a cave. Care to show me the spot?"

"Maybe in a day or two. A two-hour hike along the shore is a bit beyond me today. There's more though, Constable. I heard them mention they planned to take another ship due here in two days. That would be tomorrow."

Brown's gaze sharpened on Will's face. "Is this a ploy to distract me from my real questions?"

"And what would those questions be?"

Brown puffed on his cigar for a long moment. "Miss Eliza's disappearance. I find it an odd coincidence that her wedding gown was found right below this lighthouse." He pointed his cigar at the rocks below. "Don't you think it strange too?"

Will kept his expression impassive. "I arrived a few hours after her disappearance. I have never met the woman."

"Yet you were at her home when I arrived. And you took charge of her child. There is much more that you're not saying. Where might I find your brother?"

"He went for a walk on the beach." Will caught a movement down by the pier and tensed when he recognized Philip.

Brown turned his head and saw the figure as well. "Is that your brother?"

"Yes."

"Excellent. I shall wait and speak with him." He puffed content-
edly on his cigar as Philip drew nearer.

Philip's confident stride soon had him within hailing distance. Brown
rose and motioned for Philip to join them. The wary expression on his
brother's face made Will tense again. Though he believed his brother
had nothing to do with Eliza's disappearance, if Philip were cocky or his
answers failed to satisfy, he could find himself behind bars.

"Constable Brown. I wasn't expecting to see you here," Philip said
when he reached them.

Brown puffed on his cigar before answering. "Mr. Jesperson. What
do you know about Miss Eliza Bulmer's disappearance? I suspect your
involvement in solving the *Paradox's* disappearance is merely a ploy to
dispose of your former mistress."

Will flinched. "That's ridiculous, Constable. Philip was legiti-
mately hired by the shipping company. Telephone them and check
for yourself."

The constable didn't look at Will. "Shall we let your brother
answer for himself?"

"Look, I know nothing about Eliza's death," Philip said, splaying
his hands outward. "Our relationship was over two years ago."

"You say she's dead. How would you know that when we've found
no body?"

Philip flushed. "It certainly appears she's dead. Her dress was
found right here, and Miss Russell said she was wearing it the day she
disappeared."

"I would like to know the details of your relationship," the constable said. "How did you meet her?"

"Through a mutual friend."

"And that friend's name?"

"I'd rather not say."

Brown puffed his cigar again. "I'm afraid I must insist."

Will had to admire the constable's tenacity. Some would have done a perfunctory investigation and gone on. "You'd better tell him, Philip," he said.

Philip thrust his hands in his pockets. "Mr. Russell."

Will straightened. "Katie's father?" When his brother nodded, he wanted to strangle him. "Why have you said nothing about this?"

"It had nothing to do with me."

"You told me to talk to Miss Bulmer about Albert Russell, yet you already knew him."

"Shut up, Will," Philip said through gritted teeth.

Too late, Will realized how incriminating his words were. Was Philip trying to frame Albert for Eliza's disappearance? Nausea roiled in his belly. He wouldn't believe his brother might be capable of such a thing and yet it certainly looked suspicious.

"I only met Russell one time, at the gentlemen's club in San Francisco," Philip said. "Eliza was with him and another man. Russell introduced us and asked me to take her back to her hotel. He had a meeting he was late for. I never heard the name again until I was told she'd said he was involved in the disappearance of *Dalton's Fortune.*"

"Who was the other man? Can he corroborate your story?" Brown asked.

"Mitchell is his last name. The club could tell you how to get hold of him." Philip glanced at Will.

Will thought of the watch on his dresser. It was his duty to tell the constable about it.

Brown frowned at Philip. "Why did you send your brother to speak with Miss Eliza? Did you intend to offer her money for the child?"

"Of course not! She had contacted my employer and indicated she had information that might help me find the pirates. But you know all this. Her correspondence with the owner of the ship indicated she could tell me who masterminded the theft. She asked for a fee in return."

Brown puffed on his cigar before answering. "So she wanted to be paid for the information."

"She did," Philip said.

It was a common demand. Philip probably was used to forking over money for the clues he needed to solve cases.

"Did my brother tell you about Russell's watch?" Philip asked.

Brown glanced at Will. "What watch?"

"I found a pocket watch on the island out there." Will gestured offshore. "Engraved with the name Albert Russell."

The constable's eyes widened, and he took another puff of his cigar. "You tell Miss Katie?"

"I did."

"Bet that went over big." He puffed in silence for a moment. "It appears Mr. Russell may be involved in this even deeper than I thought. He might have disposed of Miss Eliza then tried to kill himself rather than get caught. If he recovers consciousness, he can explain much of this."

"Unless the pirates took care of both of them. Miss Russell believes her father was attacked."

Brown shook his head. "I'm still not convinced the pirates are around here. Makes no sense to me. Why not take their loot and get out?"

"How? There is no way in or out of here without going through Mercy Falls or down the coast and risk a blockade. It makes sense to wait until the furor dies down then get the gold out."

"Maybe." He put out his cigar, then nodded at the men and headed back to his horse.

Will glanced at his brother and caught an expression of relief flitting across his face. He didn't want to believe Philip had anything to do with this mess, but he wasn't entirely certain.

The luncheon had been an ordeal. It was clear by the quick, darting glances Mrs. Foster sent her way that the sunburn horrified her. By the time Bart escorted Katie outside, her eyes burned from holding back tears, and her throat was sore and tight. She longed to go to her own house.

"Are you all right?" Bart asked when the carriage pulled away from the manor. "You're very quiet."

"Were you ashamed of me, Bart?" She touched a gloved finger to her cheek. "About my face?"

"Of course not." He shifted on the seat, glanced at her, then looked away.

"But you lied to your mother. I told you I forgot it."

"There is nothing wrong with my attempt to help you put your best foot forward with my mother," he said, still staring out the window.

"There is if you feel you have to lie."

His gaze swung back to her. "I'm not sure I'm comfortable with you staying out at the lighthouse. This isn't like you. What kind of influences are you under that you'd go out unprotected? A lady just doesn't do that."

She bit back the hot words trembling on her tongue. If this man were to be her future husband, then of course he would be concerned about her reputation. "Lady Carrington is there," she reminded him. "There is no cause for worry."

His scowl turned darker. "I heard that the lightkeeper's brother is there too. It's not seemly, Katie. I think you should stay here, at the house. If we're to be married, no one would think anything about it."

"I didn't know we were to be married," she said. She chewed on her lip and wished she could recall the words. She was hardly ready to push him into a declaration when she was full of such indecision.

"I thought it was understood," he said. "Your father gave his blessing for me to court you. As soon as I'm in a position to marry, I intend to ask you to marry me."

In a position to marry? He was nearly thirty, the only son of a wealthy father. She kept a smile pinned to her face and said nothing to encourage him. If he waited a bit, she hoped to be able to summon more enthusiasm for a life shared with him. Though their future needed to be settled soon. Her parents were counting on her.

Still, perhaps he was feeling as much indecision as she. The thought did little to comfort her. If he wasn't totally enamored with her, and she had conflicted emotions too, what hope was there for a relationship? This indecision was so unlike her. All her life she'd been groomed to make a wise choice of husband. Bart would be the perfect spouse.

When she didn't answer, he rushed on. "I'll be in a position soon. I don't want to be dependent on my father when I take a wife. I intend to strike out on my own and start my own company."

His ambition encouraged her. "Doing what? Open another sawmill?"

He scowled. "Not in a million years. I hate the noise, the dirt. I want to open a Macy's."

She'd love to be part of that kind of enterprise. "Wouldn't that take an exorbitant sum?"

His earnest blue eyes sought her face. "I have some backers. It's figuring out how to tell my father I'm not following in his shoes— that'll be the tough part."

"I'm sure you'll explain it so he understands."

He pressed her hand. "You're so easy to talk to, Katie. When I'm with you, I think I can do anything."

She smiled and clung to his fingers. "I know you can do whatever you set your mind to, Bart." If only the touch of his hand moved her the way being with Will did. She was so confused. Addie's words had haunted her lately. God had a plan for her and she would feel peace when she found it. She longed for that peace but it seemed so nebulous and unattainable.

She saw a figure standing on the sidewalk, walking away from them down a side street. The men on the benches watched the woman saunter past, and Katie heard a low whistle. Even before the sun pierced the shadows under the woman's hat, she knew it was Florence.

She must have clutched Bart's hand because he studied her face. "Is something wrong?" he asked.

"N—not at all," she said. She asked him a question about the potential Macy's store to distract him, and he immediately launched into his plans, warming to the subject.

Katie had to find some way to get Florence out of town. Katie had no idea where she could find the kind of money the woman demanded. Not unless some of the papers she'd found in her father's safe were worth something. She should have examined them more closely.

"Would you mind if we stopped by my father's shop a moment? I need to get into the safe," she asked.

"As you wish." Bart leaned forward and gave the driver directions.

Minutes later the carriage stopped in front of Russell's Haberdashery. Bart exited the carriage and helped her alight. "Please, just wait here," she said when he acted like he was going to accompany her. "It won't take me but a moment." She smiled and brushed past him to the door, which she unlocked before stepping inside. The shop was closed for the day.

She stepped through to the back room, where she rotated through the safe's combination and unlocked it. The papers were on the bottom. She lifted them out and retrieved her glasses from her pocket. A brief scan showed her hope was in vain. These were all old contracts and nothing that showed any money due. She replaced them and spun the lock, and her heart was leaden as she retraced her steps.

Blinking in the bright sunlight outside the shop, she locked the door. Bart was chatting with two gentlemen, not looking her way, and the bank was just at the end of the block. She walked quickly to the bank and approached the teller.

"Good afternoon, Miss Russell," the young male teller said. His mustache twitched as he spoke. "You're quite brave to be out and about with the epidemic still raging."

Katie had been so preoccupied, she hadn't stopped to think about why the bank was practically deserted. "I'd best not stay out long. I wondered if you could give me the balance in all of my father's accounts?"

"I've heard of his condition. Me and the missus have been praying he'll awaken soon. It will just be a moment while I consult the ledger." The teller vanished down the hallway.

Katie clutched her gloved hands together. Though she knew it was a futile hope, she prayed there was more money than she'd been told. Perhaps Papa had another account where he'd saved money for their future. She turned and glanced through the plate glass window into the street. There were few passersby. She hadn't heard of any new smallpox outbreaks, but people still feared stepping outside their homes.

The teller returned and slid a piece of paper across the counter to her. "Here you are, Miss Russell."

"Thank you." She glanced at the slip of paper as she turned toward the door. When she saw the total, she stopped and glanced back. "You're sure this is all his accounts?"

"Yes, miss. I know it's not much." His brown eyes were apologetic.

Not much was an understatement. One account held only a thousand dollars and the other held two thousand. Perhaps her father would know more. She retraced her steps to the buggy and asked Bart to take her to the hospital.

"I can't allow you to go there, Katie," he said. "Not while it houses people with the pox. Surely you've been telephoning to check on your father's condition."

"Of course I have," she said. "I thought a visit from me might bring him around to a more lucid frame of mind."

"The nurse will tell you when you're allowed entry," Bart said.

"I should like to see my mother. I could speak to her through the window."

"The road to your house is blocked, and I'm quite unwilling to see you endanger yourself. I'll take you back to the lighthouse."

There was no arguing with him. Katie would have to come back by herself. She sat staring silently out the window until Bart's carriage drew up outside the lighthouse.

"I do hope you will think about moving to our house for the remainder of this smallpox outbreak," Bart said, helping her alight from the buggy.

"I shall take it under consideration," she said. When he might have bent to give her a kiss on the cheek, she stepped back. "Thank you for lunch," she said. "I must go."

She fled up the hillside before he could protest. When she reached the lighthouse, Lady Carrington met her at the door.

"Katie, my dear, the doctor called. Your father is beginning to regain consciousness. Dr. Lambertson says not to come until the smallpox is past, but he wanted you to know of Albert's improvement."

"I have to talk to him," Katie said.

"They won't let you in."

"Then I shall have to sneak in." She had to know the truth of the events swirling around her. She turned and retraced her steps. Will's bicycle was lying at the bottom of the slope, so she grabbed it and climbed onto the seat. She rode back to town and turned down the street to the hospital. The barricade ahead warned her she couldn't go through that way, so she dismounted, left the bicycle parked under a tree, then darted through several yards and down an alley to finally arrive at the hospital's back entrance.

She tugged on the heavy door but it was locked. If she went around to the front, she would be turned away. Before she could decide what to do, the door opened and a woman dressed in a maid uniform stepped out. Katie seized the handle and slipped inside, though the woman called after her.

Papa's ward was on the second floor. A back stairway opened off the hall, and she peeked into the stairwell. Empty. Lifting her skirts, she scampered up the steep steps to the second floor landing. The hallway held a lone nurse pushing a cart with bedpans. Katie lifted her head and sailed into the hall as though she had every right to be there. The nurse barely gave her a glance before disappearing through a doorway. Katie peeked in after her but the ward held only women. She hurried along until she found one inhabited by six men. Her father's bed was the last one on the right.

She approached him lying there. He bore little resemblance to the vital father she was used to. His thin hair was in disarray on the pillow. His normally florid complexion was pasty. His eyes were closed.

She touched his hand. "Papa?" she whispered. "It's Katie. Are you awake?" She noticed a curtain by the bed and pulled it closed to shield her presence from anyone passing by.

Her father's lids fluttered, and he opened his bleary eyes. He blinked then focused on her face. "Katie?" He returned the grip on her hand.

He knew her! Tears burned her eyes. She pulled up a nearby chair and put her head close to his. "How are you feeling, Papa?"

"Thirsty," he said, licking his lips.

She saw a glass of water on the table beside his bed and helped him sit up. He drank greedily then fell back against the pillow as if the effort had exhausted him.

"Papa, what happened?" she asked.

"When?"

"You were found in the pond at the base of Mercy Falls. Has the constable been over to talk to you?"

He rubbed his forehead. "I don't know, Katie."

"Did someone shove you into the falls?"

His pale blue eyes studied her face, then he nodded. "Don't ask me who pushed me. I don't know. I have my suspicions though."

"Were you involved with the theft of gold from the *Paradox*?" she asked. When he flinched, she had her answer. "You were, weren't you?" This would hurt her mother terribly.

"My business is in trouble," he said. "No one was supposed to get hurt. We were just going to take the money to survive the recession. When they killed those sailors . . ." He swallowed hard and shook his head. "I was going to turn them in."

"You can still do that."

"No, I can't. A man stopped by here last night. At least I think it was last night. It was dark and I was so confused. He said if I talked, he'd kill you and your mother."

"What about Eliza? Your watch was found on the island where her body was dumped."

He shook his head. "We argued and she slapped me. I grabbed her shoulders and pushed her away. Later I realized my watch was gone. She must have had it in her hand or pocket when she was killed. I had nothing to do with it."

"What did you argue about?"

"It's not your business."

She hadn't thought he would tell her. "Did you recognize the man's voice who called on you? If you can tell the constable . . ." She didn't want to tell him she'd received threatening phone calls.

"I can't tell anyone and neither can you. There are more people involved than this one man. If he's identified, they'll just hire someone else to take his place. I don't even know how many are a part of it. Too many."

"But the constable suspects you of killing Eliza! You'll go to jail."

"I have no choice."

She bit her lip. "There's more, Papa. Florence is in town."

His lip curled. "Your mother? So that's why you're here asking these questions? I knew the time would come when you'd revert to her ways. Like mother like daughter."

She'd heard it too many times. "She's not my mother!"

His eyes narrowed. "What does she want?"

"Money."

"I am nearly bankrupt."

Katie sat back in the chair. "I told her that, but she is threatening to tell Bart's family about my heritage."

Panic filled his eyes. "You must not allow that to happen! How much does she want?"

Katie told him and watched his eyes cloud over. "Is there any way to get that amount?"

"I don't know where. We are mortgaged to the hilt. Perhaps I can get a loan from Bart without telling him what I need it for."

"I'd rather not be beholden to him."

Her father frowned, but before he could speak, a hand swept the curtain back to reveal a scowling male orderly. He glanced from Katie to her father then jerked his thumb. "Out," he said. "No visitors allowed."

Katie rose. "Good-bye, Papa." She rose and swept past the orderly but his dark gaze followed her all the way to the door.

TWENTY-ONE

THE BABY GRABBED Will's ear and chattered something full of vowels and totally incomprehensible. He managed a smile though he'd been in a bad mood ever since Katie had left with that blond dandy.

"You are so cute," he said. He showed her the pap feeder and she grabbed it. He settled on the sofa with her and dribbled the pap into her mouth. He glanced up and met Lady Carrington's soft smile.

"You're wonderful with children, Will," she said.

He tugged on his tie and glanced out the window without replying.

"I don't expect her back for at least another hour," she said.

"Who?"

Her smile widened and her skirt swished as she walked into the room and settled in the armchair. "I'm not quite blind and doddering yet, young man. Anyone with eyes can see how you watch Katie."

"She's just a . . ." He searched for the right word. It wasn't *friend* and it wasn't *acquaintance*. His head felt a little funny when he remembered the way he'd awakened to the press of her warm lips on his frozen ones. Could he actually be harboring strong emotions for Katie?

Lady Carrington chuckled. "Love is like that, Will. It sneaks up on you." She sobered and took a sip of tea. "I've often wondered about the sadness I sometimes glimpse in Katie's face. I don't see it when she's with you. There is something special between the two of you. Nurture it and see how it grows."

Were his feelings so clear that even Lady Carrington could see? His chest tightened at the thought that he could be so transparent. "I think I'll go see if my balloon has descended, if you don't mind watching the baby. I need to run down to the harbor for a few minutes too."

Her eyes were wise and held amusement. "Run along, my dear. This will all catch up with you sooner or later."

He grabbed his hat and escaped into the sunshine with heat rising on his neck. The balloon had fallen on the beach, and he set off at a brisk jog. Once he wrote down the readings on the instruments, he glanced at the sky. Rain was coming, if his readings were correct. He dragged the remains of the balloon out of the way of the tide. He would dispose of it on his way back. The tide was coming in, and he veered away from the encroaching foam on the waves as he walked toward the harbor.

The quay teemed with activity. Stevedores hauled crates to waiting ships, and fishermen sat on the pier with their poles dangling into the water. One of the fishermen would be most likely to have the time to answer a few questions.

He walked to where an older man sat in dungarees. "Catching anything?"

With a glance from under gray brows, the man said, "Yup."

Will settled on the boards beside him. "You live around here all your life?"

The fellow jerked a bit on his line. "Born and raised."

"You hang out here a lot?"

"Look, young fellow, just spit out what you're looking for. I ain't got all day."

Will grinned. He liked the direct approach himself. "I heard there's an important shipment coming through tomorrow. You know anything about that?"

"Even if I did, what's it to you?" The man studied him from under his battered hat. "I ain't seen you around."

"I'm the lightkeeper."

The man's face changed and he actually smiled. "That's good work you do, son. The old lightkeeper saved my bacon back in '80. Storm tore my ship from stem to stern. I was clinging to a piece of the boat and he came rowing out to get me. Best sight I ever saw."

"About the ship? I want to be on my guard after the last instance of piracy."

"Can't be too careful," the man agreed. He spat a dark stream of tobacco into the clear blue water. "Way I hear it, the *Hanson Queen* is due in here late afternoon. She's carrying the pay for the navy. Don't reckon she'll be docked long, and I hear she'll have guns mounted just in case."

"That's good news. Perhaps the pirates will hear of it and stay away." Will watched the old man another moment. "You hear any scuttlebutt about the last ship? Any idea who did it and how?"

The man spat again. "Sometimes it don't pay to listen too close."

The guy knew something. Will could see it in his clouded eyes. "You think they're still around?"

"They ain't going nowhere."

"Residents?"

The man shrugged and jerked on his line. "Got a big one. Been nice talking to you, but I do believe we're done." He rose and reeled in his fish, a big rockfish.

❦

Will was out when Katie returned in the afternoon. Her spirits dragged along the ground with her skirts. She inhaled the salty scent of the sea a final time before stepping into the house.

When she walked into the parlor, Jennie squealed in delight. Katie scooped her up and kissed her soft cheek. "I thought you'd be napping," she said. Katie's smile faded. It would be most difficult to leave this place and not see the baby every day. "Where is Will?" she asked Lady Carrington, who was seated in the armchair with a book in her hand.

"Down at the harbor. Philip is in town."

She wished she could share with Will what she'd learned from her father. Katie put the baby back by the blocks. "I believe I'll change then go for a walk."

She went to her room and changed from her dress to a white shirtwaist. As she buttoned the skirt, she heard a rustle in the pocket. When she slipped her hand inside, she found a slip of paper. She pulled it out and glanced at it. It was the note she'd found in her father's safe. The one about the ship docking an hour earlier. Now she realized what this note had to be referring to. She'd forgotten all about it.

Her spirits lifted but she told herself it had nothing to do with the fact that she was going to find Will. The safest path to the beach led out to the road and back past the rocky hillside to the rocky sand. Billowing clouds carried the tang of rain to her nose. Orioles sang in the bushes along the hill.

She saw a figure striding away from the dock. The long stride and the wide shoulders brought a smile to her face. How odd that she could recognize Will from such a distance. As he neared, she realized he seemed to be gazing off into the horizon as though he was deep in thought. He didn't see her until he was five feet away. The faraway expression changed to sharp awareness that made her heartbeat race.

"You're back," he said, stopping when he reached her. "Have a splendid time?" His tone was wry.

"Very nice," she muttered, not wanting to think of Bart now. "I thought I'd take a walk and intercept you. There's something I want to show you."

A teasing smile came. "I'm crushed. I thought you came out to greet me because you missed me."

She couldn't help but return his smile, but she didn't know how to respond to his words. Was he actually *flirting* with her? Sometimes in the night she remembered the way his eyes had opened after his near drowning and he'd stared into her soul. She could taste again the salty flavor of his lips. How cold he'd been. Some connection had been forged in that moment and she didn't know what to make of it.

"What, no response?" he asked. "I guess that means you didn't miss me. So what did you want to show me?"

"This." She pulled the note from her pocket and handed it over. "I found it in my father's safe the day the smallpox epidemic broke out. At the time, I had no idea what it meant, and I quite forgot about it."

He took it from her fingers, unfolded it, and looked it over. "Your father's handwriting?"

"No. I don't recognize the handwriting."

"It sounds as though he was involved with the piracy."

She winced at the definitive tone in his voice. "I still can't quite believe it. There's more," she said slowly, the words pulled from her tongue. "I spoke with my father today. He admitted to me that he knows something of this matter." When Will's face darkened, she rushed on. "He's not a bad man. He thought no one would be harmed." Even as the words spilled out, she realized how utterly ridiculous her statement sounded. She rubbed her forehead. "He has his faults but this shocks me."

"What faults?"

Did she trust him enough to tell him the truth? Yes. "He is the kindest man on the face of the earth, as long as he isn't drinking. When he imbibes alcohol, he changes."

"Many men do." He took her hand and she allowed it, finding the warmth of his touch comforting. "He has struck you?"

"Not physically. Only with his words."

"That can be even more painful. He is kind to your mother?"

She nodded. "Always. She makes excuses for him. Often months, even a year or two, go by between bouts of drinking. He usually only drinks when things aren't going well for him in some arena of his life."

"Has he been drinking lately?"

She hesitated then nodded, still clinging to his hand. "I'd begun to hope he had tamed his demons."

"Do you know what has not gone well for him?"

"His business is struggling."

One brow rose. "Perhaps he became involved in the theft of the gold to dig his way out of a financial hole," Will said.

"He admitted as much to me today."

He appeared lost in thought for a moment. "I have to admit something, Katie. I had to tell the constable about finding your father's watch."

She flinched, and a sense of betrayal tightened her throat. "You know what he will assume. That Papa murdered Eliza and dropped his watch while he was disposing of the body."

"Perhaps that *is* what happened."

"I know my father. He would never do something like that."

He kept a tight grip on her fingers. "His involvement with Eliza may have spiraled him into something quite out of character. A beautiful woman can make a man quite lose his head."

His words were almost tender. Katie's gaze darted to his face and found him staring at her with such an intent expression that the moisture in her mouth dried instantly. His gaze dropped to her lips. His grip on her fingers tightened. He was going to kiss her.

She jerked her hand away and stepped back. "We must be getting back," she said, feeling out of breath, as if she'd just run down the beach.

The disappointment in his eyes matched an ache building in her chest.

TWENTY-TWO

WILL GLANCED AT Katie from across the table. She'd been quiet and withdrawn since they returned from the beach. Had she sensed he had nearly lost his head and kissed her, or was she still upset that he'd told the constable about the watch? The thought that she had run from him was quite discouraging. Maybe she had no feelings for him.

Jennie picked up a piece of jam and bread between her forefinger and thumb in the pincher movement he found so amusing. She looked at it then threw it to the bird, who was waiting for just such an opportunity. Paco gobbled up the tidbit. She giggled and threw down another piece. Strawberry jam smeared her face.

"It's your supper, not the bird's," he said.

She puckered at the rebuke in his voice, and he quickly gave her a sip of milk from her cup. Her milky smile as he put it back down was a reward in itself. He offered her a spoonful of potato and she accepted it, though her brown eyes studied his face. She was a most charming baby. He glanced at his brother, who was writing in a notebook. Not that Philip seemed to notice her. He shook his head. Surely there would be some sort of biological pull if the two were related . . .

"If you'll excuse me, I'm rather tired tonight," Lady Carrington said. "I think I shall retire and read for a while."

"I'll come help you," Katie said.

"I think I shall try to prepare for bed by myself tonight. My arm is getting much better. Did you see your mother when you were in town today, Katie? You never said."

"No, the quarantine is still in effect. I'm forbidden to enter the house for at least another week to ten days."

"I thought perhaps you stepped into the yard and conversed through the window."

"Bart was with me, and he was reluctant to let me endanger my health."

Lady Carrington nodded. "Wise, I'm sure, my dear." She rose. "Good night."

Will echoed the good nights. Even Jennie chattered something that sounded like "night." The tiny girl waved her chubby hands toward the older woman then tossed another piece of bread to the bird.

Philip stood and stretched. "I do believe I'll wander down to the quay and see what's going on. See if I can dig up any more information about tomorrow."

Will narrowed his eyes. He watched in tight-lipped silence as Philip gave them a casual wave, then strode out of the kitchen. He was probably on his way to play poker under the guise of doing detective work. Which was probably the best way to obtain information, but . . .

Katie seemed to sense his agitation. She stood and began to clear the table. "I'll do the dishes if you can mind Jennie for fifteen minutes."

"She's still eating. I'll help you."

That brought her out of her fog. Her eyes were clear as she glanced at him. "You want to help with dishes?"

"I'm good at washing if you want to dry."

She smiled. "I do believe I would pay to see such a thing."

"The only payment I would exact is a round of checkers after Jennie is down for the night."

"Seems cheap enough. We can discuss the case over the game."

He'd hoped to speak of his growing feelings but it was clear she wanted to avoid such a topic. "Very well."

After depositing the dishes into the sink, she took the kettle from the wood range and poured hot water into the sink. She added soap flakes and swished it. "Your turn," she said, her smile widening.

He grinned and plunged his hands into the hot, soapy water. As he washed the dishes, he handed them to her to rinse in a tub of clean water.

"How did you learn to wash dishes?" she asked.

"I often helped my mother."

She shot a quick glance his way. "Just you? Not Philip?"

He shook his head. "He was more likely to be out playing."

"Are your parents still alive?"

His smile faded. "They died in the Galveston hurricane."

She put down the dish she was drying. "Oh Will, I'm so sorry. That must have been terrible."

"The worst of it is that it could have been prevented if anyone had listened to the early weather warnings."

"Weather warnings? You mean specific to the day? Not the almanac?"

He shook his head. "There are many scientists who are working to forecast the weather. A warning was issued about the hurricane but no one paid any heed. There is still much skepticism about the accuracy of the forecasts. We are getting more accurate every day."

"*We?*" she asked. "Do you forecast the weather as well as care for the lighthouse?"

He grinned. "Sounds quite outlandish, doesn't it? Weather is my passion though."

"Is that why I saw you with a balloon?"

"Yes. It collects data from the upper atmosphere."

"How very fascinating," she said.

"I'd like to do it full time someday," he said, surprising himself with the admission.

She smiled and her eyes lit with amusement.

"What's so funny?" he asked.

"I thought you might join your brother in the investigation business. You are naturally curious. Just like me."

He grinned. "No one is that nosy. I'm only helping Philip because I saw that ship being seized."

The baby jabbered something with a lot of vowels as though in approval. He noticed her tray was empty. "Are you done, little one?" He handed the last dish to Katie.

"Done," she echoed, lifting her arms toward him.

Katie laughed. "Did you hear that? She actually said a word."

"She's smart," he said.

"I'll clean her up," Katie said. She put down the plate in her hand.

"I've got it." He grabbed a clean towel and wet it, then wiped the goo from Jennie's face. She squirmed and wailed at the indignity then gave him a smile when he removed the tray from her high chair and lifted her in his arms. She planted an open-mouthed kiss on his cheek.

He turned from the table to intercept a strange expression on Katie's face. Softness lurked in her eyes, and a half smile lifted her lips. Their gazes locked, and he saw that awareness flash into her eyes again. His pulse lurched. He wished he had the nerve to kiss her.

The log in the fireplace glowed and danced with flames. The heat was welcome with the damp chill creeping into the room from the rain sluicing down the windows. Katie arranged the checker pieces on the board table then pulled an armchair close. Will carried in a kitchen chair and set it down across from her. She draped a shawl around her shoulders and settled on the cushion.

"I play a mean game of checkers," she said.

"I've got an hour before I have to wind the light again."

She smiled, though her heart ached. The last time she'd played had been with her father. They often had a game after dinner. Would those times ever come again? So much had changed.

"Is Jennie sleeping?" he asked.

She nodded. "It didn't take her long. Is Philip still gone?"

He glanced at the window. "I wound the light and started the foghorn. I'll have to check on things in a few hours. I doubt Phillip will be back until late."

At his remote tone, she lifted a curious glance to his face. "You're the oldest?" The Galveston hurricane had been in 1900—eight years ago. Philip would have been thirteen. "Is it just the two of you?"

"And my sister, Ellen."

"Where is she?"

"Following her dreams. She's been crazy about babies ever since she was a child. She's a midwife in Boston."

She smiled at his indulgent tone. "How old is she?"

He thought a moment. "Twenty-five, I think."

"And unmarried?" Philip and Will were both handsome and she imagined Ellen was a dark-haired beauty as well.

His smile was wry. "She'd be the first to march in a voting rights for women parade. The man who marries her will have to be the adventurous, strong sort."

Ellen sounded like someone Katie would like. "I hope I get a chance to meet her."

"I've invited her to spend the summer with me."

She stacked several of her checkers together and tried to ignore the way her pulse skittered when he looked at her. Strange that she'd known him such a short time and yet he was the first thing she thought of every morning when she awakened.

He pushed a checker forward to another square. "You know this area. Are there any inlets or hidden coves along the shore where we might look for that ship? If we had found it by now, we might've had a clue on how to stop what is to happen tomorrow." He rubbed his head. "But that's not my worry, as the constable is quick to tell me. And Philip is the private eye, not me."

She sat back in the chair and considered the question. "My father owned a sailboat for a time, and my family explored the coastline from here to Oregon over several summers. There are plenty of places to hide a ship. The trees grow thick, and unless someone enters the bays and inlets, one would never see it."

"Anything in particular come to mind?"

She started to shake her head then stopped. "There is a river that is navigable in the spring floods. A side stream leads off to a small lake, but part of the year you can't take a boat in or out of the lake. Anything still there in July is stuck until the following spring. There is also a small inlet about ten miles up the coast. My family and I stumbled on it accidentally during a storm. You can't see it from the ocean until you get close."

"Those are possible places to look. Anywhere else?"

She found it difficult to think with those midnight eyes on her. They'd been to so many locations in her father's boat. "There's one other place. It's a deserted island inside a cove. On the backside, nearer to the land, is an inlet into the center of the island. Those are the only possible areas I can remember."

He moved the checkers around on the board. "Thanks. Would you mind showing us where they are after tomorrow?"

"Of course. Weather permitting." She smiled. "You're so interested in weather, perhaps you can predict what tomorrow will bring. What did your balloon indicate?"

He rose and grabbed a small notebook on the desk under the window. Flipping it open, he stepped to a spot beside her and showed her rows of neatly printed numbers. "These are temperatures, barometric pressures, and humidity."

The numbers made no sense to her, but she enjoyed seeing the way his voice rose and the color came to his face. And he was close enough that her mouth went dry. "What do they tell you?"

He jabbed at the page. "Things are pretty stable right now except for this slight dip in barometric pressure. This light rain will intensify, and a real storm could be headed our way."

"How interesting." She had trouble marshaling her thoughts with him so close. Being with Bart didn't affect her pulse or her breathing. It was disconcerting. She liked the predictable. Bart was dependable and well respected. That was better than exciting. This pull she felt toward Will was something to be fought, not embraced.

She pushed a checker to the next square. "What do you do with all those numbers?"

The light in his eyes faded. "Whenever it's possible, I call my observations in to the Weather Bureau."

"And they compile it with other numbers?"

He nodded. "There are many amateur meteorologists around."

She liked seeing his eyes lighting with passion. "Only amateur? Is it possible to make a living at weather forecasting?"

"If I moved to one of the major centers and worked there, I could make enough to live on."

The glow in his face died and she wanted to see it come back. "I see you have much passion for it. You could try for a job and see where it led."

"I've thought about it. I like what I'm doing now, but mostly because it gives me the chance to study the weather and tides. Besides, this way I'm close to Philip and can help him stay focused on making a success of his business."

"It's not your responsibility to care for him," she said. "He's a grown man."

He gave her a wry smile. "That's the pot calling the kettle black. Someone else in this room feels responsible for other adults."

Her cheeks grew hot. "That's different. My parents need me."

"It's exactly the same. Your parents should feel responsible for you, not the other way around."

"My father has always been a good provider. I'm sure he's shattered by his failure." She looked down at her hands. "I don't know what we're going to do."

"No money to live on?" His voice held sympathy.

"Hardly anything. The house is too expensive to keep up. I expect we shall have to sell it and get a smaller place in town. Mama will be devastated. She was born in that house."

He frowned. "I'll make Philip split the finder's fee with you if your tips on the location of the ship earn out. The gold will be long gone but the ship itself is worth something."

She gasped. "Seriously?"

"Of course."

"How much would that be?" She began to calculate expenses. Maybe she could pay off Florence too.

"Your half would be ten thousand dollars."

A fortune. It would care for her mother for some time even after paying Florence. "Perhaps the boat isn't at any of the places I suggested," she said.

"We shall see." He grinned and then moved a checker piece. "You could always marry Bert."

"Bart," she corrected.

"He looks like a Bert. All proper and full of starch. He wouldn't contradict his mother if you paid him."

"You don't even know him."

"What's to know? He's had a silver spoon in his mouth all his life and has never had to work for a thing."

She couldn't deny it. "You can scarcely hold his birthright against him. Besides, he doesn't plan to take over his father's business. He wants to open a Macy's."

"Just as I said. Too proper to get his hands dirty."

"You're goading me now."

He grinned. "Maybe a little. He's not good enough for you."

"You don't even know him. Or me."

"I know you better than you think. I haven't shared this house with you for about a week now without realizing you long for adventure but you're too afraid to go after it."

She shifted on her chair and glanced away from his penetrating eyes. "I like things to stay calm and controlled," she said. "Adventure is too uncertain for me."

"Nice try." He chuckled.

"I don't like surprises," she said. "If I know what's going on, I can plan for every eventuality."

"You're not convincing me. It's more than that. You jumped in that boat without a hat and came running to find me. If you were as staid as you'd like people to believe, you would have waited to let the constable take care of it." His gaze dropped to her lips.

He was remembering that kiss of life. The same way she was. The moment stretched out between them until she gave an uncertain laugh and moved a checker piece. "Your turn," she said.

Surely it wasn't disappointment that lodged in her belly when he dragged his gaze from her to the board.

Twenty-three

Will saw the ship nearly to the dock. It might be the *Hanson Queen* but it was hard to tell from here. He noticed Katie struggling to keep up with him and slowed his stride to match hers.

"Is that the ship we're watching for?"

"I think so. It's one that size." He yawned.

"You haven't slept yet. Philip should be doing this."

"He's still sleeping off his liquor."

He offered his hand to assist her onto the pier, and after a moment's hesitation, she put her gloved fingers in his palm. Once they were on the rough boards, she started to pull away but he held fast. "The walking surface is uneven."

Her cheeks colored but she let him keep possession of her hand. Her gaze darted up and down the dock, and he wondered if she was assessing the occupants for anyone who might recognize her.

She tugged her hand free then placed it on his elbow. "It's a bit more proper," she whispered.

He grinned. "I dare you to take off your hat and let your hair down from its pins."

Her full lips curved in a smile. "I don't think so."

The docking of the ship broke his bantering mood. He read the name on the bow: *Hanson Queen.* "That's it," he said. "I'm going to talk to the captain. You wait here."

Her fingers tightened on his arm. "I think not. My presence here might be misconstrued if I'm alone."

"Of course. Forgive me, I would never put you in a compromising position. I'll wait until he disembarks then approach him." He stepped to the side of the dock as the sailors poured down the gangway. Several armed men in uniform stepped onto the dock and took up position on either side. At least the ship had protection, as reported.

The number of exiting sailors slowed to a crawl. When no one had disembarked for several minutes, he straightened. "Let's talk to an officer since the captain hasn't come out."

They approached the closest officer, who gave Will a sharp look then lifted a curious smile to Katie. Will tamped down the jealousy that surged in his gut. She didn't belong to him.

"Good morning," he said. "I'm glad to see you're guarding this ship. I have information that indicates pirates may have targeted it. Could you fetch the captain?"

"You questioning our ability to protect this ship, buster?" the sailor demanded.

"Of course not. I just wanted to pass along the warning."

"Duly noted. We're allowing no loitering around the ship. I suggest you be on your way."

He wasn't going to get far with the man. "Come along, Katie," he said. He led her away. "Touchy fellow."

"At least you told him. If anything happens, it's no fault of yours. And the sailor seemed competent." She glanced over her shoulder and smiled at the fellow who was staring after her.

"He was quite taken with you."

She glanced up at him from under the brim of her hat. "He was being polite."

"I think not."

"You sound angry."

"I'm not angry. Just . . . concerned." He nearly laughed at his defensive tone. What a fool he was. If she harbored no tender feelings for him, the best thing to do was squelch the emotion churning his gut.

She said nothing for several minutes until the noise of the dock was a dull hum behind them and they were walking along the sand back to the lighthouse. "You've been engaged in my personal life but have said little about your own beyond your parents' unfortunate deaths."

"I'm touched you care," he said, his grin widening.

"Forgive me," she said, her tone frosty, "I didn't intend to pry." Her gaze stayed down and didn't meet his. "I merely wondered if we should expect a fiancée to join you soon. This town has never had a bachelor for a lightkeeper. Most have families to keep them company."

"I've never been even close to marriage," he said. When her expression didn't change, he touched her chin with his fingers and tipped her face up. "Look at me, Katie."

"We should be getting back," she said, looking away. "My shift on the switchboard is about to start."

No more games. "I care about you much more than I should," he said.

Her lids opened wide and she met his gaze. Her shocked expression delighted him. He bent his head, and his lips brushed hers. Their warmth coaxed him to kiss her again.

She jerked away and stepped back. "Mr. Jesperson!"

His grin widened. "And here I thought we were on a first-name basis."

"You're being quite forward." She swallowed but didn't look away.

"I should apologize but I'm not one bit sorry."

Her cheeks flamed with color and she put her gloved fingers to her mouth. Her eyes were sparkling and he didn't think it was with outrage. She hadn't slapped him either. He was going to make an attempt to woo her, he decided. While he might not succeed, he couldn't just give in and let that dandy from town have her without a fight.

❧

The service was poorly attended but Katie hadn't expected the church to be full with the sickness around. She sat in the third pew on the right with Will, who held Jennie, and Lady Carrington. Philip had made an excuse and disappeared down to the docks. She was very conscious of the bulk of Will's arm when it occasionally brushed hers. She had barely slept the last few nights. All she could think about was his kiss on the beach.

She could almost feel Bart's eyes drilling into the back of her head. He sat two rows back with his mother and father. She'd had to refuse his insistence on her sitting with them, since there was no room in their pew for all of them. But she admitted to herself that even if there had been room, she would have preferred to sit elsewhere. It made no sense. Every time Bart made an attempt to draw her closer into his family circle, she resisted. What was the matter with her? Bart could give her the respectability she craved, but all she could think about was Will, just inches away.

When the service ended, she spoke with friends and acquaintances. Most reported improving conditions of those afflicted with smallpox. She trailed out the front door and down the steps behind Will and the rest of her little family. *Family.* That was how she was coming to think of the group staying at the lighthouse. Such notions needed to be stamped out.

A flicker of movement by a live oak tree caught her attention. A woman stepped out from the shelter of the tree. The large chapeau obscured her face, but Katie didn't have to see the rouge on her cheeks and lips or the pompadour to know it was Florence. Her hands clenched the handle of her bag as Will turned to look at her.

He frowned and glanced back as though to see what had so alarmed her. "Is there someone you need to see?"

The woman edged behind the tree, obviously having accomplished her mission. "No, no one." Even if she was not intended for Bart, even if she fell for another, it would be devastating if her birth mother's identity came out now.

Katie reached for the baby, who gurgled her vowels at her. The soft warmth of little Jennie's body comforted her. She pressed a kiss on the baby's curls and turned her back on the woman. *Go away, please go away.* The women wouldn't be so bold as to approach her in front of everyone.

The Fosters joined them. "Is there anything I can do for your dear mother, Katie?" Mrs. Foster asked. The smile she directed to the baby appeared strained. "And how is your father?" She uttered the last word in a hushed tone, disapproval tugging at her mouth.

"I so appreciate your willingness to help," Katie said, shuffling Jennie to the other arm. "I've spoken with Mama every day of late, and she's quite improved. The servants have been taking good care of her. Papa is also growing stronger."

"Would you care to join us for dinner?" Bart put in.

His mother shot him a quick glance, which Katie interpreted as a rebuke. A few drops of rain plopped onto the sidewalk. "Thank you, but I must get the baby out of the weather. It's beginning to rain."

Bart nodded. "Things will be back to normal soon. This quarantine will end and you'll be back home. I'll be able to take you to dinner and the nickelodeon." His voice held deep satisfaction.

His mother's smile was stiff. "And we'll have a dinner party to announce your engagement."

Katie saw Will tense. She clutched the baby to her chest a little too tightly, and Jennie squirmed. "We—we're not engaged, Mrs. Foster."

The woman's brow lifted, and she glanced at her son. "After you're engaged, of course," she said.

Had Bart told his parents they were engaged? Maybe even purchased a ring? Katie's throat closed at the thought. She wasn't ready.

It was one thing to think about marrying him, but another thing altogether to actually take that step.

The woman under the tree moved again, and Katie realized that even if she were ready to marry Bart, she might not have the option if the woman told anyone the truth. Everyone, even Will, would think she had withheld the truth of her heritage. And she had. She needed to get Florence out of town before the Fosters and everyone else in town found out about her. But Katie had no idea how to accomplish it.

Jennie reached for Will. He took her, and Katie turned away. "I'm going inside the church a moment." She desperately needed the release of tears and to seek God's succor right now. There was no one to talk to, no one to share her problems with except God.

"We'll be in the carriage. Take your time," Will said.

Through a rapidly building blur of tears, she directed a pleading glance at Bart, and he nodded stiffly. If she'd offended him, she was most sorry, but she couldn't stand here making small talk another moment. She lifted her skirts and hurried across the wet grass to the church door.

The scent of old wood and wax greeted her when she stepped inside and approached the altar. The solitude of the holy place descended on her. She sat on the front row in the wash of light from the stained glass window above the pulpit and clasped her hands in her lap. With her head bowed, she pleaded for strength to do whatever was necessary to care for her parents and for Florence to leave town before the truth came out.

Was that even something she could pray for? Wasn't God all about truth? She'd been living a lie for twenty years. No, not a lie. Her true parents *were* the Russells. The woman who had birthed her was no more than a brood mare. Katie's allegiance was to the mother who had soothed her hurts and braided her hair. Calm washed over her. What gain would Florence receive from revealing Katie's heritage? All leverage would be gone. The woman had as much to lose as Katie.

The door creaked behind her, and she turned to see a figure slip through the door. The wide chapeau betrayed her identity. "You shouldn't have come. Someone might see you."

"They'll just think I was a fancy woman who is finally repenting," she said with a saucy laugh.

Katie winced at such crude talk. "Why are you following me?"

Her satin skirts swishing, Florence drew nearer. "I thought about what you said when we spoke before. I think you need to know the truth now. My dear sister probably never told you the whole story, has she?"

Katie stared at the woman, willing her to tell what had happened so long ago. "Truth?"

"Albert was mine first. My sister was his second choice. I wanted to be an actress and Albert couldn't deal with it." Her beautiful face scowled. "No one tells me what to do. I was determined to show him I could succeed, so when I had the opportunity to join a vaudeville show, I took it. It was only after I left that I discovered you were on your way, but I wasn't about to go back to Albert and hear his 'I told you so.'"

Katie passed her hand over her forehead. "Y–you mean he's my real father?" She'd always believed her parents were really her aunt and uncle. It explained so much. Why her father constantly said what trash Florence was. Every thought of her brought up memories of his own indiscretions.

Florence's eyes flashed with triumph. "I knew you were an innocent to my sister's scheming ways."

Florence was close enough now for Katie to smell the perfume she wore. It was something spicy and overpowering. Strong enough to make Katie's eyes water. Florence had left the gentle fragrance of lily of the valley behind.

Katie stood and faced the woman. "Yet they raised me and you didn't."

Florence's eyes flashed. "Come now, you appear to have fared just fine."

She reached out and touched a curl of Katie's hair. It took

everything in her not to shy away from her touch. "If you're smart, my darling, you'll run far away from that uptight man in the tweed jacket. I've seen his type before. He'll expect perfection. What will he do when he finds out your real mother is a woman of the world?"

There was so much more to it than Florence was saying. Katie had to know all of it. "Why were we even in Mercy Falls? To ask for money?" Florence winced and Katie realized she'd guessed right. "That's it? You wanted money?"

"Raising a kid isn't cheap! It was time he paid his share. But he paid up. Oh yes, indeed. My dear sister was determined to have you since she couldn't have any of her own. It was the perfect time for them since only your father had arrived in town." Florence fumbled with a sequined bag and withdrew an embroidered hanky. She dabbed at her eyes. "It wasn't easy for me, Katie. Not easy at all. I love you. I always have."

For a moment Katie almost believed it until Florence put down the hanky and Katie saw a hard shine in her eyes. "If you loved me, you wouldn't want to cause trouble for me. You'd leave and never come back rather than try to ruin my life."

"I wish I could, but I'm broke, darling. I don't like putting the squeeze on you, but I have no choice." Her voice took on a wheedling tone. "Surely your loving father has put the money I need at your disposal."

Katie shook her head. "He has not. I'm not even sure how we will survive on the little left in the bank. It will be a while before Papa is back to work. His business is failing. We may have to sell everything."

Florence's placating manner vanished. "I know a lie when I hear it, Katie. I'll give you a few more days. If you won't give me the money, I'll see if your intended can spare some for the mother of his wife-to-be."

Katie watched Florence saunter toward the door and knew the woman would do exactly as she threatened, if only for revenge against Mama.

TWENTY-FOUR

THE RAIN SETTLED into a drizzle. Will peered through the curtain of gray toward the church. Still no sign of Katie. Jennie slept on Lady Carrington's lap. The horses stamped their hooves impatiently. "I'll be right back," he told her. He shoved open the carriage door and stepped out into the rain.

The cold drops bounced off his hat. He skirted mud puddles and hurried to the door of the church. In the vestibule he shook the moisture from his clothes and glanced toward the sanctuary door, where he heard the low murmur of voices. He recognized Katie's voice but not the other woman's. Interrupting them might not be a good idea.

The woman drew closer to the door and said, "I know a lie when I hear it, Katie. I'll give you a few more days. If you won't give me the money, I'll see if your intended can spare some for the mother of his wife-to-be."

He stepped around a pillar and caught a glimpse of a gaudily dressed woman as she moved through the vestibule and exited the church. The smirk on her face raised his ire. He puzzled over the words he'd heard. It sounded as though she had demanded money from Katie. What had she meant about being Katie's mother? She resembled Katie, but the woman didn't seem to have any pox on her face, and she'd been out in public when she was supposed to be quarantined. But why would she attempt to blackmail Katie?

He moved back through the vestibule then opened the door to the sanctuary. The sound of soft weeping made him pause in the doorway. He saw Katie kneeling at the altar under the stained glass window. Sobs shook her shoulders and she fumbled for a hanky in the sleeve of her dress. She dabbed at her eyes then rose and turned toward the door.

She stopped when she saw him. "How long have you been there?" The skin around her eyes was reddened.

"Long enough," he said gently. "That woman was your mother?"

"She's not my mother!" Katie clasped her gloved hands together.

"But I overheard her say—"

She walked toward him. "Whatever you heard, it's no business of yours."

"Fair enough, but if you're in some kind of trouble, I'd like to help you."

She reached him and paused. "Why would you think I'm in trouble?"

"I overheard her try to blackmail you."

Color stained her cheeks. "You listened?"

"I came looking for you and was in the vestibule. I didn't intend to eavesdrop."

Her shoulders slumped and she grabbed the back of a pew. "Oh what am I going to do?" she whispered.

"Let me help you, Katie. Who is that woman?"

She bit her lip and raised moist eyes to his. "The woman who bore me. *Not* my mother."

"I don't understand."

"She abandoned me when I was five. She's Mama's sister. A–and it appears Papa is my real father. I'd always thought it was one of Florence's men friends." She bit her lip. "I'm sorry. I didn't mean to tell you all of that."

"I know how to keep a secret. But why is it a secret? If you were five, surely people know you are not Mrs. Russell's daughter."

She shook her head. "We couldn't bear for people to know I was born to a woman who danced and entertained men. No suitable man would want anything to do with me. My reputation would be gone. I'd have to leave Mercy Falls in disgrace."

He wanted to object to her conclusion but she was right. "You moved here after the Russells took you in?"

She nodded. "Papa had just moved to Mercy Falls. I assumed it was coincidence that Florence brought me here. Now I know it was because she wanted money from him. Mama wasn't here yet, and we went to visit my father. I liked him right away. Perhaps I always knew . . ." She paused, lost in reveries, then shook her head and continued, "A few nights later Florence left me alone, something frightened me, and I found my way back to the Russell house. My father took me in, and when Mama showed up the next morning, everyone in town assumed I was their child. I never knew what happened to Florence."

"Perhaps your father paid her off."

She nodded. "I think that must be what happened."

"And now she's back, wanting more money."

She tucked her hanky back into her sleeve. "She didn't believe me when I told her Papa's business was in trouble."

"So she is threatening to ask Mr. Foster for money."

She paled. "Yes, and she mustn't. Mama . . . I would be ruined."

He studied her panicked expression. "The truth usually comes out sooner or later. If Mr. Foster loves you, it won't matter." The thought of her marrying that fellow made him thrust his hands in his pockets.

"It matters to me."

He offered his arm and she took it. He guided her toward the door. "So now I understand a little more about you."

Her fingers tightened on his arm. "Whatever do you mean?"

A wave of tenderness surprised him. "Your intense desire never to be faced with a surprise. I understand now."

Her smile was weak. "Would you care to translate?"

"You feel the need to control things so you're never faced with a situation like that again. But you should remember that your real friends will stick by you. If others don't, they never really cared about you."

She thrust out her chin. "It must not come out."

"Truth always comes out, Katie. Who you are has nothing to do with who bore you. God rejoices over you and who you are as a person. That's where your worth comes from. Not from fickle men. Or women."

"I know that."

They reached the door and he opened it for her. "Then put it into practice."

She glanced up at him. "You don't understand how important this is to me."

He didn't answer as she preceded him out the door. With her real mother in town, she hadn't a hope of keeping this quiet. He'd seen the resemblance. It wouldn't be long before someone else did too.

⋘⋙

The rain pattered on the carriage top and the scent of wet ground filled the air. Katie pointed out the road to Will, who nodded and turned the horses. He sat hunched on the driver's seat in a rain slicker. Rain sluiced off the brim of his hat. She thought she could trust him with her secret. What did it say about their relationship that she was so comfortable with his knowledge of her background? And moreover, that she so feared Bart and his mother finding out?

"Katie, dear, are you sure this is wise?" Lady Carrington asked. The baby slept in the crook of her arm.

Katie craned her neck to see through the downpour. The house would be visible any moment. "I must see how Mama is doing."

"But the quarantine," the older woman protested. "Your mother is still contagious."

"I'll stay well away from the window." Ever since Mrs. Foster had mentioned it, she couldn't get it out of her mind. The carriage had barely come to a halt when the rain slowed then stopped. Katie flung open the door and stepped down before Will could assist her. "I won't be long," she said.

His dark eyes held sympathy and concern. "Would you like me to come with you?"

"That's not necessary," she said before he could jump down from the seat. "I need to do this alone." Though he knew much of the story, there was more he didn't know. She told herself it was best to keep it that way.

The wet grass soaked her feet before she reached the house. She stopped about five feet from the window, which was open a crack. "Mama," she called. "Are you awake?"

"Katie? Is that you?" her mother's voice was weak but clear.

Katie whispered thanks to God at the sound of her voice. She didn't dare move closer. "It's me, Mama. Can you come to the window?" Though they'd spoken by phone, she needed to *see* her mother. And she needed to tell her of Florence in person, not over a buzzing line.

A few moments later the window rose higher and her mother's face appeared. "Katie, darling, I've missed you." Red pox marred the creamy complexion of the older woman. She appeared thinner and her hair lay in disarray on her shoulders, but she was smiling.

Katie didn't know where to even begin. Her mother's frail appearance gave her pause. Perhaps it should wait. Nubbins came running from the backyard. The kitten was drenched and mewing. Katie scooped him up and held her against her chest. "Poor kitty, I think I'll take you home with me. I've missed you." There was that word *home* again. How peculiar when she was standing in front of her home and felt no real inclination to move back into her room.

She studied her mother's face. "You're healing, Mama."

Her mother smiled. "I'm getting stronger by the day. How are you, Katie? You look pale. Are you well?"

"I'm fine." She wetted her lips. There was no way to navigate this story in a delicate manner. "We have a–a problem though." She hated to burden her mother when she was so sick but what else could she do? "I need some guidance, Mama."

Her mother's smile faded. "What is it? Your father has died, hasn't he? You must tell me. Oh dear, I spoke to him on the telephone today and he seemed to be getting stronger."

"Wh–what? No, of course not, Mama. He's fine. I saw him." Her mother's question drove thoughts of Florence from Katie's head. "Why would you say that?"

"Your father would never try to kill himself." Her mother leaned her head out the window. "I've thought this over. Someone had to have tried to hurt him. You know he's a good man, Katie. It was only when he's drinking that things are . . . difficult."

"I know, Mama. He's doing fine though." She couldn't tell her mother what Papa had revealed.

"He would never deliberately leave me to face the problems ahead without him. Your father isn't a coward. He's a fighter."

"Mama, please listen," Katie said, trying to keep a desperate edge from her voice and failing. "Florence is in town. Demanding money."

Her mother's eyes widened. She grew even paler and her mouth hung open. She disappeared from the window. Katie heard something scrape on the floor, and then her mother's face appeared again, a bit lower. "I had to sit down," she said, her voice quivering. "My sister came to see you?"

"Yes. She's after more money, Mama."

"She deserves nothing from us," her mother said in a trembling voice. "In twenty years she has not even so much as sent any of us a Christmas greeting. We didn't know if she was dead or alive. She simply vanished."

"I know."

"What makes her think we would give her money?"

"To keep her quiet. Otherwise, she will go to Bart and ask for money. She'll tell him she's my mother." Katie could barely even say the words *my mother*. Florence had no concept of what being a real mother entailed.

Her mother put her hand to her throat. "She can't do that! Bart's parents would put a stop to his courtship if they knew."

"I know." She blinked back the moisture in her eyes.

"How much money does she want?"

"Five thousand dollars."

Her mother gasped. "Katie, whatever shall we do? There isn't that kind of money."

"I could offer her what we have, but if I give it to Florence, there won't be anything left to live on."

"She doesn't deserve one penny!" her mother cried. "Oh if only Albert were here. He would soon put a stop to her shenanigans."

The rain picked up and Katie felt the dampness to her bones. It added to her weariness and despair. "But he's not. And you need to guard your health. It's up to me, and I don't know what to do."

Her mother leaned farther out the window. "You simply *must* get Bart to propose. Soon."

A lump formed in Katie's throat. "Is it fair to him, Mama? I mean, what happens if he finds out the truth after we're married?" She couldn't believe she was arguing for telling him the truth. But Will was right. The truth always came out. And when it did, she didn't want her husband to think she betrayed him.

"Don't you dare whisper a word of it!"

"All right, Mama," she said, trying to soothe her mother's agitation.

"Get rid of that woman, Katie. Somehow!" Her mother's voice rose nearly to a shriek. She broke off and began to cough.

Katie checked her impulse to spring forward. "Mama, are you all right?"

The fit of coughing stopped. Her mother wiped her mouth with a hanky and seemed to gather herself again. "I don't know what we shall do if it becomes known in town. It's not only Bart and your chance to become a Foster, you know. All of society will shun us. Because we passed you off as my own child. No one likes to be hoodwinked. I couldn't bear the pity either. We would have to leave Mercy Falls."

Katie nodded, though the thought made her cringe. "We have a total of three thousand dollars, Mama. We can't give her all our money."

"Perhaps we could get a loan from the bank."

"We have no assets to put up."

"The haberdashery," her mother suggested. "I don't think there is a mortgage on it."

"Papa told me it was all mortgaged," Katie said. She glanced back at the carriage. "I must go, Mama."

Her mother reached out a hand through the open window, as if she longed to touch her. "Are you getting along all right? How curious that you're staying at the lighthouse."

"I'm enjoying caring for the baby."

"Oh yes, the child. Might I see her again? From a distance?"

It was one thing to risk her own health, but Katie wasn't willing to risk Jennie's. "I think that we should wait until you are well. Will has taken responsibility for now and we really have no money to raise her."

Her mother's brows rose. "Will? You are on a first name basis with the man?"

"It seemed sensible."

Her mother shook her head. "Oh Katie, my dear. Watch yourself. Your future is planned out already. There is no room in it for a poor lightkeeper."

"I know, Mama. I know my duty."

Her mother frowned. "Duty? But surely you want to marry Bart, do you not?"

The dark clouds seemed lower than they'd ever been. The rain drenched her, and the wet grass chilled her toes. "Of course I do," Katie said before the fear grew in her mother's eyes. "I am praying for your rapid recovery, Mama. I'll talk to you soon." She turned and fled back to the carriage with the kitten in her arms for comfort.

TWENTY-FIVE

KATIE HADN'T BEEN able to stop shivering since they'd arrived back from town. Will had built a roaring fire and she sat as close as she dared in dry clothing. A now-dry Nubbins lay sleeping on her lap. She'd towel-dried her hair and it lay still damp on her shoulders. The rain continued to come down outside, sometimes in a drenching downpour and sometimes in a gentle patter. The scent of oatmeal cookies drifted from the kitchen and she heard Lady Carrington banging pots.

Will kept staring at Katie from the sofa then looking away when she glanced in his direction, and Katie wished she was the one who had insisted on making dinner.

Jennie had fallen asleep on the rug. "I'll go put her in her crib," Katie said.

"Let her sleep," Will said. "If you move her, she'll awaken in a grumpy mood."

"I don't want to move anyway," she said. "This chair is just now warming up."

He rose and grabbed the knitted afghan that was draped over the back of the sofa. His eyes were soft as he laid it over her. "Better?" he asked.

She nodded, her mouth drying at his nearness. Pulling her hands from under the wrap, she willed him to head to the lighthouse and not confuse her even more. "Nubbins will like it too."

He rolled his eyes. "A cat. We have quite the menagerie here." As if in answer to his remark, the bird meowed in the kitchen. Nubbins sprang to full alert, his ears flicking. He jumped from the sofa and crept toward the kitchen. "Good thing the bird is in his cage," Will said.

Her gaze drifted to the window, where raindrops still sluiced down the glass. "You were right about the weather," she said.

He smiled. "I like being right."

To her relief, he moved over to the window, giving her room again to think straight. "Do you want to talk about what happened today?"

Katie strained to hear what was going on in the kitchen. It sounded as though Lady Carrington was chopping vegetables. "There isn't much to say about it. I can't pay what she's demanding."

"I wouldn't pay her anyway."

She pressed her lips together. Did he want her to be humiliated? "I must help you and Philip find the ship and the missing gold."

"And then what? Pay her off and worry about the next time she wants money?"

He was right. This situation could be never ending. "I'm not sure I have the courage to just let it be known."

"You're the bravest woman I know. People who care about you will stand by you. I'll be one of them."

She swallowed hard and didn't look away from the intensity of emotion in his face.

"The woman's appearance changes nothing, Katie. You are still your own dear self. Courageous and beautiful. Fiercely loyal. Why is respectability so important to you?"

He thought she was dear? Courageous? And . . . beautiful? No one but her mama had ever told her that. "My father, he–he often intimated I would turn out poorly. I want to make him proud of me."

He scowled. "Did he throw this Florence in your face?"

The penetrating knowledge in his eyes made her glance away. "You are most astute," she said, her throat tight.

"Your desire for respectability is really a desire for peace, I think. That comes from being comfortable in your skin—with who God made you to be. Not trying to be something you're not. Being willing to be transparent, without airs."

Her pulse raced even thinking about such transparency. "What if people reject who I really am?"

He leaned forward. "They won't, Katie. You're beautiful, inside and out. And if some do, so what? We answer to God. We belong to him. We are his children. His bride. His brothers and sisters. You can rest in that. Peace is a beautiful thing."

His eyes held a mysterious tenderness that drew her. She wanted to be able to rest in the peace he and Addie talked about. To turn over control. Would marrying Bart bring that or just make her more fearful of letting anyone see the real Katie Russell? "How do you learn to rest in that? To make that enough?"

He glanced at the baby. "Do you think Jennie thinks she must hide who she is? She knows she has our total love and acceptance. We have God's in that same way. That can give us confidence to put down the masks and be who we were created to be."

She shuddered and tried to tell herself it was from the cold and not from sheer terror. "Sometimes I dream that the whole town knows who I am. I see people point and turn their backs on me. Whisper about me when I'm not looking. I can't bear pity."

He knelt in front of her then clasped her hands in his. "So don't accept it. Hold your head high. You are not Florence. You are your own self."

His hands were warm. Steady and strong. Just like the man himself. "I'll try to remember that."

He lifted her hand to his mouth and turned it over, then kissed her palm. His intense gaze stayed locked with hers. With his lips pressed against her skin, she couldn't think, couldn't breathe. Bart never affected her this way. What did it all mean?

All she would have to do was lean forward just a bit, show her attraction to him, and he would take the lead. He would draw her into his arms and kiss her again. She knew from the experience on the beach that all thought left her when he kissed her. Was that the place to find peace?

But no, it had to be more than sheer attraction, didn't it? Addie said God had a plan for her life and that finding it would bring the peace Katie sought. Peace wasn't in a man, but in God.

Mrs. Carrington appeared in the kitchen doorway. "I need a day off, children. When this atrocious weather breaks, I suggest we go for a sail up the coast. We can take Jennie out for some fresh air."

Will moved away from Katie and stood near the fireplace.

"It sounds like a lovely idea," Katie said. "I can point out some coves Will and Philip might want to investigate. Any idea when this storm will end?" she asked him.

"By my readings, I think it will break tomorrow and turn beautiful."

"We can make a picnic. It should be quite pleasant to take my boat along the coast," Lady Carrington said.

"Can I do anything to help you tonight? You've been quite mysterious about what we're having for dinner."

"The stew is my specialty secret. I haven't even shown Addie how to make it yet, though I will do so when she comes home. Enjoy the fire a few more minutes. I'll call you when it's ready." She stepped away with a satisfied smile.

Katie glanced up to see Will watching her intently. A sail with him sounded quite lovely.

⌘

The foghorn tolled its warning into the night. Katie rolled over and stared at the dim light shining in the window, wondering why she was awake. As Will predicted, the storm had passed and the moon was out, but the storm surge still crashed against the rocks. She sat up and pushed her heavy hair from her face.

Katie wasn't sure what had roused her, but the skin on the back of her neck prickled. The cat leaped from the bed to the floor, but Nubbins was silent in his movement. She held her breath and listened to the night sounds: the surf crashing on the rocks, the owl that roosted in the light tower hooting, and the blare of the foghorn.

Was that a shout? She leaped from the bed and ran to the window. She stared out to sea. The sliver of moon outside illuminated a boat riding the waves toward the rocks. It listed to one side, and she realized it was damaged. A man pulled a dinghy toward the water. Will was going to attempt a rescue. He needed help.

She grabbed her robe and thrust her arms into it. With her robe belted, she ran for the stairs. Should she rouse Philip? She peered through the open door of his bedroom and saw the covers still smooth. He wasn't home from his night at the quay yet. She rushed down the steps and made her way outside. When she reached the porch, she paused and saw Will was already out on the rolling sea. He was rowing with all his might toward the ship that was breaking apart on the rocks.

It took a lot of courage to do what he was doing. She wished she'd been able to get out there in time to help him. While she couldn't put her back to the oar, she could pray. She gripped the porch post and prayed that he would rescue the three sailors, that all of them would return safely to shore. Will had reached the boat and was pulling a man from the waves. Another man leaped into the dinghy and nearly capsized it. A few minutes later there was nothing much left of the boat, and Will was rowing back to the beach.

Katie leaned against the post and whispered a thank you. She thought of the medical kit, and as she turned back to the house to fetch it, she saw a shadow flit by the end of the porch. She froze.

"Philip?" she asked, her voice quavering. When no one answered, her sense of unease grew. "Who's there?"

An inner warning bell rang. She should get inside. Turning, she stepped toward the door, but before she got more than two feet, hands grabbed her and she was pulled back against a hard chest.

The man's hand went over her mouth. "Did you tell the constable?" he hissed in her ear.

She couldn't speak with his hand smelling of horse over her mouth. All she could do was shake her head. If only she had her shoes on, she'd try stomping on his instep. He dragged her toward the edge of the porch, out of the beam flashing from the lighthouse lens.

She couldn't breathe, couldn't think. If she could get her mouth free, she'd scream, though she doubted anyone would hear her over the sound of the surf. She seized the man's wrist with both hands and yanked downward. She opened her mouth until she saw the glitter of a knife blade.

"Scream and you're dead," he said in a hoarse whisper.

She was good at recognizing voices because of her job, but she'd never heard this one before: guttural with an East Coast accent.

"What did you tell the constable?" he demanded.

"N–nothing," she choked out.

"He showed up to talk to my boss. You must have told him something." His fingers tightened on her throat. "I want to know what you said."

"I told you—nothing."

The man's grip tightened, and he swore. "You tell your father that if he talks, you're dead. You and your mother both."

Several men came stumbling up the path from the beach. The man's hand fell away and Katie reeled at her sudden release. She could only see the broad back of a man melt into the darkness. She thought he might be dressed in overalls but she couldn't be sure. The survivors of the shipwreck moved past her as she stood in the shadows.

"There are dry clothes in the well house," Will called to them.

"Thanks," one of the men said. They all went around the corner of the house, and the door to the shed creaked open.

At least the men were unhurt. When at last she saw Will's broad shoulders crest the top of the hill, her feet seemed to move of their own volition.

A trace of whiskers darkened his chin. His tired eyes sharpened when he saw her. "What's wrong?" He reached out and grasped her shoulders.

She nestled against him. All she wanted was to inhale his musky scent and rest in his strength. "There was a man with a knife," she said, her voice barely above a whisper.

His fingers tightened. "Where?"

"On the porch, but he's gone now."

"He threatened you?" His voice was a low growl.

"Yes. He wanted to know what I overheard. And what I told the constable." She didn't repeat the threat against her and her mother.

"Did you tell him you didn't know anything?"

She nodded. "I don't think he believed me." Her fists grasped the cotton of his shirt and she buried her nose into it even more.

"I'll look for him."

"No!" she said as he started to pull away. "Just hold me a minute." Shudders wracked her shoulders as she remembered the knife. Will embraced her more tightly and she rested there a few more moments before she lifted her head. "I'm okay now. I don't think I've ever been so frightened."

His rough hands smoothed her hair. "I wouldn't let anything happen to you."

"You weren't there," she reminded him.

"God was, though."

She heard the smile in his voice and smiled too. "Of course."

Waves lapped at the sides of the boat. The sails billowed with air above Will's head. He smiled as he saw Katie sitting on the deck with Lady Carrington. Jennie played with blocks at their feet. The seas were calm today, blue and beautiful. They had a picnic lunch aboard. He'd invited Philip to come, but after the attack on Katie the night before, his brother decided to speak with the constable and see who he'd interrogated.

The mynah rode the waves on one of the crossbeams as if he were scouting for land. "Six steps, matie," he squawked. Nubbins hissed from under Katie's seat when the bird meowed. Will grinned. They were like a family out for a pleasure ride. The thought made him turn his gaze from where it wanted to linger . . . Katie's face.

"Ahoy," Katie called. She joined him at the helm and pointed. "Just past that thickly forested finger of land, there is a tiny inlet that looks as though it goes nowhere. It does. Veer into it and angle the boat around to the left. Don't worry how tight it is. The passage is deep and will widen soon enough."

He nodded and concentrated on guiding the boat. Katie grabbed the railing with one hand as the sailboat, leaning with its sails full of wind, veered toward the passage she'd indicated. He would have missed it if it hadn't been for her. In fact, it appeared so narrow he would have guessed the boat couldn't fit. The trees on either side nearly brushed the side of the boat, but he could see the water was as deep as Katie promised. A few more feet and they were through the narrowest part. The shores on both sides receded and the passage grew wider and wider. A small bay opened in front of him. The few feet of rocky sand soon gave way to heavy forest.

"Isn't it charming?" she asked. "We used to come here every Sunday when I was small."

"Lovely," he said, looking at her. The pink in her cheeks was most becoming. Her blue dress deepened the color of her eyes. He forced his attention back to the inlet ahead of him. It was clear and empty. There was a nice beach to his right. "How about we have lunch there?"

"Looks good to me. I'm hungry," she said.

He steered the boat toward the shore until just before he would scrape bottom, then dropped the anchor overboard. They had no dinghy attached, so he leaped over the side into the cold water. He held out his arms for Lady Carrington then carried the older woman to the beach, where he set her on her feet, before returning for Jennie. The baby wound her fingers in his hair and smiled, showing her small teeth. He grinned back and carried her to Lady Carrington.

His pulse was running away in his chest when he returned to the yacht for Katie, and he told himself it was the exertion of slogging through the water from the boat to the shore. Katie's smile was a bit uncertain, but she slipped over the side and he caught her. The top of her bonnet brushed his chin and she weighed hardly anything in his arms. He caught the scent of lavender. It made him want to hold her closer. Her arms came around his neck and she slanted a glance into his face. The little point of her chin and the way her eyes tipped up at the corners intrigued him.

"I'm sorry you have to carry me," she said.

"I'm not." The words were out before he could stop them. He grinned at the way the color washed up her neck. He liked the feel of her in his arms, the way her breath stirred the hair at his sideburns, the smell of her. They reached the shore, but he didn't put her down right away. Instead, he carried her onto the sand to where Lady Carrington stood with Jennie at her feet, scooping up sand.

He set Katie down and waded back to the boat where he climbed aboard and grabbed the wicker basket of food. As he jumped back into the water, he saw movement off to his right. Narrowing his gaze, he saw a flutter of red. A shirt? He rushed the rest of the way to shore, dropped the basket at Katie's feet, then took off at a run to where he'd seen the flash of color. He heard a noise behind him and realized Katie was on his heels. It would do no good to tell her to go back.

He reached the black sage clumps and glanced around. The vegetation here was matted down with footprints. Large ones. A man, maybe two, had milled about in this area. A chill ran down his back. He stooped and picked up something glinting in the sun, nestled among the matted weeds. A knife. It had a snake's head on it. Just like the one from the night they discovered Miss Bulmer's wedding gown . . . and were attacked.

He wheeled to face Katie. "Get out of here!"

Twenty-six

"What's wrong?"

He turned her toward the beach. "It's dangerous. I'll take care of it."

She turned back around and folded her arms. "I'm coming with you."

A forest mist curled around Katie's feet. The dankness of the vegetation filled her nose. This place felt sinister, but she pushed away her sense of foreboding and tried to see what Will was trying to hide.

His arm came out and blocked her forward movement. "You are the most inquisitive, bullheaded woman I've ever met," he said.

Katie managed not to smile at his peeved tone. She peered around him at the flash of silver in his hand. "Is that a knife?"

He thrust it in his belt then took her arm and turned her back toward the beach. "I shouldn't have brought you out here." He glanced over his shoulder toward the thick forest. Tension etched the line of his shoulders.

She tried to see where he was looking but all she noticed were tall redwoods that blocked out the light and ferns waving in the breeze. That sensation of being watched intensified. "What's wrong?"

"Let's get out of here." He propelled her away from the coolness of the woods toward the beach.

She tried to look around him. "I think those footprints were fresh. Whoever left that knife might still be around."

"The very reason that I should get you to safety."

They stepped out into sunshine. Gulls cawed overhead and her earlier sensation of danger seemed overblown.

He stopped and pulled out the knife he'd found. "This knife. The guy who attacked me on the island the night we found Miss Bulmer's wedding dress had it."

She shuddered and stared into the coolness of the tall trees. "You mean he's been here?"

"He had to have been there just a few moments ago. I saw his shirt. That's what made me go look."

She quit trying to resist. "We should get Lady Carrington and Jennie out of here."

"You too. I'll have you take the boat out a safe distance."

"Now wait a minute." She dug her heels into the sand. "You're going to investigate it, aren't you? Yes, we'll get them to safety, but when you go to check it out, I want to help."

"I don't want you hurt."

The concern on his face warmed her. "That fellow nearly killed you. You need me." His lips twitched then stilled, but she saw the amusement in his eyes. "Really. You need assistance. You don't even have a weapon, do you?"

He moved her closer to Lady Carrington. "I have his knife."

"What if he has a gun?" They were nearly within earshot of Lady Carrington, and Katie didn't want to worry her. "Please, let me help you. I led you here in the first place. You can't take my help one minute then shut me out the next."

The frown remained crouched between his eyes. "I won't have you in harm's way, Katie. I–I care too much about you."

Before she had time to respond, something whizzed over her head.

"Run!" He grabbed her arm.

She picked up her skirts with her other hand and dashed across the sand with her feet barely touching the ground.

Bullets spit at their feet and Katie nearly stumbled, but Will's hand on hers kept her moving until she regained her balance. The sharp retort of the gun stopped.

"What's happening?" Lady Carrington asked as Will scooped up Jennie and grabbed the older woman's good arm.

"Danger! Run!" Katie splashed through the water toward the sailboat. The water dragged at her skirts and she nearly lost her balance. She glanced back to see Will coming with Jennie in his arms and Lady Carrington at his side. There was no sign of the shooter and she thought they were far enough away from the woods that bullets couldn't reach them unless the man was ready to be seen.

She finally reached the boat but had no strength to climb the rope ladder, so she stood panting in chest-high water until Will reached her. He boosted Lady Carrington onto the ladder and the older woman clambered slowly up the rope then took the wailing baby he handed up to her.

"Your turn," he told Katie. His big hands spanned her waist and lifted her.

She forced herself up the ladder. Lady Carrington was sitting at the top and reached out to her with her good hand. "I can make it," Katie said. She hauled herself up until she stood on the deck, Will right behind her. The bird fluttered and squawked above her head. Will cranked the anchor up and hurried to set sail.

"I don't see anyone," Katie said, taking Jennie, who was reaching for her. The little one lay with her head on Katie's shoulder and one fist clutched at her neck.

"I think they just wanted to scare us off. They could have hit us. We were close enough."

She peered toward the woods. "Maybe you're right." She hoped so. It was one thing to investigate with Will herself, but she didn't want Lady Carrington in any danger.

"Step away from the cake!" the bird squawked. "Six feet back."

She jumped at the loud noise. "Stupid bird," she muttered. The wind blew a salty breath into her face as the boat got underway. She moved to the bow and watched the blend of redwood bark and deep green leaves recede as Will took it through the inlet. A hundred yards offshore, he trimmed the sails and threw out the anchor. He shucked his shoes and removed his belt and shirt.

"Why are we stopping? Where are you going?" She had a sinking feeling she knew.

"I'm going to swim back and investigate."

She grabbed his arm. "You can't go by yourself. It's too dangerous."

"I'll be fine, Katie. If there's a chance to end it now, I want to take it. You were accosted last night. He could have killed you."

Before she could respond, he leaned forward and brushed his mouth across hers. The sensation of his lips on hers was intoxicating. Of their own volition, her fists grabbed his shirt and she returned his kiss.

His hand cupped her cheek and he smiled into her face. "If I'm not back in an hour, take the boat back to Mercy Falls and contact the constable."

"But—" Before she could finish her protest, he was gone over the side. She heard a splash then saw his head, dark and sleek as an otter, moving through the water. She ran to the rail and prayed for his safety. He had to come back safe and sound. She couldn't bear it if anything happened to him.

With the realization that she loved him, she put her fingers to her lips where the taste of his mouth still lingered.

❧

The fifty-degree water chilled Will's skin through and through by the time he rose dripping from the sea. A brisk wind rustled the treetops and left him shivering. He skirted the rocks and headed for the forest where he'd found the knife. Not a twig snapped under his carefully placed bare feet, and he flitted from trunk to trunk, stopping often to listen. He heard nothing other than birdsong and the rustle of leaves in the breeze.

A smile lingered on his face from the way Katie had kissed him back. He sobered and reminded himself to focus on his objective so he could return to kiss her again. Pausing, he inhaled the dank loam of the forest and focused his senses on the task at hand. He reached a small clearing and paused behind a rock. The remains of a campfire lay scattered in the center of the space, and a few logs had been pulled up for seating. He stepped from behind the shelter of the rock and approached the ashes. The scent of campfire still lingered. Kneeling, he put his hand over them. Warm.

He rose and scanned the area. He saw two different sized shoe prints. Whoever they were, they'd taken their belongings and departed. He followed the beaten path to the other side of the meadow. The faint trail continued through a stand of redwoods. As he walked through the forest, he heard the sound of surf. The woods gave way to beach and he saw waves lapping onto a rocky shore. It was another bay, different from the one they'd entered. A small rocky island jutted out of the water in the distance.

And a large sailing vessel was anchored in the water offshore. His pulse jumped. The *Paradox* floated just before him. He'd found it.

He hung back in the shelter of a redwood and let his gaze roam the ship. The pirated boat looked intact. The sails were tied down and he could see no breaches in the wooden sides. No one stood on the abandoned deck either. He glanced around the rocky shore. There was no sign of the men whose trail he had followed here. A flicker of movement caught his eye and he saw a smaller boat in a narrow channel leading away from the *Paradox*. Squinting, he realized one of the figures aboard wore a red shirt.

He cautiously exited the shelter of the forest and picked his way across the sharp rocks. The men hadn't seen him. Wading out into the cold water, he walked as far as he could toward the ship then plunged in and swam toward the boat rocking in the waves. He edged to the starboard side and climbed the rope ladder. When he reached eye level of the deck, he glanced around and listened.

The ship was a silent, floating tomb. Not a sound except the flitter of the hanging sails came to his ears, so he heaved himself aboard. He shuddered with the chill. It wasn't just the swim and the wind but the knowledge of what had happened to the crew aboard this boat. Bloodstains marred the deck as a testament to the brutality of the pirates. There had to be more of them than the two he'd seen. Two men couldn't have dispatched the entire crew by themselves. He listened again before he made another step but the ship was silent. Whoever had assisted the men was no longer aboard. He was certain he was alone.

His bare feet slapped along the planking and left an echo hanging in the air that was a bit unnerving. The flapping of the loose sails added to his sense of unease. He found the door to the hold and descended a few steps until the light gave out. There was no lantern around, so he retraced his steps. His best option was to summon the constable and bring him to this location. But first Will needed to inform Philip that the ship had been found.

He shielded his gaze and stared out across the water. There was no sign of the two men in the boat. His heart paused then pounded painfully at a sudden thought. What if this inlet fed into the same area as the other one? The men would come out by the boat where Katie, Jennie, and Lady Carrington waited for him.

Will ran to the edge then paused, forcing himself to think. It would take longer to swim to shore then traipse back through the forest. If there was a vessel anywhere near the *Paradox*, he'd make better time by sea. He did a quick scan and found a lifeboat with oars. A few moments later he was on the water and rowing with all his might. With every flex of his arms, he prayed he would reach them in time.

TWENTY-SEVEN

KATIE GLANCED AT the watch pinned to her blouse. Will had been gone nearly forty-five minutes. She was not going to leave him behind. If he didn't come in a few minutes, she was going to go looking for him. Her fingers strayed to her lips again. Every time she thought of that kiss her pulse raced. She wanted to see if the love she'd felt in his arms would swell again at the sight of him.

"I don't care for your expression," Lady Carrington said. "You're planning something."

"I'm going after Will," Katie said, making her decision. She put Jennie on the other woman's lap. "It's been nearly an hour. I'm not leaving him behind."

Lady Carrington pulled the sleeping child to her. "Katie, you're no match for men with guns. We would help Will much more if we garner help for him. Do you know how to sail well enough to get us back to Mercy Falls?"

"We can't just sail away and leave him behind!"

The mynah squawked. "Step away from the cake! Six feet!" He fluttered his wings as Nubbins stalked him.

Katie scooped up the kitten. "Oh do be quiet," she muttered to the bird. They had thought this would be a pleasant day for a sail. How distressing that it had turned into a dangerous foray into enemy territory. "Don't you know any other words?" She glanced around for any weapon she might take with her. There was nothing here. She was going anyway.

Starting toward the rope ladder, a movement caught her attention. Squinting, she stared at the boat that had appeared from around the spit of land ahead. At first she thought it might be Will and he'd found someone to help him return by sea, but as the dinghy neared, she realized one man wore a red shirt. A flash of red was what had attracted Will to the place where he'd found the knife. Her unease deepened when she realized the men seemed to be rowing straight at them.

"Lady Carrington, I think the men who shot at us are coming our way."

"Oh my," Lady Carrington said. She rose and stepped beside Katie. "What shall we do?"

"I'm going to try to get us out of here." Katie reached for the anchor winch and cranked it, keeping an eye on the approaching vessel. She rushed to the sails and began to raise them, but one pulley got hung up. She yanked on it, it swung free, and then caught again. In terror, she looked back to the boat. Her pulse raced when she saw how close they were. "We're not going to make it," she said. "Get below!" She rushed Lady Carrington and Jennie into the hold and followed them down.

She glanced around for anything she might use as a weapon. There was a bed and some cupboards. She threw open the cabinet doors and flinched at the strong odor of mildew. Nothing but enameled tin plates and cups. A glint caught her eye, and her gaze landed on a knife back in the corner. She grabbed it then rushed up the ladder to the deck. The boat was eight feet away when she reached the railing at the bow.

Keeping the knife in her right hand hidden in the folds of her skirt, she raised her left hand. "Are you in need of assistance?" she asked with a smile.

"Ahoy! Yes, we need help."

At the sound of the man's voice, Paco squawked and fluttered his feathers. "Eight feet down!"

The man in the bow was dressed in trousers and a vest. His mustache was neatly trimmed and waxed. His dark good looks with the gray wings at his temple would turn the head of most women. Her memory flashed back to the description of the man at the skating rink who had called her. Could it be the same man? Her attention veered to the second man in the boat. He wore a red gingham shirt and dungarees held up with suspenders. Maybe the man who had attacked her the night before? They were clearly from very different social standings. And they also matched Will's description of the two men he'd seen talking and pointing to the sea. Her fingers tightened around the knife when she saw the sun glint on the rifle in the bottom of the boat.

The fellow in red kicked an oilcloth over it and smiled. "Ahoy there. We're about worn out and could use a ride back to Mercy Falls. Can we board?"

"I'm sorry, but no," she said. "We're not heading to Mercy Falls." At least not until she had Will safely aboard.

"Could you take us to the nearest town then?"

Again she shook her head, softening it with a smile. "I'm sorry, but we're not going to town anytime soon."

"We can wait," the man in the vest said. He clutched his stomach. "I'm not feeling well and I would appreciate some assistance."

"In that case, I must insist you keep your distance," she said. "I cannot run the risk of exposing myself or my friend to the smallpox that has been spreading."

The man in red reached under the oilcloth and brought up the rifle. "You'll do as you're told, miss."

The small dark hole of the gun barrel focused on her. Her chest squeezed, but she shook her head. "You're not coming aboard," she said, diving to the deck.

She crawled to the rope ladder. It clanged against the side of the boat as though one of the men had grabbed hold of it. Working furiously, she sawed the knife against the rough hemp. When the knife cut through the last strands, the ladder splashed into the water. One of the men shouted an oath. It wouldn't slow them down for long, but if she could untangle the sail, they might be able to get away.

Scooting along the deck, she reached the mast and began to work on the tangled sail. She heard a *thump* and knew the dinghy had touched her sailboat again. The angle would be wrong for them to fire on her until they got to the deck. Stepping up her efforts, she jiggled the ropes, and the sail finally rose into the air. The wind billowed into the white canvas and the vessel began to move.

But not soon enough. Katie saw a hand slap the top of the boat, then another one. She ran to the bow of the boat intending to slash the hand with the knife, but she couldn't bring herself to do it. Instead she stomped on his fingers with her boot. "Go *away*!" she screamed.

"Yeow!" The man dropped back into the boat.

Before she had time to rejoice, hard hands seized her from behind. She felt hot breath on her neck and she twisted in the brutal grip. The man in the red shirt sneered at her, then dragged her back away from the rail.

"Come on up, boss," he called. "I've got this little she-cat corralled." The bird squawked again. "Shut up, Paco," the fellow snapped.

Katie twisted in his grip without hope. She had to save Lady Carrington and Jennie.

⌒⋇⌒

His palms ached and so did his back. Will put all his strength into fighting the waves. He reached the thickly forested point and rounded it, straining to see the sailboat in the distance. There it was, but the boat had moved from its original location. Frowning, he lifted the oars from the water and stared. Katie's dress was clear but two other figures moved on deck. Neither of them was Lady Carrington, and with a sinking sensation in his belly he recognized the red shirt.

He'd been right. The men had gone straight for the sailboat. The women were at their mercy. The dinghy bobbed in the waves as he considered his options. If he rowed right up to the sailboat, he'd be seen. His best option was to swim. The distance appeared daunting but God would be with him.

Leaving the boat behind him, he slipped into the sea. As soon as the cold slammed into his bones, he realized how weakened he was from his previous swim. The frigid water sapped his energy and slowed his movements. The sailboat seemed to recede in the distance as he put himself into stroke after stroke toward it. It seemed an impossible task at first, but as his body cut through the waves, a bit of warmth crept into his limbs from the exertion.

A seagull dove toward him then veered at the last minute. He wished he could swim as effortlessly as the three sea lions whose sleek heads passed him in a blur. He paused and treaded water a few moments. The boat still seemed impossibly far away. Voices carried over the water, but he was breathing too hard to be able to make out the words. Katie's defiance was clear in the tone, though, and he feared for her.

Once he caught his breath, he struck out for the boat again. *Stroke, kick, stroke, kick.* His methodical movements finally began to draw him near enough to the boat that he thought he was going to make it. As he neared, he switched to a breaststroke to create the least amount of noise. He was now close enough to make out the conversation.

The sound of the men's raised voices carried over the water. "Tell her to open the door!" The man's anger nearly vibrated the air.

"Don't you unlock that door!" Katie yelled.

Was that a slap he heard? Will reached the aft side of the sailboat.

"You want more of that, you little witch?" the man demanded. "Get that door open or I'll use my fist next time instead of my palm."

Rage coiled in Will's belly. The man had struck Katie. He would pay. Will grabbed the line on the anchor and rested a moment to gather his strength to board. He needed to explode over the side with enough force to overpower the man with the gun he'd seen glinting in the sun.

"You're just as independent as your mother," another male voice said.

"Florence is not my mother!" Katie spat.

Will heard a tussle, and under the cover of the commotion, he began to climb up the rope that held the anchor to the boat. His arms ached dully and so did his back. He gained the railing and peered over the deck. The men had their backs to him. He hoisted himself onto the boards and crawled behind the bulkhead.

Katie's eyes flickered and he knew she'd seen him, but the men noticed nothing amiss. Her right cheek was bright red from being struck and his anger reared again. The only weapon he possessed was the knife tucked into his belt. The man in the red shirt still held a rifle loosely in his right hand. If Will could figure out a way to gain possession of the gun, he'd have the upper hand. He stepped out from his hidden place and mimicked jabbing a fist in someone's stomach.

Katie didn't respond but he knew she'd seen him. He waited until she raised her voice.

She shook her finger in the businessman's face. "You imbeciles! If you think for one minute I'm going to allow you to lay a finger on Lady Carrington, you are sadly mistaken." She turned as if to walk away. The man in the vest caught her by the arm and she whirled. Her right fist came up and arced into his midsection. He collapsed to his knees and gasped for air.

Will leaped onto the back of the man with the gun. One hand got caught in the fellow's suspenders, but Will succeeded in getting it free. The man bucked him off then dived on top of Will. Will grabbed the fellow's throat and squeezed then brought up his knee and kicked out. The man went flying, without the rifle in his hand.

Will leaped up and seized the gun. He was breathing hard as he stood over the man in the red shirt.

Katie ran to him, and he put one arm around her waist. An emotion he didn't want to name clutched at his chest at the sight of her. "Lady Carrington and Jennie are below deck?" he asked. When she nodded, he held her tighter in relief.

The mynah squawked and ruffled his feathers. "Six steps," he croaked.

Both men rose and faced him. "Who are you?" Will demanded.

The businessman's eyes flickered but he said nothing. He shot a warning glance at his accomplice, who abruptly shut his mouth.

"You're going to jail," Will said.

The businessman smiled. Perspiration dotted his handsome face, and he mopped his brow with the sleeve of his tweed jacket. "Look, we can cut a deal. Let us go and I'll see you get a share of the money."

"That's not how it works. You killed the crew. That kind of barbarism has to be punished."

"We had nothing to do with that. The men I hired took things into their own hands."

Will saw the flicker of falsehood in his eyes. "I don't believe you."

The bird sidled to the edge of his post. His feathers fluttered as one leg slipped over the edge of the railing where he perched. He squawked and fluttered his wings but didn't catch his balance. The mynah's weight landed on Will's shoulder, and the bird's wings fluttered in his face.

Will tried to catch himself, but he was weak and standing off-kilter. He fell onto one knee. Before he could react, both men were over the railing. Two splashes sounded. He ran to the bow and saw them swimming toward shore.

"Stop!" he shouted. Raising the gun, he sighted down the barrel then lowered it. He couldn't shoot any man in the back, not even murderers like these two.

Katie joined him at the railing. Her fingers crept into the crook of his arm. "I was so glad to see you. I couldn't have held them off much longer."

"I heard you face them down. You were very brave."

"I couldn't let them harm Lady Carrington or the baby."

He stared into her eyes. The emotion in them caused his throat to close. He didn't know much about women, but even he could recognize love when he saw it. Did he dare to do something about what he felt?

TWENTY-EIGHT

THE WARM PRESS of Will's fingers on her waist was a sensation she wanted to savor—as was the intense look in his eyes. Katie allowed herself to lean against him for a moment and remember the kiss they'd shared. But it was best not to think about that.

She pulled away. "I'd better get Lady Carrington." She went to the hatch and called through the closed door. "You can unlock it now."

When she heard the older woman throw back the lock, Katie lifted the door open. Lady Carrington's eyes were wide with alarm.

"Where are those men?" Lady Carrington asked.

"Overboard," Will said, helping her up to the deck.

"Y–You made them walk the plank?" the woman quavered.

He grinned. "No, they went of their own volition." His smile faded. "We have to fetch my brother and the constable. They will try to move the *Paradox* and I can't stop them."

Katie gasped and shuffled the baby to her other shoulder. "You found it?" She couldn't keep her eyes off Will. He seemed taller, broader, more handsome than she'd ever seen him. Like a knight in shining armor, he'd come barreling over the railing to save the day.

His gaze lingered on hers. "Sure did. In a second hidden bay. Hard to find, but it's there."

The finder's fee. He'd promised half to her. She could pay off Florence. "They mentioned my mother," she said slowly. "Florence must be involved in this somehow."

"Maybe that's another reason she's here," he said.

Katie's throat felt tight. For some reason, she felt near tears. Florence's visit to Mercy Falls had nothing to do with her. She was an afterthought. A convenient way to get more money. Well, she didn't care.

Will's charcoal eyes studied her face. "She's not worthy of causing you a moment's pain, sweetheart."

The endearment was pleasant to her ears. The tenderness in his eyes made her eyes well, and she turned her gaze before he could see. "We'd better get to Mercy Falls and summon help." She nearly winced at her frosty tone. Did she want to push him away? Maybe so. If she let him get close, she might be forced into a decision she wasn't ready to make.

"Of course." His tone lost its warmth.

Retreating to the stern, she found a deck chair and settled in. Her feelings for Will changed nothing even though she wished it would. For just a moment she imagined life as Will's bride. There would be no placid days where life moved in expected patterns.

Lady Carrington joined her. "You care about that young man, Katie Russell," she said. "I saw him kiss you before he dived over the side."

"I don't want to," Katie forced herself to say. "I plan to marry Bart Foster."

"Somehow I doubt that will happen. Love comes when it's least expected." The older woman had a faraway look in her eyes.

Katie shot her a quick glance. "I want to please my parents, to take my place in society as they expect. I don't want to upset anyone."

The older woman's smile was sad. "I made the wrong choice for the very reasons you mentioned, Katie. I wanted to stay close to my parents, and I wanted my pleasant life to continue to run like a placid stream."

"You had a second chance with Lord Carrington," Katie pointed out.

"God blessed me with that, but it's rare we get a second chance." Lady Carrington's expression was kind. "The ups and downs in life are good, my dear. They keep us from boredom."

Katie captured a stray lock of hair and pinned it back into place. "I don't like surprises."

"Do you think God wants you to never grow? Surprises can be both good and bad. You can't control everything. That's God's job."

"Surprises can hurt. They come out of nowhere and slam into you like a Pacific storm. Sometimes you never recover."

"God is our husbandman. Sometimes he makes a snip there, a cut here. It's all designed for our good, though it can be painful at the time."

Katie tapped her forehead. "My intellect knows you're quite correct, but I like things to be controlled and expected."

Lady Carrington smiled. "Controlled can be quite stifling. Think of how your handsome lightkeeper makes you feel. More alive in his presence than you ever felt?"

Katie couldn't deny it so she said nothing at first. Then she said quietly, "What if he drowns saving someone? What if he leaves me?" She wanted to add, "Just like my mother left me," but she clamped her teeth against the admission.

Lady Carrington's eyes filled with compassion. "Darling, what if that fear keeps you from really living? Surely ten years or even one year experiencing life to its fullest is better than never knowing what real love is like at all."

Katie shook her head. "I'd rather avoid pain."

The older woman chuckled. "Life can be quite untidy, can it not? You think you have it all mapped out, then God plants a vine next to you, and the next thing you know, everything has changed. Embrace what God has for you. Somehow I don't think it's Mr. Foster." She closed her eyes and sighed. "I shall take a nap. The circumstances have exhausted me. But I wouldn't have missed it for the world, would you?"

With the woman's eyes closed, Katie knew no response was necessary but one welled in her throat anyway. "No," she said. "I wouldn't have wanted to miss it. It was quite . . . exciting."

Lady Carrington smiled but didn't answer, and Katie was left to ponder the admission she'd made. A lack of surprises also meant a lack of excitement. Her fingers crept to her lips again. Though he'd never kissed her, somehow she doubted that Bart's kiss would affect her the way Will's had. Suppose she found the courage to change her life's course. Nothing was set in stone yet. That option dangled in front of her dazzled eyes, but she very much feared the love for the handsome lightkeeper that swelled in her bosom.

Will tied up the boat and helped the women alight onto the dock. "I'll telephone the constable," he said. "I fear the men will be long gone, though," he told Katie.

She nodded and said nothing as she walked up the beach to the lighthouse. She'd been distant on the way back. Their earlier closeness seemed as transient as the fog beginning to waft down from the wooded hillsides. As he'd steered the sailboat back to harbor, he'd decided he was going to pursue Miss Katie Russell. He'd convince her he was a far better choice than that dandy from town.

The roar of the sea was the only sound as they traipsed to the lighthouse. He glanced at his pocket watch. It was only four o'clock, though it felt much later. His job was the lighthouse. Philip would have to pursue the criminals. He stepped into hall. "Now to telephone the constable."

"I'll just call on the switchboard," Katie said. "It will be faster." She settled in front of the switchboard and connected the proper jack.

Will watched her as she told the constable what had happened. Her beautiful face was animated and alive. How did she think she would ever be happy burying herself in a mediocre life with a man she didn't really love? It wasn't what she wanted, not deep down.

Convincing her of that fact would be his goal over the next few weeks. He was a patient man. She couldn't tell him she had no feelings for him. Her response to his kiss had proven that.

Katie spun around on the stool. "He'll meet Philip at the dock. He's quite excited."

"He should be. This is a huge break." He frowned. "You're sure you've never seen those two men before? They seem to be from the area."

"I don't know them. The businessman matches the description of the man who used the telephone at the skating rink to threaten me."

"I never would have guessed our pirates would be businessmen."

"Nor I. Perhaps the depression has them searching for a way to stay afloat."

He nodded. "I need to find Philip before the constable arrives. Will you be all right?"

She tipped up the pointed chin he found so adorable. "We'll be fine," she said.

There was a distance in her gaze he found disconcerting. "What are you planning?"

She didn't meet his eyes. "Nothing."

Nothing he could do about her mood now. He went in search of Philip. He only found his brother down at the dock after asking around. Philip was aboard a beautiful sailing yacht that looked as though it had fewer than ten hours on it. Pristine condition with white sails and an immaculate deck. Will motioned to his brother. Philip frowned but joined him on the dock.

"I found the *Paradox*," Will said. He told his brother what they'd discovered. "Katie called the constable. You're to meet him in an hour to go out looking."

Philip shook his head. "Can't do it tonight, Will. I have a chance for something big." He hooked a thumb toward the man in the dapper suit aboard the yacht. "Hudson Masters sent his man to hire me.

He wants me to track his missing wife. We've got a lead on her. We're about to talk it over on the yacht."

"B—but what about this job? You're so close to wrapping it up and collecting the finder's fee." Katie would get her share too. He had to make sure that happened.

"It's a minor detail to take the constable out to the ship. Surely you can handle that. This is a huge opportunity for me, Will. If I come through on this, he'll funnel enough work to me that I'll be able to afford anything I want."

Will struggled to keep the disappointment out of his voice. "This is your job, Philip. Not mine."

Philip's gaze was pleading. "If this comes through, we're sailing to Hawaii. I've always wanted to go."

"Fine. I'll take care of it." Like always.

Philip's smile faltered then he shrugged. "I'll make it up to you, Will. I'll have to shove off right away though."

"I just don't understand. Why not see this through first?"

"Hey, you should be happy! I'm handing off a payday to you. Just be sure to cut me in, all right?" He paused, looked down at the floor, then back to Will. "I'm not like you. I'd rather have some fun and take my pay as it comes. And *this* job is bound to make the missing *Paradox* pale in comparison." He tipped his hat. "I'll see you tomorrow."

TWENTY-NINE

THE FOGHORN SOUNDED in the night, and the glow from the light tower added to the last of the sunset. Katie had lit the light early because she had to run to town and Will wasn't back yet. She pinned on her hat and told Lady Carrington she would return as soon as she could. She wound the light to allow herself a little more time, just in case, then hitched the buggy and went to town.

It was only seven o'clock, but Mercy Falls was quiet, still in the grip of the smallpox scare though the danger was mostly past. Katie disembarked the buggy outside The Redwood Inn. The gaslights lining the street hissed as they illuminated the decaying neighborhood. Katie's chest was tight as she squared her shoulders and walked up the front steps. The smell of cooking cabbage wafted out the open windows of the café next door and her stomach clenched uneasily. She'd barely managed to get down a mouthful or two of food at supper with this facing her.

Holding her head high, she marched up the steps to the large building. It was only as the bell tinkled over the door that she realized people might wonder what her business was with Florence. And she had no idea what name the woman was going by this time. She nearly retreated to the buggy but the man behind the reception counter looked up from the ledger.

"Miss Katie, what brings you to the neighborhood again?" he asked.

She forced a smile at the grizzled proprietor. "Good afternoon, Mr. Wilson. Is the hotel full these days?"

He shook his gray head. "Most folks skedaddled at the first sign of the smallpox."

She advanced to the desk across the worn red carpet. "Has your household escaped it?"

"We have indeed. Even the missus has stayed well, though she's been working at the hospital. I heard your mama was not so lucky. She is doing better?"

She glanced at his open registry book. "Recovering nicely. Papa too." When he lifted an expectant expression to her and said nothing more, she cleared her throat. "Um, I'm looking for a woman, but I'm unsure of her name. In her early fifties. Dresses rather indiscreetly."

His mouth tugged downward. "Ah, you mean Mrs. Muller."

So she still used the same name. "Is she here?"

"Far as I know. She came in just after lunch, and to my knowledge, hasn't left. Room ten. Up the stairs and clear to the back on the right."

"Thanks, Mr. Wilson. Give your wife my regards." Ignoring the curiosity in his eyes, she lifted her skirts and went up the wide staircase to the second floor. The red carpet was even more worn on the treads, though clean.

She marched down the hall. The rose wallpaper was faded but still tightly adhered to the wall. The wide woodwork was battered. She paused outside room ten. Listening, she heard no sound from behind the wooden door. Confronting the woman wasn't something Katie really wanted to do. She squared her shoulders, took a deep breath, and then rapped on the door.

Moments later the door opened, and Florence peered out. "Oh, it's you."

She stepped out of the way to allow Katie to enter. Her green dress showed too much bosom, and her hair was a bit disheveled and loose on her shoulders. Katie stepped into the room. A sweetish odor hung in the air and she couldn't quite place it. She glanced around. The bed was unmade and discarded clothing lay in a tumbled heap at the foot of it. Toiletries covered the dressing table. A tray of partially eaten food was on the floor by the door.

Florence shut the door behind her. "Did you bring my money?"

Katie winced at the rapacious excitement in the woman's voice. "I told you I have no money to give you."

Florence flounced away to sit in a chair by the window. She picked up the hairbrush and tugged it through her unbound hair. "Then why are you here?"

The deeper she penetrated into the room, the heavier the scent became. It nearly sickened Katie. "What is that odor?"

Florence smiled and put down the brush. "My happy smoke."

Opium. Katie took a step back when she saw the pipe on the table beside Florence. "I know why you're really in Mercy Falls," she said.

"Oh?" Florence picked up the pipe and then put it down again.

"You helped with the piracy. We found the ship. And some men who know you."

Florence coiled her hair around her head. "I have no idea what you're talking about."

"I don't believe you."

Florence shrugged. "You may believe what you wish. Piracy? This isn't the 1700s, daughter."

"I'm not your daughter!"

"You even look like me." Florence finished pinning her hair. She rose and touched Katie's chin. "From your heart-shaped face to the way your eyes tip up. Albert used to call them 'cat eyes.'"

Katie loathed the thought of her father whispering to anyone but Mama, yet studying the woman's face, she knew it was true. "I didn't come here to speak of my appearance."

"Then get on with it and let me get back to what I was doing." Florence glanced at the pipe again with longing in her eyes.

"I know you have plenty of money. You were surely paid handsomely for your part in stealing the gold from the ship."

"A woman can never have too much money, my dear."

Katie grew tired of the dance around the truth. "I'm giving you no money so you might as well leave town with what you've gained from your piracy. I won't be blackmailed."

Florence smiled. "So it's quite acceptable for me to pay a visit to Mr. Foster?"

Katie decided to call her bluff. "Do whatever you like. He won't pay you anything either." She retreated to the door. In spite of her bravado, her pulse kicked up. What if the woman did just that—went straight to Bart?

She twisted the knob on the door. If she ever saw the woman again, it would be too soon.

"Wait!"

Katie turned to face Florence again. "We have nothing more to say to each other."

The woman rose and approached her. "I regret many things, Katie, but nothing more than the fact I wasn't allowed to raise you. I quite dislike seeing how much you despise me."

Katie's throat closed. "You always cared more about yourself than you did about me. I remember many nights going to bed to the sound of you laughing with a male visitor. You seldom noticed I was in the room."

The softness in Florence's eyes vanished. "Did you think I didn't deserve a life too—a little fun?"

"All I knew was that you never noticed me unless you wanted me to fetch your shoes or something. No child deserves to be cold and lonely."

"You were so young. I doubt you can remember much of those days. You always had a vivid imagination."

Faced with Florence's emphatic statement, Katie paused. Was it possible her memories were faulty? But no. The night she ran to the Russells was seared into her mind. No coal for the fire that night. No food in the room. Her mother had promised to bring her back something, but it had been hours. That dreadful man's appearance had been the final straw.

"Good-bye, Florence." She stepped through the door and shut it behind her.

A crash sounded in the room as though Florence had thrown something at the door. The words Katie heard from the woman would have made a sailor blush. With that much rage, she feared Florence would go straight to Bart. For a moment, Katie almost hoped for such an outcome.

It would make her path much clearer if marrying into the Foster family was no longer an option.

✁

The mynah squawked a greeting as Will walked up the hillside to the lighthouse. His steps dragged with fatigue but he was smiling. He'd heard the foghorn while still in the bay and the light had pierced through the haze as well. Since Philip was gone, Katie must have done it. Dear girl. The ship had still been there when he led the constable to the location, but the men were long gone. He'd also placed a call to the owners to let them know it had been recovered. The finder's fee would be deposited in his account. But his smile faded when he remembered the lives lost could never be recovered.

He heard the sound of horse hooves and turned to see Katie arriving in the buggy. The sight of her lifted his fatigue. Reversing his direction, he headed to the road to greet her. When he reached the buggy, he realized she'd been crying. Her reddened eyes and stained cheeks made him wince.

He reached up to help her down and she hurtled into his arms. He embraced her and held her close, resting his chin on top of her head. "What's happened, love?"

She retreated and pulled her hanky from her sleeve then dabbed her eyes with it. "I went to see Florence. She is such a liar. Of course, she claimed to know nothing about the piracy."

"I think it would take more than that to make you cry," he said. He stuffed his hands in his pockets to keep from pulling her close again.

She nodded. "She tried to make me think I didn't remember my childhood clearly. I thought I'd dealt so well with her neglect, but I realized it still hurts to know the woman who bore me cared for me so little."

A declaration of his love trembled on his tongue, but he reminded himself she seemed set on staying in Mercy Falls. If he followed his dream of a career in weather, there would be no soaring edifice of a house or servants. Still, there would be enough to care for her. He opened his mouth then shut it again. Maybe she would be better off with Foster.

"Did you find the ship?"

"We did. You'll be getting a nice finder's fee. You can pay off Florence and keep your secret intact." He wanted to add *for now* but clamped his teeth against the words. She already knew his opinion.

"I'm giving her nothing," Katie said.

His pulse leaped. "You've broken it off with Foster?"

She shook her head. "I don't think Florence will do anything. I called her bluff."

He swallowed his disappointment. "She might do it to spite you. Then what?"

"Then it was meant to be."

He offered his arm. "You sound very philosophical about it. I fear your attitude will change if she goes to see Foster."

"I shall deal with it if I have to."

Their gazes locked. The glow in her eyes held Will. Her lips parted and he took it as an invitation. His left hand went around her waist and his right drew her close. She closed her eyes and he bent his head.

The taste of her was intoxicating. Sweet and pure. She fit into his arms perfectly, as though made only for him. He chose to believe that was true, despite her seeming reluctance to put Foster aside. They belonged together. Her arms crept up to his neck and he deepened the kiss, savoring her response. Whether she wanted to admit it or not, she cared about him.

When she finally pulled away, he was loath to release her. Her right hand stayed on his chest and he covered it with his. "I don't think you should marry Foster," he whispered. "Not when there is this emotion between us."

Pain darted into her eyes. "I have to care for my parents. I fear Papa will go to prison."

He knew there was a good possibility that would happen. The constable knew Russell had something to do with the piracy. "I'll take care of your mother," he said.

"A lightkeeper's salary wouldn't pay for the upkeep on the house." Her voice rang with sadness.

He could tell her of the money in the bank, but he wanted more than her gratitude. "I love you, Katie. I believe you love me. You wouldn't kiss me like that if you didn't." He willed her to hold his gaze, but her lids shuttered her eyes. She started to withdraw her hand, but he held it place. "Look at me, Katie."

"I can't," she said in a choked voice. "You make me weak. I must be strong."

"Be strong enough to do what's right for you. For us. I never thought I'd want to marry, but I can't see my life without you in it." Her lids flickered, and he caught a glimpse of their blue depths before she lowered them again. "I know you love me," he said.

Her eyes opened then, blazing with color and passion. "What

difference does it make, Will? It would kill my mother to take her from her home. She's done everything for me. How can I not sacrifice for her?"

"I understand about duty, darling. It's driven me my entire life. But duty is a cold companion. You haven't even talked to your mother about your true feelings. I can't believe she wouldn't want to see you happy. I might not have a fortune, but I'm respectable too."

She bit her lip. "She loves me," she admitted. "But she thinks she knows what is best for me."

"I'd like to see her myself."

"I–I don't know. I wouldn't want her to suffer a relapse."

"I promise not to upset her."

"Very well." She tried to withdraw her hand again.

He lifted her fingers and kissed her gloved palm. "I want to hear you say you love me, Katie."

Her eyes widened. "I–I cannot say it yet, Will. Not until I know if our situation can be resolved. Once words like that are spoken, I can never go back."

"We can't go back now."

"If it's necessary, I can try," she said in a barely audible voice.

She tugged again and he let go of her hand. He watched her lift her skirts and run for the lighthouse. She might not have admitted it yet, but he knew love when he saw it. And he wasn't willing to give it up. He'd woo her with kisses and an outpouring of love that she couldn't resist.

THIRTY

THE FIRE FLICKERED in the fireplace. The scent of popcorn still lingered in the air. The house felt empty to Katie with Will up in the tower. Jennie played at Katie's feet with the kitten. The little one grabbed Katie's skirt and pulled herself up then toddled across the floor to where Lady Carrington sat on the sofa. The baby plopped on the floor and grabbed at the ball of yarn at the older woman's feet. As her wrist healed, she'd gotten back to knitting a bit.

Lady Carrington glanced at Katie. "You're very pensive this evening, my dear. Is there anything you'd like to talk about?"

Katie put down the copy of *McCall's Magazine* she'd been reading— or not reading—and forced a smile. "Life can be so confusing."

"Your color was high when you came in this evening. I saw you speaking with Will when you arrived."

"He wants to speak to my mother. About . . . us."

Lady Carrington put down her needles. "He's declared himself?"

Katie nodded. It had been all she could think about since he'd told her he loved her.

"And how did you respond?"

Katie laced her fingers together. "I–I'm not sure what I think."

"How did you feel when he told you of his intentions?"

"Terrified of making the wrong decision," Katie admitted.

"You love him, my dear. It's written all over you."

Katie lowered her gaze to the floor. If she didn't admit it, she wouldn't have to deal with it just yet. "It's so very difficult to think about disappointing my mother."

"You are so bound up in meeting your mother's expectations. And that young Mr. Foster's, too, I fear." The older woman glanced at the baby on the floor. "If you were this child's mother, would you withhold love from her if she didn't do exactly as you said?"

"Of course not. I adore her."

"How much more should you become the bride of a man who loves you for yourself and not for some preconceived idea of what a wife should be. A husband is to love his wife as Christ loves the church. With a sacrificial love. Can you say that is what Mr. Foster feels for you?"

"No." Bart liked her looks and thought she would be a good adornment on his arm. When he looked at her, she never felt as though he saw inside to her soul. Not like Will did.

"Will sees the real me," she said. The baby tugged on Katie's skirt and she picked her up. Staring at the beloved round cheeks and brown eyes, she prayed this baby would only know total love and acceptance. How had Katie gotten so far off track?

"I'm not sure I've ever experienced that kind of love," she said slowly. "Even Mama has high expectations."

"God loves you that way."

Katie nodded. "Of course. I meant human love." Will loved her that way. No wonder her soul responded to him with such passion. A love like that was most difficult to resist.

"Will you let him speak to your mother?"

Katie nodded. "Would you pray with me that Mama accepts him and sees the goodness in him?"

"You know I will, my dear." Lady Carrington rose and picked up her yarn. "I believe I shall retire. It's been a most grueling day."

"I think that's an understatement." Katie smiled as the older woman dropped a kiss on Jennie's head then exited the room. "It's about time for bed for you, too, little one," she told the baby.

"Ah-ah, do-ee," Jennie said. Using her index finger and thumb like pinchers, Jennie picked up a piece of lint from the floor and started to put it in her mouth before Katie took it away from her. She puckered up her face to howl and Katie picked her up. "How about a bath, sweetheart?" The baby gave a jerky nod and smiled. Katie carried her into the kitchen past Paco, who squawked at them.

"Step away from the cake!" he screeched. "Six feet back."

She scowled at the bird. Why on earth would someone teach a bird such a ridiculous thing to say? She shook her head and lifted the teakettle from the stove. As she poured the hot water into the sink then pumped in cold water, she thought back over the day. They'd found the ship but the gold was still out there somewhere. The pirates too. She paused. She'd recognize them again, though, and they had to know that. Would they come after her? They knew who she was because they mentioned her mother. One of them might even have been the one who dared to attack her here, before.

The bay by Wedding Cake Peak should have been one of the places she'd thought of. When Will described the cove where he'd found the boat, she'd remembered it. The passage to it was difficult to find and wasn't always open this time of year. At least she'd have the money to let her mother keep the house. And what if she turned that money all over to her mother? Then she could marry Will and not fear that her parents would lose their home. But her mother was a spendthrift. What if the money ran out? Her way would be clearer if she could help Will find the missing gold as well. Then there would be plenty of money to do both. Care for her mother and marry Will. But where could the pirates be hiding with it?

She didn't have long to find out. Hope stirred in her heart. If she could get the money to care for her mother, she would feel freer to follow her heart.

Will watched Katie stir the porridge and lift it from the stove before ladling a bowlful for him. Her hair was still down on her shoulders and the sun lifted the brown to honeyed highlights. He needed to get some sleep this morning after tending the light last night, but he'd rather stay up and watch her. Lady Carrington had fed Jennie then taken the child into the parlor to rock her for a bit, though pieces of bread and jam still littered the linoleum floor. He meant to use these few moments alone to discover if Katie would allow him to speak with her mother today.

He'd never expected it to consume his every thought. As he'd tended to the light last night, he'd spent most of the time thinking about her and how he could convince her to marry him.

Their eyes caught and held when she turned toward the kitchen table. Color rushed to her cheeks. "Don't look at me like that," she said.

"Like what?" he asked, enjoying the sparkle in her eyes.

"Like you might . . ." Her blush deepened.

"Do something like this?" He rose and took the bowl of oatmeal from her hands and placed it on the stove. She entered his arms with no resistance. When he broke the kiss, he inhaled the sweet aroma of her breath. "Let's talk to your mother today."

"If you wish," she said softly. She stepped back and picked up the bowl of oatmeal.

He took the bowl from her, then carried it to the table. He'd rather kiss her again. The bird squawked on his perch by the door. "I wish Philip had never gotten that bird," he muttered.

"Where did he get it? I assumed he'd had it a long time."

"Did I hear someone mention my name?" Philip walked into the kitchen with his hair uncombed and his tie still askew. He yawned and dished up some oatmeal on the stove then joined them at the table.

"We were talking about your mynah," Will said.

"Good old Paco. He's something, isn't he?"

Will regarded the bird with disfavor. "If you like him so much, why am I stuck with him?" He watched his brother, who flopped into a chair in cocky fashion. "So did your big deal come through?"

Philip flashed a smile his way. "Sure did."

"Then you can take your bird with you. He loves being on a boat. We took him out yesterday."

Philip shoveled a spoonful of porridge into his mouth. "He came from this area, or so I'm told."

Will frowned. "What are you talking about?"

"I told you this," he said, glancing at Katie as if he didn't want to go into it in front of her.

"No you didn't."

"Those men yesterday," Katie said slowly, her eyes widening. "The bird got all excited when they came aboard. He was squawking and fluttering his wings. I just remembered the man in dungarees called him Paco. I assumed he'd been watching us. I didn't consider Paco might know him."

"What difference does it make?" Philip's head was down as he took another spoonful of food.

"Philip, tell me everything you know about this bird."

Philip shrugged and finally met Will's gaze. "I won him in a game in San Francisco. The guy was a businessman from this area, or so he said."

"What did he look like?" Katie put in.

"Description of the man? Do you know his name?"

"Just his first name. Ethan. Dark hair with wings of gray on the side. A mustache he kept waxed. Wore a bowler. Very distinguished and quite a hit with the ladies at the party."

Will exchanged a glance with Katie. "Sounds like the man, doesn't it?" She nodded and he stared back at his brother. "Anything else? Why did he put the bird up?"

"He was losing. His man had the bird on his arm and I admired it. He threw it in rather than end the game to go after more money. He lost anyway." Philip's voice was pleased.

"What did his partner look like?" Will asked.

"Older than Ethan, maybe in his fifties. Bald. Wore dungarees with suspenders."

It had to be the same two men. Will sensed Katie's excitement too. "They said they were from Mercy Falls?'"

Philip frowned. "Now that you mention it, they said they were heading home. I heard one say something about Mercy Falls, so I assumed that's where home was."

Katie shook her head. "I know most of the people in town and neither of these men were familiar."

"Did you get a sense for this Ethan's profession?" Will asked.

"I thought maybe he was a banker," Philip said.

Will had been expecting a railroad tycoon or some other kind of high roller. "What made you think that?"

"He said something about 'my bank' as though he owned one."

Will waved his hand in a dismissal. "I've said that myself."

"It was something in his tone. I could be mistaken though."

"Anything else you can think of?"

Philip shook his head. "Not really. He seemed cut up about losing old Paco here. Asked if he could buy him back. I told him I'd consider it."

"Did he ever show up again?"

"I left town a little early."

"Why was that?"

Philip rose and carried his bowl to the sink. "I didn't like the looks of this man. Something told me he might try to do me harm."

"And you didn't say a word about this to me."

"It's my investigation, as you've been quick to point out," Philip said.

"I think this bird belongs to the men who took the gold," Will said. His brother seemed unconcerned with what Will had just told him. "Where are you going?" he asked as Philip headed toward the door.

"I have to pack. The boat is pulling out tonight."

"Tonight? That's crazy, Philip. I need some help with this case. You're the one who dragged me into it and it's about to get wrapped up."

His brother gave a heavy sigh. "You can finish up the details and collect our money. I'm leaving tonight, Will. If there's anything I can do in a few hours, I can help out, but that's it."

Will pressed his lips together. "I was up all night tending to the light. I need some rest. You could poke around in town. See what the constable found out after he took custody of the ship."

Philip wrinkled his nose. "I'll pack, then go to town and ask around."

Will was tired, cranky, and fed up. "Never mind. Do what you want. That's all you've ever done."

Philip folded his hands across his chest. "You have no idea who that guy is who hired me for this new job, do you?"

"Does it matter?"

"Of course it matters! If I solve this, I'll have enough work to keep me solvent for ten years. He's Hudson Masters, who owns the biggest newspaper conglomerate in the country. He's always digging into dirt. If I come through for him, I'm set."

Wide-eyed, Katie glanced from Will to his brother. "So you're leaving, Philip? Just like that? When your brother needs you?"

Philip laughed. "You two are just alike. All bound up with what others expect of you. Life is too short to live it for duty. Sometimes you have to follow your own dream, not someone else's."

"When have you ever followed anyone else's?" Will demanded. "You don't know what *duty* means."

Philip spread his hands. "I'm grateful you knew your duty, Will. But I'm not like you. I'm never going to fit into the mold you want. I'm not a younger version of you. I'm just not." Philip threw up his hands. "Oh what's the use? You never listen." He stomped out of the room.

Will opened his mouth to call after his brother, then clamped it shut. His brother looked so much like their father that Will had often caught himself expecting him to act the same way Dad did. What did Will himself want from his life? He'd never asked that question. It hadn't seemed important with his duty before him.

He glanced at Katie. "Do you see the resemblance, Katie?"

She met his gaze. "I've tried to see either Philip or my father in her, but I've never been sure."

"You think Philip is right?"

Her gaze went soft. "You're a caretaker, Will. It's quite admirable."

"You're not answering my question."

"He might be."

"Then who does Jennie belong with?"

"I'm not quite sure," she said softly. "I don't think either one of us wants to give her up."

THIRTY-ONE

MAYBE SHE WAS wrong. Katie stood outside Will's bedroom door and studied the hallway wallpaper with flowers and birds on it. Her hand was still raised to knock. She should let him sleep. He'd only come up here three hours ago. But this was important. Surely she was right.

Excitement curled in her belly and she couldn't wait any longer. Her fist fell on the door. "Will?" There was no answer so she knocked again. "Will, I'm sorry but I need to talk with you." She thought she heard a muffled groan, then the pad of bare feet.

The door opened and Will stood in the doorway with his hair askew. He wore a robe and slippers. A stubble of whiskers darkened his chin, and the muskiness of his skin nearly enticed her to step closer, but she held her ground. "I'm sorry to awaken you, but I think I know where we can find the gold!"

He rubbed this roughened chin. "Honey, what are you talking about?"

The endearment in his voice caused pleasure to curl up her spine. She was hopelessly in love with him. So much so that tears filled her eyes. She couldn't speak to even tell him why she'd come. It didn't even seem important with the emotion flooding her right now. She couldn't marry Bart.

"Hey, hey, what's wrong?" He drew her into his arms.

She allowed herself the luxury of leaning into the sanctuary of his strength. "I–I'm fine. I'm just overwrought."

His rough hand smoothed her hair and he kissed her forehead. How had she endured life without him in it? His warmth enticed her to burrow deeper against him, but she must be strong. She closed her eyes and composed herself, then drew away and lifted a smile into his face. "I know you're exhausted but I believe I know where we should look for the gold!"

He raised a black eyebrow. "What have you discovered?"

She clasped her hands. "The bird had the clue all along."

"Paco?" He frowned. "What are you talking about? That dumb bird only knows two things to say."

"Exactly. It's the cake." She knew it sounded quite ridiculous so she rushed on. "Wedding Cake Rock. The rock out in the bay where we found the ship."

"I remember seeing it."

"The bird says, 'Step away from the cake.' And 'six feet back.'"

"Over and over," he agreed, his smile coming quickly.

"What if it's a clue to where the gold is hidden?"

"You mean the cake refers to that rock?"

She nodded. "Indeed. I think we should check it out."

He crossed his arms over his chest. "Katie, that's hardly likely, is it? That thing is all rock and gets lashed with storms. I can't see where they could hide anything there."

She hadn't thought of the storms. Her certainty faltered. "Still, there could be something there."

"It's possible, I suppose." He yawned again. "Let me get some rest and we'll run out there this afternoon."

His tone indicated he was only humoring her. "All right. You get some sleep." She stepped away and his arms fell to his sides.

"A good night kiss?" he asked, reaching for her.

She went back into his arms willingly and lifted her face for his kiss. He bent his head, but she heard footsteps coming up the steps and drew back.

He dropped his arms. "Later," he whispered and shut the door.

She stepped briskly forward toward the stairway and met Lady Carrington at the top. The older woman had Jennie in her arms. The baby reached for Katie and she took her. Jennie grabbed at the comb in Katie's hair. "I think I'll go see my mother," she told Lady Carrington.

"I thought Will wanted to speak with her."

"I'd like to warn her so it isn't such a shock. Will and I have something else to do when he gets up anyway."

"Splendid idea," the other woman said. "I was about to put this little one down for a nap."

Katie kissed the baby's pudgy cheek then handed her to Lady Carrington. "I shall return in a couple of hours. Do you need anything from town while I'm out?"

"I believe we're fine, my dear. Give my regards to your dear mama."

"I will." Katie went down the stairs and out the door where she hitched the buggy and started to town.

When she'd talked to her mother last night, she'd discovered the doctor said she no was longer contagious. Katie was eager to see her well. As the buggy rolled through town, she noticed more people out and about. People waved and called to her. She stopped to speak with Nell a moment and discovered the other telephone operator was eager to get back to the office. The infection truly seemed over.

Which meant she could move home within days.

The very thought filled her with dread. Her mother would expect her to come home. She *should* go home. But the thought of leaving Will and Jennie . . . It was no use. Lady Carrington was bound to want to return to her own home, tomorrow or the next day at the latest. And Katie couldn't stay at the lighthouse without her.

Smiling stiffly at passersby, she turned the horse onto her road. Moments later, she pulled up outside her house and clambered down. Adjusting her hat, she put on a happy expression and went up the steps to the front door.

The house was quiet when she entered the foyer. "Mama? Where are you?" She crossed the polished wood floor to the parlor and found her mother seated in the chair by the front window. Her head dipped to one side and she snored lightly. The pox on her face had faded, though some were still an angry red against the pale skin. A wave of love washed over Katie as she watched her mother. She crossed the few steps to the chair and knelt by it.

When she touched her mother's hand, the older woman's lids fluttered up. "Hello, Mama," Katie said softly.

Her mother straightened and clutched at Katie's hand. "Darling, I'm so glad to see you!"

Katie embraced her. "I've missed you so much."

Her mother fingered the fading marks on her cheeks. "I still can't believe they're gone." Her eyes brightened as her gaze roamed her daughter. "You look quite well, my dear. Blooming, in fact. Has your young man declared himself?"

Katie had intended to tiptoe into the subject, but the words spilled out before she could help herself. "Mama, I love Will Jesperson."

A frown crouched between her mother's eyes. "The lightkeeper? Oh no, no, Katie, that's ridiculous. You're much too precious for me to allow you to marry a man with no prospects."

Katie managed to keep her smile in place. Her mama just didn't know Will. "Wait until you meet him. He's quite wonderful."

Her mother took her arm in a firm grasp. "You haven't broken it off with Bart, have you?"

"Well no, not yet. There's been so much going—"

"Oh, good. And what about my sister? Is she still in town?"

"She is. But Mama, I didn't come to talk to you about them. It's about Will. He wants to speak with you himself."

She heard a footfall in the hall and turned as her father entered the room. "Papa, you're home too?" She embraced him and found him thinner and much more frail. "How are you feeling?"

He dropped heavily into a chair. A livid scar still marred his forehead. "What are you saying about the lightkeeper, Katie? I've already promised your hand to Bart. He asked for my permission. Of course, I was delighted."

"Without even discussing it with me?"

"I thought you had feelings for Bart," Albert said, frowning. He shook his head. "You've always been a good girl, Katie. Your mother and I have done so much for you." He passed his hand over the beads of perspiration on his forehead. "Don't fail us now over some silly romantic notion."

"It's not a silly notion, Papa."

"You must talk her out of this, Albert," her mother said.

He patted her hand. "Katie has always done her duty. I'm sure she will do so this time as well."

"What about Florence?" Katie's mother asked.

"I'll handle Florence," he said, his voice grim.

"I love Will," Katie whispered.

"It's out of the question." Her mother smiled. "Let's not continue to speak of such unpleasant things. Let's celebrate being a family again." She smiled at Katie and Albert, her eyes bright. "I'll ring for tea."

The sun refused to be restrained behind the curtains, which meant the bright rays kept coaxing Will from any kind of restful sleep. He groaned, rolled over, and glanced at the clock on the fireplace mantel in his bedroom. Only a little after twelve. He hadn't shut his eyes for more than fifteen minutes at a stretch. Every time his lids closed, he saw Katie's face. So earnest and excited about her so-called "clue" and he'd disregarded her conclusion.

He swung his legs out of bed, quickly washed and dressed, and then went in search of Katie. He saw Lady Carrington in the yard with Jennie. Lady Carrington was rolling a ball and Jennie was trying to toddle after it. The kitten pounced after her.

A family man. That's what he'd become in this past month. And it felt good. His brother and sister had been teenagers when he took over their care. This was different. Jennie was as much his child as anyone's, and he couldn't imagine giving her up now. But what court would grant custody to a bachelor?

He grabbed his hat and stepped into the yard. The baby squealed when she saw him and lifted her hands. He scooped her up and she planted an open-mouthed kiss on his face. He grinned, quite ridiculously pleased at her obvious affection.

"Katie isn't here?" he asked Lady Carrington.

She shook her head. "She went to town to see her mother."

She hadn't waited for him. What did that mean? "I believe I'll join her if you're all right with the baby?"

"I'm doing splendidly. We just had lunch, and we're enjoying the sunshine. Run along, dear boy."

He handed Jennie off to her and went to the barn at the foot of the hillside. Katie had taken the horse, so his only option to get to town was to ride the bicycle. He set off on it. It was hard going in the gravel at the side of the road, but he reached the edge of town and found it thronging with people, all eager to get out now that most had been let off quarantine. By the time he reached the main street, he was hot and thirsty. Hungry too. He parked the bike at the café beside the roller rink and went inside. He ordered ham and potato salad. Halfway through eating his lunch, he noticed Katie's beau two tables over by the window.

Bart saw him at the same time. He rose and walked to join Will. "Mr. Jesperson," he said. "It's not often we see you in town. Is Katie with you?"

"No," Will said. He could have told the smiling young man where she was, but he had no intention of allowing the man to interfere in the coming interview with Katie's mother.

"A shame," Bart said. "I'm quite eager to speak with her." His smile beamed out. "I picked this up a few days ago and it's burning a hole in my pocket. I'm quite eager to see how she likes it." He pulled a small box from his pocket and opened it to reveal a glistening diamond ring nestled in velvet. "I've been waiting on some backers for my new business. The groundwork has all been laid and I can finally see my way clear to supporting a wife."

Will recognized when he was being warned off, but he didn't have to like it. "Congratulations," he said, his tone sharp.

Bart seemed not to notice Will's curt manner. "This union of our families was something both of us have wanted for several years."

"An arranged marriage? How archaic."

Bart flushed then. "Hardly just an arranged marriage. I quite adore her. Any man would be most fortunate to have Katie as a wife. I received her father's consent yesterday."

"Congratulations," Will said shortly. "I must go."

"If you see Katie, don't tell her," Bart called after him. "I want to surprise her."

Will didn't answer as he strode out the door. Did Katie know her father had made these arrangements? She'd never mentioned it. He mounted the bicycle and rode out to her mother's house. The buggy was still parked in front of the stately manor by the ocean. The roar of the sea soothed his agitation. He laid his bicycle in the grass and went up the walk to the front steps. The windows were open, and he heard the low murmur of female voices, though they were too soft to make out any words. Then a man spoke. Her father? His gut tightened at the coming confrontation.

He rang the bell. A maid in a white apron over her gray dress opened the door to him. He gave her his card and she had him wait in the entry while she went to announce his presence. A few moments later he heard Katie's light step.

She rushed into the hall. "Will, what are you doing here?"

"I understood you to say we were going to speak to your mother together," he said.

She practically wrung her hands. "I'm not sure today is the right time," she whispered. "Papa just returned home and—"

As if to contradict her, her mother's voice floated from the parlor. "Katie, bring that young man in here."

Katie pressed her lips together and she looked near tears. "I don't think this is a good idea."

He took her arm. "Let's just see, shall we?"

"Very well," Katie said.

She led him down the hall with its richly flocked wallpaper to a large parlor papered in green silk. The woman seated in the damask armchair wore a stern expression. Her back was straight and her chin high. He recognized the challenge in her gaze and knew this interview was not going to go well. Her husband was in an armchair. He seemed to look Will over and dismiss him.

Katie glanced from her mother to Will. "Mama, Papa, this is Will Jesperson." She stepped into the room and settled on the sofa.

When Will started to sit beside her, her mother gestured for him to take the other armchair closer to her. Will glanced at Katie then did as he was bid. "It's good to meet you, Mr. and Mrs. Russell. We've prayed for you both every night during family prayers."

"Family prayers?" Mr. Russell blustered. "Hardly, Mr. Jesperson. Katie is not part of your family, and neither is Lady Carrington."

Will glanced at Katie. When he saw the appeal in her face, he bit back his initial heated response. "I meant nothing by the comment, sir. Just that we prayed for you and your wife. We've been very concerned."

"Thank you," Mrs. Russell said, her tone frosty.

Will leaned forward and concentrated on the woman. Surely she could be swayed by how much he loved Katie. "Mrs. Russell, I love your daughter very much."

Her father interrupted with his hand held up. "Enough, Mr. Jesperson. You're hardly of the same social standing as Katie."

"My grandfather was Thomas Jesperson, founder of Jesperson, Texas, Mr. Russell. He came from very old money. I assure you that I can provide for a family."

His smile was condescending. "It's all been arranged, Mr. Jesperson."

Katie visibly swallowed. Will didn't like the way she wilted in her chair. He understood duty, but this was something more.

THIRTY-TWO

KATIE AND HER parents stood on the front porch as Katie took her good-byes. There was no room in the buggy, so Katie had to let Will ride his bike back to the lighthouse. She'd read the disappointment in his face as he said his farewell.

"He's a nice enough young man, but he's not for you, Katie," her mother said when Will was out of earshot. She patted her daughter's arm. "I must lie down for a bit. Go collect your things and I'll arrange for the groom to pick you up."

"I can't leave Jennie," Katie said.

Her mother looked at her father. "You deal with this, Albert. I'm exhausted." Her mother went inside.

"You need to stop this nonsense. Your mother is quite right," her father said. "Bart will make a much better husband. He's going to take over the haberdashery and turn it into a Macy's. You own a quarter of the block, and it's the perfect location."

"*I* own it? Whatever do you mean?"

"I put it in your name some time ago."

"Why?"

He shrugged. "Tax reasons, my dear. It was expedient."

"Does Bart know this?"

"Of course."

"So he is courting me for the property?"

His brows drew together. "For such a smart girl, Katie, sometimes you're a silly child with your head full of dreams and fluff. Just like your mother."

She stuffed her hurt and focused on her father's words. "I thought it would be a while before he got the money to build his Macy's. He hadn't mentioned it to his father."

Her father cut his gaze away. "He's found the money."

She studied his expression and the way he wouldn't meet her gaze. Businessmen. The pirates had been businessmen. "Was Bart in on your scheme as well?"

He laughed. "Daughter, you have a vivid imagination."

"I don't understand something, Papa. If you received your portion of the gold, why are you in such desperate straits financially?"

His mouth grew pinched. "My partner has withheld my portion of the money. I can hardly complain to the constable, can I? And he knows it."

"Has the constable been to see you?"

Her father nodded. "I told him nothing."

"Papa, you must!"

He shook his head. "I'll not risk you and your mother. I know these men, Katie. They would seek revenge. There are too many for the constable to get them all before they carry out their threat."

She shuddered, remembering the harsh tones of the man who had grabbed her on the porch. She'd believed him too. "God will take care of us, Papa. But you must do the right thing." His jaw flexed and she knew he wouldn't tell the constable. "Does the constable suspect you in Eliza's death?"

He shrugged. "He was pleasant enough. I assured him I had nothing to do with it. I think he believed me."

Katie hadn't been sure what to think, but staring at her father, she believed him incapable of murder. "Who killed her, Papa?"

He held her gaze. "I don't know for sure, but I suspect one of my partners found out she was selling her information."

"How was she involved in this?"

"She was hired to get close to the ship captain when the boat docked here a few months ago. She was to find out when *Dalton's Fortune* was making its money run. She transmitted the information and the heist was successful."

"So successful you all decided to do it again with the *Paradox*."

"Unfortunately, yes."

"Why was she selling the information?"

"Because she was greedy." He swayed where he stood. "I must rest."

He had a lot of room to talk. She wished she had the courage to say it to him. "I'm not coming home, Papa. Not yet. I must think about this." Ignoring his angry blustering, she went to her buggy. She had a lot of thinking and praying to do. Will had said little as they'd left, and she was thankful he was not pressing her. This was a decision she had to make on her own.

The clopping of the horse's hooves melded with the chirps of the birds in the shrubs as the buggy rolled along the road. Mercy Falls was just ahead. If only Addie were here to talk things over with. Katie missed her dreadfully. When she thought of marrying Bart, she felt no peace. Only disquiet in her soul.

She rounded the curve into town and slowed the horse. The buggy's wheels rolled along the cobblestone surface and the thumping drowned out her thoughts. On a whim, she parked the buggy outside her father's shop and went inside. The scent of pipe tobacco and men's clothing surrounded her when she stepped inside. The two men shopping nodded at her, as did the clerk who worked for her father. She wandered the front display room, pausing occasionally to touch a hanging jacket or adjust a hat display. What would this place be worth? There was still a good amount of stock here and the shop was the only haberdashery in town. Surely someone other than Bart might want to buy it. The town needed the shop to stay open.

The bell tinkled on the door and she whirled to see Bart step into the store. "Bart, what a surprise," she said, forcing a smile.

"I saw you come in. I was across the street at the bank." He crossed the few feet separating them and took her hands. "I've missed you, Katie. I was going to call to take you to dinner and the nickelodeon. You've been cooped up with that baby for too long."

"How sweet of you," she said. When he frowned, she realized he'd expected her to say she missed him too. But she had barely given him a thought all week.

I can't marry him.

Katie knew it with every fiber of her being. He was pleasant enough. Handsome, rich, respected. But she loved Will Jesperson. And she couldn't live a lie anymore.

"I talked with your father. He seems to be doing quite well," Bart said, drawing her to a quiet corner of the store.

"Yes, he is," she managed to get out.

"Has he said—what happened?" His mouth twisted.

"It wasn't a suicide attempt," she said, reading the distaste on his face.

Doubt still lurked in his eyes. "I certainly hope not."

"He didn't try to kill himself," she insisted. What would he say if he knew what her father had done was so much worse than an attempted suicide? Her father somehow hoped to keep it all quiet, but truth had a way of coming out. Especially something this big.

Bart's face cleared. He released her hands then reached into his pocket and withdrew a small velvet box. When he withdrew his hand, a piece of paper fluttered out. He didn't notice it as he glanced toward the door as one of the customers exited.

She scooped it up. "Wait, Bart, this fell from your pocket." She glanced at the paper and saw the handwriting. She'd seen the writing before and she struggled to remember. She gasped when it became clear.

He turned at the sound of her distress. "What's wrong?" he asked.

Her fingers clutched the note and she pulled it away from his out-stretched hand. "Is this your handwriting?"

"Yes." He reached for it again but she stepped back. He frowned. "Whatever is the matter?"

"My father had a note in his safe," she said. "It was from you."

He shrugged. "Perhaps, but what of it? We often did business. I bought all my wardrobe from him, and surely you know by now that I hope to buy the haberdashery."

She clamped her teeth against the accusations cascading through her mind. Bart was in on the piracy. Maybe the mastermind. Katie nearly took another step back. She frantically searched for something to say that would make him put that velvet box away but her words dried on her tongue. In a daze she noticed the showroom was empty now. The clerk had put the CLOSED sign out and had left with the last customer, as if he had figured out that Bart was about to propose. They were alone.

When she didn't answer him, Bart opened the box to reveal a mar-quis engagement ring. He went to one knee and took her left hand in his. "I'd intended to do this over dinner and candlelight, but I can't wait. Katie Russell, would you do me the honor of becoming my wife?" His blue eyes were earnest and warm. He released her hand long enough to pluck the ring from its case, and then he took her hand again and slipped the ring on her finger.

The touch of his hand sent shivers through her. He was evil. She pulled her hand from his and shook her head. "I'm sorry, Bart. I can't marry you." She tugged the diamond from her finger and pressed it back into his hand.

Bart shot to his feet. "I should have waited," he said. "Any woman wants to be romanced a bit. We've been apart too long, with the quarantine and all. I was too eager."

She had to get out of here, away from him. "It's not that at all. I'm honored you would ask me. I've just realized I can't marry a man I don't love."

His face clouded. "I care very much about you, Katie. I thought you felt the same way about me. But no matter. We have a much better basis for marriage than mere love: respect, equal social standing, the same goals for our lives. Our marriage would be steady and quite happy. I'm quite certain you will come to care for me in time as I care for you."

"I think I want more than that," she choked out past a tight throat.

"Your father promised . . ." He broke off and cleared his throat.

"My father promised what?"

"That I could marry you."

This square city block was perfect for his Macy's. Her father had lied to her about Bart's involvement. No, that wasn't right. He'd never answered.

Staring into his face, she searched for the truth. "It's clear you don't love me either, not really. You said you *care* for me. That's not love. We get along. Our union is suitable. That might be enough for you to agree to marriage, but I've discovered it's not enough for me. There is no spark between us."

His brows drew together. "Of course there is. You're overwrought. I love you, Katie. I'm sorry if I wasn't clear."

Katie heard no ring of truth in his voice though. His eyes were evasive, crafty. As she stared, his face changed. His eyes grew shuttered and his mouth twisted. He put the ring back into his pocket.

"Something has changed you. It's that lightkeeper, isn't it? You must marry me, Katie. It's been decided." He took a step toward her.

The hard light in his eyes made her stomach plunge. "You aided the pirates. You and Papa took the gold," she said, backing away.

❧❧❧

Will rode the bicycle back toward the lighthouse. His spirits dragged at how it had gone with Katie's parents. Katie had been impossible to read, but he knew how she treasured her mother. It would be difficult for her to go against her parents' wishes. Could he even ask her to? It would cause a break in their relationship.

He pedaled out of town toward the coast. The going got harder and harder until he realized he had a flat tire. He dismounted and kicked the tire. A team of horses pulling a heavily laden wagon lumbered toward him. As it drew near, the driver reined in the horses and stopped beside him. He was a portly man in his forties with a grizzled beard.

"You from around here?" the driver asked. "I'm looking for the old Houston place. I hear it's hard to find."

"I'm new here," Will said, straddling his bicycle. "I've never heard of it. As you can see, I have a flat tire. Could I get a ride back to town?"

The fellow looked him over then shrugged. "If you don't mind waiting while I make this delivery."

"Not a problem. I'll just throw my bike in the back of your wagon." Will tossed his bike on top of some boxes covered with a tarp then climbed up next to the driver. "I appreciate it. Where is the property you're looking for?"

The driver consulted his notebook. "The driveway is off Oak Road."

"This is Lighthouse Road," Will said. "Oak Road is back to the highway then four miles down." He'd seen the road but had never been on it. "What is this fellow's name?"

"Hudson Masters."

The name was familiar. It was the fellow who had hired Philip.

The driver continued to talk. "I hear he owns a bunch of newspapers. He's opening a new one over at Ferndale."

"It sounds like his place is about halfway between Mercy Falls and Ferndale. Where are you based?"

"Ferndale," the man said.

Will directed the driver to the road and the lorry lumbered around the corner and down the highway that traced the coastline. The driver spotted the turnoff to the estate. He turned the big wagon into the narrow lane. The house was a three-story brick mansion with peeling paint and a few broken windows. If Will had seen it from the road, he would have assumed it was uninhabited.

"Looks vacant," he told the driver.

"It's been empty for years. The renovations are going to take a year. A businessman from the city bought it a couple of months ago and has been renovating it."

"He's living in this shack?"

"I heard he's living in two rooms when he's there. He conducts much of his delivery by telephone and telegram. He's there today to take delivery of the floor tile himself."

Will studied the derelict building. It could be magnificent. When the wagon came to a stop, he leaped down. "I see no buggy or horse," he said. His senses tingled the way they always did when something didn't feel right. A businessman from the city. Could it possibly be the man who had taken the ship?

The driver jumped down and tugged the tarp off the boxes of tile. "He might not be here yet. I'm an hour early."

"I'll give you a hand." Will helped the driver haul boxes of tile to the front porch. It was still sound structurally, but the paint had peeled from the redwood boards. The men stacked the tile to the right of the door.

"I have to wait around," the driver said when they were done. "He's paying me for this load when he arrives."

"I think I'll look around," Will said, his senses on full alert. He brushed his hands off on his pants and went around the side of the house.

There were two barns, a chicken coop, a well house, and another shed in the weedy expanse behind the home. This place had been quite the estate back in the day. He shoved open the first barn door.

Dust motes danced in the air as he stepped inside. Rusty tack hung on the walls. The stalls were empty except for old hay. He poked around until he was satisfied that the structure held no secrets. Shutting the door behind him, he went to the second barn. It appeared to have been in more recent use. The tack on the walls was new and a gleaming buggy sat in one stall. There was a horse in one enclosure and droppings in another so the man must own two horses.

He examined the barn but found no gold or other clues. When he stepped back into the sunshine, he heard voices. The owner must have returned. Taking care not to be seen, he sidled around the side of the house. Two men stood talking by the porch. Though the businessman had his back to him, Will recognized the dark-haired man immediately.

He'd found his pirate.

THIRTY-THREE

SHE'D THOUGHT HE was so mild-mannered and kind. Katie stared at Bart and wondered how she'd been so deceived. "You killed all those sailors."

He held out his hands. "I had nothing to do with that. No one was supposed to be harmed. The men we hired took it into their own heads to deal with witnesses."

More than ten men had died that day.

She doubled over and breathed through her nose. She tasted bile in the back of her throat and willed herself not to throw up. When her nausea passed, she slowly straightened and stared at Bart. "Why did you kill Eliza?"

He reached out to her. His face darkened when she flinched. "It wasn't me. I cared about her. My partner got wind that she was going to sing about who was involved in taking the gold. He had her killed."

She put her hand to her head and thought it through. The baby. "You cared about Eliza? Then Jennie—"

"Is my daughter," he said, finishing her thought. "But it means nothing. You're the one I love." His voice rose.

She stared at him. "She looks nothing like you."

"She looks exactly like my mother," he said.

Katie nodded, remembering his mother's flashing dark eyes. "But I heard Eliza try to blackmail my father. Why would she—" Katie took a step back. It was all clear when she thought about it. "I understand. He wanted a marriage between you and me. Eliza was going to tell me about the baby and ruin everything if he didn't give her money."

"She wouldn't have done it," he muttered. "She wanted us to leave, start over somewhere else. Nothing I told her could make her understand I wasn't marrying her."

"No, you wanted this property to build your Macy's," she said.

"It's more than that, Katie. Things can still work out. No one has to know about this. I have plenty of money to help your parents."

"I'm not marrying you!"

"Then your parents will be destitute."

She stared at him. "You refused to pay Papa unless I married you," she said. "That's why he's still pushing me toward this."

He reached for her and she stepped back again. He dropped his hands to his sides. "I care about you, Katie, but make no mistake. I mean to have this property."

"No. You can't have it. Or me." She lifted her chin in defiance but the menacing look in his eye made her take a faltering step backward. "I'll scream," she tossed out. "The constable will come running."

"You won't tell him," he said, his voice calm, still advancing. "You have no proof and I will testify that I saw your father kill Eliza. That would destroy your mother."

Her back touched the glass display case. "You're despicable. You allowed your own daughter to be abandoned."

Pain darkened his eyes. "My, uh, associate didn't realize she was there. When I heard about her disappearance, it was nearly midnight. I arrived to look for the baby and found the house empty."

"I'm sure you were quite happy you were spared your duty."

"This is getting us nowhere," he said through gritted teeth. "You'll sign that deed. Now."

"I don't have it," she said.

"It's in the safe. Your father told me that much." He took her arm in a punishing grip and pulled her toward the back room. "You're going to open the safe and get it for me."

No amount of twisting lessened the tight grip on her arm. She finally gave up and allowed him to propel her forward. "My signature would need to be witnessed."

"Then we'll go to the county recorder and get that done and the deed transferred at the same time." He shoved her, and she fell to her knees in front of the safe. "Open it."

She rose and faced him. "No."

"You'll be an orphan by nightfall if you don't do what I say," he said through gritted teeth. "Open the safe!"

How could she have been so deceived? This man was a monster. "What's to prevent you from killing us the moment you have the deed in your possession?"

"Because you'll know that if you say anything, you'll all be dead." He touched her chin. "I don't want to hurt you. Don't you see? This didn't have to come down this way. You could still marry me. I'd make you a good husband, I swear."

"Don't you touch me." She slapped his hand away. "Don't you ever touch me again."

His eyes grew cold again. "Open the safe, Katie."

"Very well," she said. She twirled the dial until the safe clicked open.

Bart pushed her aside when she threw the lever and opened the door to the safe. "I'll get it," he said.

She watched as he riffled through the documents inside and then emerged, a small grin of triumph on his face. "Now we'll get it transferred."

She smiled, glancing at the clock. "It's too late," she said. "The county office is closed. Today is Wednesday."

His face reddened and he swore. He raised his hand as if to strike her but she refused to cower and lifted her chin to stare him down.

He dropped his hand and grabbed her arm. "Then we'll have to get your signature witnessed elsewhere."

She still didn't trust him not to dispose of her once he had control of the property. As he shoved her out the back door, she prayed for a miracle.

⌁✳⌁

Will froze when he realized who the property owner was. He started to shrink back behind the corner of the house when he felt a hard metal object in his back.

"Hands up," a hard voice said in his ear. It was a dauntingly familiar voice. Will raised his hands. The fellow shoved him forward. "Move."

Masters turned as they approached. His eyes flickered but he said nothing when he saw Will. Will glanced at the driver and saw he was unaffected. Apparently, his boss was paying too much for him to notice Will's compromised situation.

"Mr. Jesperson, you've caused me untold misery lately," Masters said. "But your interference has come to an end today."

The man behind Will grabbed a rope. Will flexed his wrists as best he could as the man bound his hands behind him and shoved him toward the lorry. "Take him to the mine and shoot him. You can dump his body down a shaft."

The driver nodded toward the lane. "Wait a second, boss. Someone's coming."

A horse pulling a buggy came cantering up the drive. The sun was in Will's face so he couldn't see who was in it until the conveyance stopped and the occupants stepped out. His gut clenched when he saw Katie's white face. Bart had hold of her arm and she winced as he marched her toward the group. Will clenched his fists.

Bart shoved her and she fell to her knees in the dust. Will started to leap forward but the man behind him grabbed his arm and pushed him the other direction. He stumbled and went down on one knee then struggled upright. "Katie, are you all right?"

"I'm fine." She rose and brushed the dirt from her skirt. "That was unnecessary, Bart," she said.

Will had never seen the urbane young man so agitated. His face was flushed and he was breathing hard. Bart clenched and unclenched his fists. Katie started toward Will but Bart grabbed her arm again, the muscles in his jaw flexing.

"What's all this?" Masters demanded. "Why is she here?"

"She turned me down!" Bart said, his voice aggrieved.

Masters snickered. "You weren't as charming as you thought. What about the deed?"

Bart held up a paper. "Right here. But her signature needs to be witnessed. Then I can get it recorded."

Masters sighed heavily and pinched the bridge of his nose. "Foster, once again, you've brought me into something that you should have handled yourself."

Bart faltered. "I'm sorry. I wasn't thinking. I only—"

"You have two witnesses right here," the businessman interrupted, flinging his hands in agitation. "Just get your foolishness resolved so we can move on. Do you have a pen?"

Bart felt in his pocket. "No."

Will had no idea what they were talking about but his pulse leaped when he heard Katie had refused Bart's marriage proposal. His gaze locked with hers but his elation faded when he saw the despair in her eyes. They were both in mortal danger and his hands were bound behind his back. She was free though. And Katie was a fighter.

Masters motioned to the driver. "Get a pen from my desk." The big man nodded and headed for the house.

That left three against two. If only Will had his hands free. "What deed are we talking about?"

"Shut up," Masters said, his voice bored. "If he says anything else, shoot him."

If Will could free his hands, he'd disarm this guy in a second. He twisted his wrists. Did they give just a bit? He thought so. The other guy was watching his boss, and Will flexed his arms again. Nothing.

The driver returned. "Here's the pen." He handed it to Bart.

Bart grabbed Katie's arm and thrust the pen into it. "Sign."

"No."

He struck her and she fell to the ground. Will leaped forward, driving his chest into the other man. "Big man," Will yelled in Bart's face before the man in overalls could drag him off. "Hitting a woman. Does that make you feel strong? You're scum!"

Katie was back on her feet. Her cheek was red but her head was high. She put her hands behind her back.

"Don't sign it," Will said. "It's the only way for you to stay alive."

"A lot you know," Bart said. "If I have to, I'll get her signature forged. But I'll make sure she sees her parents are killed in front of her. She'll go to her grave knowing what she caused."

Tears leaked from Katie's eyes. "I can't believe you'd do something so horrible," she said, her voice low.

"I will," he hissed. He grabbed her arm and took a few steps toward the buggy. "Come on. We'll go fetch them right now. They're expecting the happy couple anyway."

"No," she said, wrenching her arm from his grasp. "No. I'll sign it."

"Don't do it, Katie!" Will burst out. "He'll kill you the minute you've signed."

She looked at him with regret and resignation in her eyes, then took the pen Bart handed her and signed the document.

Bart grabbed it from her hands. "Get rid of both of them," he told Masters. "I'll get this recorded tomorrow."

"What about Jennie?" Katie asked. "What will happen to her?"

Will glanced from her to Bart. "Why would he determine what happens to her?"

"She's his daughter," Katie whispered. "What about Jennie, Bart? Don't hurt her."

Bart shrugged. "Maybe your friend Addie will adopt her. If not, I suspect she'll end up in an orphanage. Or perhaps I can convince your mother she is Albert's daughter." He laughed. "I have no interest in her."

THIRTY-FOUR

THE SEA BREEZE ruffled Katie's hair and tugged at her bonnet. The sky showcased hues of magenta and indigo as sunset approached. The boat rounded a finger of land and she saw Wedding Cake Rock looming in the distance. Terror replaced her elation from earlier in the day when she thought the rock might be a clue. But now the only thing ahead of them was certain death.

She sought solace in Will's gaze. If she had to die, at least they would die together. He smiled but his eyes were dark pools of regret. The sailboat dropped anchor in the bay and Bart lowered the dinghy.

"You first, my dear," he said, smiling. He grabbed Katie's arm and helped her down into the boat. "Now your poor knight." He practically shoved Will into the boat, and he fell heavily onto the bottom. "Chesterton, get down there and make sure they don't jump overboard." The man in overalls nodded and jumped into the boat.

Katie knelt beside Will. She helped him to a seat as Bart and Masters descended to the dinghy. The men guided the boat past Wedding Cake Rock to the wild shoreline.

"Try to loosen my ropes," Will whispered.

She sat closely beside him and slid one hand around to his wrists. Her fingers tore at the rough rope, but if she'd managed to loosen them at all, she couldn't tell it.

"Get away from him," Bart ordered.

Katie moved to the center seat. It was only moments until the boat scraped bottom at the shore. The men piled out and Bart helped her into the water. The waves soaked her skirt to her knees as she slogged to land.

"That way," Masters said, pointing to a barely perceptible trail through the ferns and weeds.

Their captors marched them through the vegetation that crowded in on every side. Birds were beginning to find their night perches in the trees and the forest was silent except for the snap of breaking twigs and the tromp of feet. In a clearing up ahead, Katie could just make out the remains of the old gold mine. How long before the men shot them? Surely they would wait until they were close to the shaft that they intended to hide their bodies.

She prayed to meet death with courage. Now that it faced her, she found the peace she'd been looking for. It had been here all along. All she'd had to do was trust in God and remember that her future wasn't here in this place but in heaven. She'd looked at this temporary world too much and at eternity too little. Such a revelation, and it came too late to change her actions with other people. The control she sought had all been an illusion.

Fred stepped past them to what appeared to be a cellar door. He heaved it open to reveal a yawning darkness. When he turned back around, his pistol was up and pointed at Will's chest.

"No!" she screamed, throwing herself in front of Will. Her movement was mistimed and she barreled into Will. They both went down in a heap as the revolver discharged. She felt the wind of the bullet as it passed.

"Imbecile!" Masters snapped. "Get them in front of the shaft. I don't want blood on the ground."

He moved toward them but Will erupted in a flurry. He leaped onto Chesterton and both men fell into the shaft. One of the men shouted as they fell and Katie's throat closed. She scrambled to her feet and ran to the open shaft.

"Perhaps we can let the mine itself do the job," Bart said. He moved toward her.

Katie knew he intended to throw her into the shaft as well. She could do nothing for Will now, so she dodged Bart and ran for the forest. The darkness was falling fast. Perhaps she could escape Bart and Masters then circle back to the boat and get help. She found a thick swath of ferns and dived into them, burrowing into their covering.

Holding her breath, she listened for footsteps. She was about to think they'd taken another path when she heard the stealthy snap of a twig three feet from where she lay. Barely daring to breathe, she strained to see through the deep shadows. There, was that a boot? Yes. The man moved on past her then came back. It wasn't until he spoke that she realized it was Bart.

"I know you're here somewhere, Katie. I can smell your cologne water." His boot came up and he brushed his foot across the vegetation four feet away. "Come out now and I'll make sure you don't suffer. It will be fast, I promise. I wish you'd said yes. I care about you, I really do. This saddens me that it has to end this way."

His footsteps slowed and he turned toward where she hid. He was coming straight for her. He would find her. She refused to be run to the ground like a quaking rabbit. Her muscles coiled to rise from her hiding place, but before she could move, she heard a shot then the sound of two shots in rapid succession. Bart whirled and ran back toward the camp.

Nearly sobbing with relief, Katie rose from her hiding place. Maybe Will wasn't dead after all. He needed her help. She grabbed up a stick nearly as thick as her wrist and ran for the clearing herself.

❦

The shots echoed in Will's ears but the bullets had missed him, praise God. He crouched in the darkness. The fetid air of the mine shaft made him want to cough but he suppressed the urge. His adversary would find him if he did. He strained to hear where Chesterton might be crouching, waiting to shoot at him again.

A stone rolled to his right. Then a sliding, scraping sound. It was now or never. Will rose from a crouch and launched himself at the sound. His body collided with another one and he realized he was at Chesterton's back. He reached out and grabbed at the man's right arm. His fingers grazed the gun and it fired again. The flash left spots dancing in his vision in the darkness, but he managed to wrest it from the man's hand.

He stuck the barrel against Chesterton. "Don't move."

The man stilled. "You won't shoot me."

"In a heartbeat," Will promised even though he wasn't sure he could really do it. He climbed off Chesterton but kept a hand on his arm and the gun in his neck. "Move."

The way up was past fallen timbers and loose boulders. They'd fallen a good twenty feet, and Will's body stiffened in a hundred places. The men shuffled toward the dim glow, and fresh air began to replace the fetid stench of the mine as they climbed. The last vestiges of twilight illuminated the tunnel as they neared the shaft's opening. "Not a word or I shoot," he whispered to Chesterton. He shoved him up the final few feet until his head was out of the shaft.

Whack! Chesterton slumped to the side of the shaft and Will shot through the opening and tackled the figure waiting at the top. It was Masters. The two men wrestled until Will got the older man pinned beneath him. He jammed the pistol under Masters' chin. "One more move and I'll pull the trigger."

He heard something behind him and turned to see Katie with a thick stick in her hands. She'd hit Bart over the head as he was about to bring a rock down on Will's head. He leaped to his feet and dragged Masters up.

"Where's Chesterton?" Katie asked, her voice breathless as she joined him.

"Masters beaned him. He probably thought it was me, coming out. Good job on Bart." He couldn't keep the satisfaction from his voice.

Katie grabbed a rope and brought it to Will.

"We can make a deal," Masters said as Will bound his wrists behind him. "We'll cut you in for a portion of the profits. The gold we took from the ship will get this mine up and going again. It's a sure thing. We'll all be millionaires."

"You're like a snake," Will said. "You'd bite me the minute my back was turned." He took out his pocketknife and cut part of the loose rope off. There should be enough to tie up Bart too.

"No, no, I wouldn't," Masters said quickly. "We can make this work."

"You can make it work in jail." Will shoved him toward Bart's inert form. "Here," he told Katie, handing her the remaining rope. "See if you can truss him up."

She tied the unconscious man's arms behind him. "He's out cold," she said. "I don't think we can get him to the boat."

"We'll send the constable back for him. Chesterton too."

"I hate to leave him here. What if there are bears or other wild animals?"

"They'd spit him out the minute they tasted him." He shoved Masters toward the path to the bay.

Will had so much he wanted to say to Katie but not while he had an audience. They reached the beach, climbed into the dinghy, and headed out. "You were so brave, Katie," Will said. "I am proud of you."

"Save the hearts and flowers for later," Masters said, his voice thick with disgust. "This isn't over yet."

"I think we shall have no trouble proving our case," Katie said. "Where is the gold you pirated? If you give that back, maybe it will go easier on you."

They reached the sailboat and Masters leaned back and shook his head. "I'm not getting on that boat."

"You'd rather drown?" Will asked. He grabbed the man and yanked him forward.

"You aren't like Bart, Mr. Jesperson. You have too much integrity to kill an unarmed man. Just let me go. I'll disappear and you'll never hear from me again."

"I can't do that. I think you know it too," Will said.

"I'll not bring disgrace upon my family," Masters said, his voice tinged with desperation.

Before Will could react to the intent in the man's voice, Masters dived over the side of the dinghy and disappeared in the dark water. Will leaned over the side of the boat. "Masters!" The man would never be able to swim in the dark, rough seas bobbing the boat. A storm was moving in and the waves would only get worse. "Do you see him?" he said to Katie, above him in the sailboat.

"No, not a sign of him!" She rushed to the other side. "Not over here, either!"

Will climbed into the sailboat and walked the perimeter. When he returned to her side, he said, "He's gone. Just like that."

THIRTY-FIVE

STANDING BESIDE WILL in the bow of the boat with the sea breeze in her face, Katie could forget the terror of the night before. Jennie played with blocks on the deck as the boat rode the crest of the waves toward the bay. She squealed with delight every time a block was knocked over. Lady Carrington sat in a deck chair knitting while Nubbins pounced on her ball of yarn.

"Still no sign of the gold," Will said. "Constable Brown says Bart isn't talking."

"What about Masters?"

"They recovered his body."

Even though he hadn't lived to see it, the news was splashed all over this morning's paper. "So much for sparing his family the pain."

The mynah squawked on his perch. "I still think the bird is giving us a clue," Katie said. "We're going to find the gold today."

His smile lingered on her face. "I hope you're right."

Would his smile always make her heart sing? Since they'd come back from the bay, he hadn't spoken of his love. Maybe her parents had discouraged him too much. Or maybe he'd realized he didn't love her after all. She'd been too shy to bring up the subject. He raised her hand to his lips. Katie's heart caught in her throat.

"We need to talk. Very soon, Katie," he said.

She nodded then looked toward the black rock formation thrusting its head from the sea. Wedding Cake Rock. Waves foamed and receded on its sides. Gulls swooped and dove after the crabs clinging to its rocks. It appeared so inhospitable, she wondered if she'd brought them out on a wild goose chase. "I'm not sure where we can anchor."

Will peered over the side. "Looks shallow here. I'll drop anchor." He threw the anchor over the side. The boat slowed then rocked on the waves. He lowered the dinghy.

Lady Carrington put down her knitting and rose. "I shall get lunch out while you're gone so we can eat when you get back. I can feed the baby to keep her busy."

"It shouldn't take long," Katie said.

Will tossed the shovel and a lantern into the dinghy. He helped her onto the boat and clambered down to join her. She sat in the bow as he rowed them toward the forbidding rock. The boat scraped bottom and he leaped into the water and dragged the dinghy ashore on a flat spot of rock. Katie scrambled out and stood looking at the sea-lashed landscape while he retrieved his tools.

"Well, Miss Detective, where do you suggest we look first?" Will's smile lit his eyes.

Katie shielded her eyes from the sun that pierced beneath the brim of her bonnet. "That's what we call the wedding cake," she said, pointing to the rock that appeared to be a three-tiered cake. "Let's go there and see if we can figure out what the bird is saying." Will's warm clasp kept her from stumbling over the slick rocks. They picked their way through the loose boulders and slick deposits of seaweed to the base of the rock.

"This appears to be the only place where the wedding cake is accessible," she said. "The other avenues are straight up." She no longer cared about her finder's fee but the joy of solving the case and returning the stolen property.

"Paco always says, 'Step away from the cake,' and 'six feet down,'" Will said. He thrust the shovel into the shallow, rocky soil. "I doubt we can even dig in this stuff."

Katie stared at the various boulders and ledges. She'd hoped to find a cave or something similar that would house the gold. The space would need to be large enough to hold stacks and stacks. She stepped forward and scrambled a few feet up onto the side of the lopsided wedding cake. When she looked back toward Will she saw it. A jutting rock prevented spying the opening from below. "Will, a cave," she called. It was to her right and down three feet.

"Wait for me." Will scrambled up the sliding rocks to join her. "You can't see it from below," he said when he saw the slit of the opening. "Wait here."

"Oh no, I insisted we come out. I wish to see it with my own eyes." She slid down after him until they stood at the opening to the cave. The only way in was on her hands and knees.

Will lit the lantern and thrust it into the cave. A golden gleam bounced back at them. Stacks of gold lay in front of Katie's dazzled eyes. "So much gold," she breathed.

"It would have stayed here forever if you hadn't been so sure the bird knew about it," Will said. "Let's get to town and tell the constable to come retrieve it."

"We did it, Will," she said, turning to him. "We found the gold and the ship. Everything."

He touched his fingertips to her chin and stared into her eyes. "It's amazing. And it's largely due to you."

Katie wished he would kiss her, declare himself, but he just rubbed his thumb along her chin, dropped his hand, and turned back toward the boat. Maybe her indecisiveness had cost her his love.

The buggy rolled through Mercy Falls. The town looked different to Katie now. She'd wanted so desperately to *be* someone, to be a person who was looked up to. Now she knew who she really was. Her worth was not in an earthly husband but in her heavenly one. Even if she never married, she would be who God created her to be. She vowed never to forget that.

Will stopped the buggy in front of the constable's office. "I'll be right back. Do you want to come?"

She spied Florence across the street. "There's something else I need to do first," she said. When he disappeared into the building, she climbed down from the buggy and stepped across the street to where the older woman stood examining a dress display in the department store window. She paused. They were all dignified, respectable dresses, nothing like what she was wearing. Could her mother be yearning for something . . . different?

Florence turned and saw her. "Well, you certainly fell on your feet," she said. "I wish I could say the same for myself. I expect the law to arrest me any time. It's a good thing you didn't marry that man."

"God was looking out for me," Katie agreed.

Florence studied her face. "Something has changed about you. You don't seem as angry."

"I wanted to tell you that I forgive you," Katie said. Her hand went to her mouth when she realized what she'd said and that she actually meant the words.

Florence's smooth face didn't change but her eyes did. First there was a slow blink then a gathering of moisture in their blue depths. Her mouth trembled a little. "That's very good of you, Katie," she said, her voice husky. "I did the best I could."

"I know that now. Things could have been much worse." Katie reached out and embraced the woman who bore her. "Thank you for that." The familiar scent of the older woman's lilac sachet brought a wave of nostalgia.

Florence clutched at her and a sob burst from her throat. "I'm sorry for everything. Sorry I tried to get money out of you. I'll do just fine on my own. I always have."

She saw Dora Curry approaching. The woman owned the soda

shop and was the biggest gossip in town. Dora's brows rose when she saw Katie speaking with a woman dressed like Florence, and Katie smiled. "Good afternoon, Dora. I'd like you to meet my real mother, Florence Muller. She is Mama's sister and has been gone from town a long time." She felt rather than saw Florence start with surprise.

Dora's steps faltered a moment but she stopped and extended her hand. "Delighted to meet you, Mrs. Muller. Katie is a wonderful girl. We love her very much."

Katie saw how much Dora meant her kind words and her throat tightened. She'd been so worried about impressing people that she'd failed to see genuine love and respect when it was right in front of her face. "Thank you, Dora," she said, her voice choked. "I realize more and more how very blessed I am to have grown up in this town."

Dora pressed her hand. "I must get back to the shop." She glanced at Florence again. "You have a very special daughter."

"I think so too," Florence said.

Katie saw Will step out of the constable's office. She waved to him, and he started across the street, dodging a fast-moving horse and wagon. "I want you to meet my young man, M–Mother," she said. "He's the handsome one across the street."

Florence's eyes brightened at the term. "I'd be most honored."

Will reached them. His dark eyes went from Katie to Florence. "I do believe this must be your mother, Katie. You look very much like her."

Katie didn't even wince. "Yes, Will. Florence, I'd like you to meet Will Jesperson. He found the pirates and the ship."

Will took Florence's gloved hand. "I'm delighted to meet you, but I don't deserve all the credit. Thanks to Katie, the gold was recovered today as well."

Florence's expression turned flirtatious. She glanced at Katie. "You said your young man was handsome, but I do believe he looks like a pirate himself. No wonder you're quite smitten."

Will grinned. "She said I was handsome? I like the sound of that. I like *smitten* even more."

Heat rushed to Katie's cheeks and she avoided the light dancing in his eyes. "We must go. It's nearly time for tea and I don't want to interrupt Mama in the middle of it."

"Do you think I might come as well?" Florence asked tentatively. "I should like to see my sister."

"I–I'm not sure she would be ready for that without preparation," Katie said. She could only imagine the explosion when the two sisters reunited.

"I think she should come," Will said. "It's time the old feud was laid to rest. They are sisters."

Katie clutched her hands together. "Very well. As long as we are all prepared to face a situation that might not be what we'd hoped."

"I'm ready," Florence said, adjusting her hat. "Thank you for making it possible. Perhaps Inez can forgive me as well."

As they walked back to the buggy, Katie prayed they would find her mother in a forgiving frame of mind. She cast a sidelong glance at Will. If only he would declare himself so she could broach that subject with her parents as well.

THIRTY-SIX

THE SCENT OF chocolate wafers wafted on the breeze when Will helped the ladies down from the buggy. He longed to have Katie to himself, to discuss their future, but there hadn't been the right moment.

Katie led the way to the front door. "Wait here a moment," she told Florence. "I want to prepare them."

Will nodded and escorted the older woman to a rocker on the porch. "We'll be right back," he said. "Enjoy the birdsong and the sound of the sea." He took Katie's hand and they stepped inside and found her mother in the parlor. The tea had not yet been brought out from the kitchen.

Her mother saw her and held out her hand. "Katie, my dear girl. Did you just arrive?"

Katie crossed the plush carpet and took her mother's hand. "Just in time for tea, I hope. I smelled the chocolate wafers."

"You're always in time. I suspected you might come by and instructed Agnes prepare for guests."

"Where is Papa?"

Her mother's eyes filled with tears. "He went to see the constable. To confess."

Katie gasped and turned to Will, groping for him. He stepped to her side and put his hand on her back. He wanted to embrace her but feared offending her mother.

"He'll go to jail," she whispered.

Her mother nodded. "After you were nearly killed, he couldn't stand by and say nothing." Her eyes welled. "I shall never be able to hold my head up here again."

"Your friends know and love you, Mama. I've discovered what God thinks of us is more important than admiration from mere acquaintances."

Her mother dabbed at her eyes with a hanky then glanced at Will. "I thought you might come with her."

Katie sank onto the sofa beside her mother. "I wanted to make sure it was all right to bring him in. You're still not quite well and I didn't wish to overtax you."

Mrs. Russell reached up and took Will's hand. "I want to thank you for saving Katie's life. After she called last night, I lay awake for hours wishing I'd been kinder to you." She shook her head. "I can't believe Bart would behave in such an uncivilized manner. I quite misjudged him. And you, too, young man."

It was a start. When she released his hand, Will shoved them in his pockets. "It's quite all right, Mrs. Russell. Katie is very precious to everyone."

Katie leaned forward and took her mother's hands. "There's another visitor, Mama."

Her mother's smile faded. "You sound so serious, Katie. Who is it?"

"Your sister."

Her mother paled. "Florence is here?"

"On the porch."

Her mother rose and wrung her hands. "How could you bring that woman here?"

"I realized she made mistakes, but she did the best she could, Mama. I think it's time for all of us to sit down and talk. To forgive and forget. I'm thankful she didn't stand in the way of letting me grow up with you and Papa."

"I can't see her," Mrs. Russell said, her voice rising.

"You can and you will," Florence said from the doorway. "You stole my daughter from me, Inez. That's the real problem you don't want to admit."

Bright spots of color appeared on Mrs. Russell's pale cheeks. "I have no idea what you're talking about." She glared at her sister again. "I'd like you to leave, Florence. I told you I never wanted to see you again, and I meant it."

Tears glistened in Florence's eyes. "You stole her, Inez. You had Albert pay me to disappear."

"You took the money," Katie's mother said. "You could have come here and demanded her back but you didn't."

"You'd been waiting for a chance to get your hands on her from the day she was born."

"You didn't deserve her! Always gone with your men friends. Never a thought for what Katie needed. She was better off with us."

"I don't deny that," Florence said. "But you can at least be grateful. Thanks to me you had a daughter you were never able to bear yourself."

Will stepped between the two women. "Let's all sit down and have some tea," he said. "I think we can all agree that Katie turned into a remarkable young woman. The past is over. Let's all move forward." To his relief, the women moved stiffly to separate sides of the room like boxers squaring off. At least the verbal sparring had ended. Katie sat with her mother on the sofa while Florence took the armchair by the fireplace. He decided to play it safe and sit on Katie's other side.

The maid entered with a tray of chocolate wafers and a teapot with teacups. She served them all through a silence as thick as the fog on a cold night. Will balanced the ridiculously tiny teacup on his knee and wondered how he might help mend the breach dividing them.

Florence put down her cup. "No one can ever say I lacked courage, so I'll say it, Inez. I'm sorry. I've made some poor choices in my life, but it was my life to ruin. Not yours."

Mrs. Russell said nothing at first. She sipped her tea. "Mama?" Katie said, her voice encouraging. "I forgive her. I want you to do the same."

"Leave us, Katie," Mrs. Russell said finally. "I wish to speak to my sister in private. Take your young man for a walk. Show him the azalea garden."

Katie put down her tea. "Very well." She glanced at Will.

He rose and extended his hand. She took it and rose from the sofa. "Call us when you are ready." She led him down the hall to the back porch and out into the garden. The azaleas were in bloom. Her destination was a stone bench in the middle of the garden. "I hope they don't come to blows," she said when they reached the bucolic spot.

He kept hold of her hand. "I think they'll work it out. They both care about you." How did he bring up the subject of their future? Just launch into it or ease up to it gradually? He decided to take his cue from her. If she didn't care for him, he'd fade into the background and do whatever made her happy.

❧

Hummingbirds darted from red blossoms. Katie plucked a white azalea bloom and caressed the silken petals. She couldn't look at Will. He'd said nothing and there had been ample opportunity.

She plucked the blossoms. *He loves me. He loves me not. He loves me. He loves me not. He loves me.*

"Katie, are we going to talk about us?"

She hardly dared to raise her gaze to meet his. He looked so handsome in his white shirt and black pants. His dark hair gleamed in the sunlight. "Is there an 'us,' Will?" she asked.

"I've told you how I feel. Several times. You've skirted the subject. Is it that you don't think I have the means to provide for you?"

She smiled. "Since last night, I've realized that only God can provide for me in the end. Anything we have is from his hand. This life is temporary, and I was too focused on the here and now."

"I see peace in your eyes," he said, taking her hand. He tossed the remains of the flower to the grass.

"It's about time, don't you think?" She clutched his fingers. "I love you, Will. I didn't want to say it because I was afraid, but I've loved you for a long time."

His black eyes lit with joy. He raised her hand to his lips and pressed them to her palm. "What if I tell you that we're moving to Texas to take a lighthouse there?"

"I'll go wherever you go," she said, keeping her voice steady even though her heart sank within her.

"What if I want to move to Chicago to work with the Weather Bureau?"

"I think you'll have to buy me some new clothes to deal with the cold," she said.

His grin widened. "What if I tell you I'm staying in Mercy Falls?"

She just barely managed not to squeal when she saw the assurance in his eyes. "Really?" she whispered.

He nodded. "The new Weather Bureau has asked me to provide them with data from the coast. It doesn't pay much, but it's a nice supplement to my salary as lightkeeper." He leaned over and kissed her nose. "Your parents will be able to live on our reward money."

"You wouldn't mind? By rights, it is ours."

"I'll provide for my own wife," he said. "I rather like the sound of the word *wife*."

Her pulse stammered at the smoldering passion in his eyes. She leaned forward and brushed her lips across his. He slipped his arm around her, and in the next moment, she found herself on his lap. His kiss intensified and she wound her arms around his neck and kissed him back with every bit of love she'd longed to express. His hands took the hat from her head and removed the pins from her hair until it all lay on her shoulders. She knew she should object. Her mother would be quite horrified when she went inside in obvious disarray, but she didn't care as she kissed him back.

He suddenly jerked his mouth from hers and stared into her eyes. "We need to slow down or I fear I might lose my head," he said.

She leaned her head against his chest and heard its wild pounding that matched the beat in her own. Gulping in air, she finally lifted her chin and stared into his tender eyes. "So do I get to help you tend the lamps and rescue people?"

"I don't think I can keep you safely in the parlor now that you've learned to let your adventurous side go," he said. "Jennie will learn early to explore her world."

Katie's elation faded. "What about Jennie? What if Bart's parents want her?"

He shook his head. "I saw them in the constable's office and they were quick to take me up on my offer to keep her. They promised to have the papers drawn up quickly if I would keep quiet about her real parentage."

"So she is ours?"

"She is indeed. We shall see about adding some brothers and sisters for her."

Heat ran up her neck at the expression in his eyes. Though things were a bit uncertain right now, she realized she rather liked the unknown. One thing was quite sure, life with her lightkeeper would shine as bright as his Fresnel lens. "I think I should have another kiss," she said, pulling his head down to hers. "A budding bride needs the practice."

ACKNOWLEDGMENTS

IT IS SUCH a privilege to do another project with my wonderful Thomas Nelson family. Publisher Allen Arnold (I call him Superman) is so passionate about fiction and he lights up a room when he enters it. Senior Acquisitions Editor Ami McConnell (my friend and cheerleader) has an eye for character and theme like no one I know. I crave her analytical eye! It was her influence that encouraged me to write a historical romantic mystery, and I'm glad she pushed me a bit! Marketing Manager Jennifer Deshler brings both friendship and fabulous marketing ideas to the table. Publicist Katie Bond is always willing to listen to my harebrained ideas. Fabulous cover guru Kristen Vasgaard (you *so* rock!) works hard to create the perfect cover—and does it. And of course I can't forget my other friends who are all part of my amazing fiction family: Natalie Hanemann, Amanda Bostic, Becky Monds, Ashley Schneider, Andrea Lucado, Heather McCoullough, Chris Long, and Kathy Carabajal. I wish I could name all the great folks who work on selling my books through different venues at Thomas Nelson. You are my dream team! Hearing "well done" from you all is my motivation every day.

My agent, Karen Solem, has helped shaped my career in many ways, and that includes kicking an idea to the curb when necessary. Thanks, Karen, you're the best!

This was my first opportunity to work with Lisa Tawn Bergren, and it was a wonderful experience. I was initially a little intimidated because Lisa is such an accomplished novelist in her own right. Her expertise with historical settings (her latest books are *Breathe, Sing,* and *Claim*) was a great asset. Thanks so much, Lisa!

Writing can be a lonely business, but God has blessed me with great writing friends and critique partners. Hannah Alexander (Cheryl Hodde), Kristin Billerbeck, Diann Hunt, and Denise Hunter make up the Girls Write Out squad (*www.GirlsWriteOut.blogspot.com*). I couldn't make it through a day without my peeps! Thanks to all of you for the work you do on my behalf, and for your friendship.

I'm so grateful for my husband, Dave, who carts me around from city to city, washes towels, and chases down dinner without complaint. Thanks, honey! I couldn't do anything without you. My kids—Dave, Kara (and now Donna and Mark)—and my grandsons, James and Jorden Packer, love and support me in every way possible. Love you guys! Donna and Dave brought me the delight of my life—our little granddaughter, Alexa! Though I tried my best to emulate her cuteness in the scenes with Jennie, I'm sure I failed!

Most importantly, I give my thanks to God, who has opened such amazing doors for me and makes the journey a golden one.

READING GROUP GUIDE

1. Have you ever discovered something about a loved one that had been so hidden you didn't believe it at first? How did this make you feel?

2. Will believed in taking responsibility for our actions. If his brother wouldn't do it, Will would. What did you think about that? Was he right?

3. Katie didn't want anyone to know of her real background. What are the advantages and disadvantages of letting out the truth in our lives?

4. Katie's feelings for Will were revealed when she forgot her hat. Actions speak loudly. What is the most loving thing someone can do for you?

5. Stepping into criminal activity can happen in small steps. What steps led to Katie's father getting involved in something criminal? What should he have done to stop?

6. Katie didn't like surprises. Do you like them or do they frighten you the way they did Katie? Why do you feel this way?

7. Have you ever been torn between duty and love? How do you decide the right course of action?

8. Katie had a plan for her life. How can you tell if your plans parallel God's plans?

9. Do you crave adventure or for the days to flow by evenly? What can you do to step outside of your comfort zone?

10. Katie realized that God was the one who was her ultimate Provider and this life is temporary. Do you hold to things here too tightly? What can you do to begin to have an eternal perspective?

Lonestar Sanctuary

THE RODEO CROWD, REEKING OF BEER AND PEANUTS, FINALLY REELED OFF into the night. Allie Siders heard their good-bye calls faintly through the faded cotton curtains. The twin bed sagged under her weight as she sat down and slipped off her worn cowboy boots. She smelled like horse—not a bad smell, but pungent nevertheless. A hot shower would ease her muscles, taxed with riding around barrels all day.

Her five-year-old daughter, Betsy, slept with one fist curled under her cheek in the youth cot next to Allie's bed, and Allie watched her sleep for a moment. So innocent, so beautiful.

So damaged by the blows life had dealt.

But things would get better soon. They could hardly get worse. Once Allie won the barrel-racing championship, the money would come rolling in, and they'd have a better place to live than this old, broken-down trailer.

Allie dreamed of the day she and Betsy would have a real home again. They had one once upon a time, until the rough seas washed the sand castle away. But she'd find a way somehow. Betsy deserved more.

Allie slipped out of her dusty jeans and padded to the hall in her bare feet. The floors of the tiny travel trailer creaked and groaned under her weight as she tiptoed toward the bathroom. She left the door open a crack in case Betsy called out for her, though the chance was unlikely. The little girl hadn't spoken a word in nearly a year.

The tiny bathroom was spotless except for the rust stains Allie couldn't get off the worn fixtures. The Lysol she'd sprayed still lingered in the air, and she resisted the urge to sneeze.

She stared at her reflection in the mirror. The rodeo queen's smile was one that vanished with the crowds.

She went to the tub and turned on the shower. The hot spray sputtered from the rusty showerhead and struck her sore arm, soothing it, enticing her to step fully into the welcoming warmth.

Straightening, she tugged her shirt over her head. A creak like someone stepping on the weak floor came from beyond the door. She whirled in time to see it slam shut. Allie jerked her shirt back down. Gooseflesh pebbled on her arm when the creak came again.

"Yolanda, is that you?" she called.

Her friend's cheery voice didn't answer. Allie wet her lips. She was being a nervous Nellie tonight. The noise was probably the old trailer settling. Her hand gripped the bottom of her shirt again to remove it.

Something scratched at the door, and she caught her breath.

"*Aaaallieee,*" the taunting voice whispered through the door. The scrape sounded once more. "*Aaaallieee.*"

A man's voice, low and guttural, maybe even deliberately pitched so she wouldn't recognize it. A sharp edge under the low, cruel voice vibrated. That voice could cut to the bone without a weapon.

Allie took a step away from the menace, her back pushing away the wet shower curtain until water sprayed her neck. It was like a wet slap, bringing her back to what mattered most.

Betsy!

She grappled with the embrace of the wet shower curtain and managed to disentangle herself from it. She leaped to the door and grabbed the doorknob, yanking hard, but the door didn't move. With her hand on the cold metal knob, she could feel his movements on the other side.

"Let me out!" she screamed, pounding and kicking at the door.

"You want out?" He chuckled, the razor edge of his voice contrasting with the smooth laugh. "Your sister wanted out."

The room felt close, airless. Her lungs strained to pull in enough oxygen. She wanted to scream for Betsy but didn't dare call the man's attention to the fact that her daughter was in the bedroom.

"You sure you want out, Allie?" he whispered.

Terror whirled inside like a mounting tornado. She forced it deep, down to the dark place where she kept all the things she feared. For Betsy's sake she had to keep herself together.

Maybe she could get out, circle around to Betsy's window, and get to her. She spun around and ran to the bathroom window, but it was too small to allow even her tiny frame to exit. She turned back to the door and tried to open it again. It opened a crack against the force of his hand holding it to on the other side, then slammed shut before she could get it open wide enough to get her leg through.

"Let go of the door!" She tugged harder, kicked at it. Her fear morphed into a cold anger. If she could face him, she'd tear at his face with her nails. She would allow no one to hurt her baby girl.

The man's laugh—if such an evil sound could be called laughter—whispered through the door again. "Your sister was so pretty. Not nearly as pretty as you, though. Especially not now." A knife poked through the crack. "She screamed when she saw the knife. Are you going to scream, Allie?"

Allie stared at the blade slicing through the door. It wasn't true, couldn't be true. He was just trying to scare her.

Tammy had walked in on a burglar.

The knife blade danced in the crack, moving forward, then pulling back long enough to make her think he was leaving. Then it reappeared, the edge sharp and dangerous.

She pulled on the knob again. "You coward," she yelled. "Face me like a man! Quit hiding behind whispers and phone calls."

"You might faint if you saw my face," he whispered. "Just like Tammy did."

The fear tried to surge out of the box she'd stuffed it into, but Allie tightened her control. Her sister's face flashed through her mind, and sorrow welled in her eyes. Had this man really been the one? She couldn't let herself believe it.

Allie laid her head against the door. "What do you want?"

"I want you to pay," he said, his whisper harsher. "I'm going to take everything you love, just like you destroyed the things that mattered to me. What matters most to you, Allie?"

Betsy, he would take Betsy!

Allie's frantic gaze ran around the room. What could she do? Though she knew it was so late no one would be out there to hear, she ran to the window and screamed, "Help, somebody help me!" Her cries fell into the silent yard. No one answered her scream.

"Don't do that," he growled.

Allie ignored his commanding tone and raised her voice so loud it hurt her throat. "Help! Please, someone help me!"

Then she heard the sweet sound of another voice. A shout answered her, feet shuffled through the dust toward her trailer. Help was on its way. She whirled and leaped back to the door. The knife was gone. This time the knob turned easily under her fingers, and the door flew open.

The hallway was empty.

Allie bounded from the bathroom and raced across the hall. "Please, oh please, God, let Betsy be all right." She rushed into the room and saw Betsy's tousled dark curls on the pillow. "Bets?" she whispered.

Betsy stirred and rubbed her eyes, then rolled over and went back to sleep.

Allie sagged against the doorframe. Her legs trembled, and she wanted to crawl into the bed herself, pull the covers over her head like she used to when she was afraid of the boogeyman.

But this was a real-life monster.

Someone pounded on the front door hard enough to make the whole trailer shake. She tottered down the hall and threw open the door.

Her best friend, Yolanda Fleming, stepped through the door. "Allie, what's wrong?"

Allie clutched her. "He was here, in my house!" Aware she wore only her shirt and underwear, she backed down the hall. "My sister. He said he killed Tammy!"

Horror began to dawn on Yolanda's face. But even as Yolanda hugged her, Allie knew none of her friends would be able to protect her and Betsy. There was only one thing she could do.

ESCAPE TO
BLUEBIRD RANCH

With the lies of the past behind her,
Addie finds love . . . and discovers
her true Father.

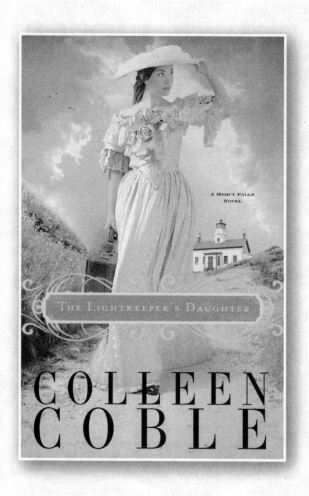

A MERCY FALLS
NOVEL

THE LIGHTKEEPER'S DAUGHTER

COLLEEN
COBLE

A Mercy Falls Novel